Finding the fairytale in Storybook Lake . . .

Grace Wade left Storybook Lake hoping to escape her crazy family and the demands of her job as a defense attorney. But not twenty-four hours after landing in a small Texas town where she hopes to find new beginnings, Grace instead finds herself in the middle of an investigation that's turning the town inside out. Once she agrees to be the defense attorney on the case, Grace suddenly finds herself torn between twin brothers Blane Sheperd, the bad boy prosecutor on the case, and Jamie Sheperd, the sweetheart town Sheriff . . .

Grace thought life in a small town would be simple, but simple has a way of eluding her. To find her way to a happy ending, she'll have to master the art of following her heart . . .

Books by Melissa Shirley

Storybook Lake Series
Here He Comes Again
Falling Grace
Breaking Hearts

Published by Kensington Publishing Corporation

Falling Grace

A Storybook Lake Romance

Melissa Shirley

LYRICAL PRESS
Kensington Publishing Corp.
www.kensingtonbooks.com

Lyrical Press books are published by
Kensington Publishing Corp. 119 West 40th Street New York, NY 10018

All Kensington titles, imprints, and distributed lines are available at special quantity discounts for bulk purchases for sales promotion, premiums, fund-raising, and educational or institutional use.

To the extent that the image or images on the cover of this book depict a person or persons, such person or persons are merely models, and are not intended to portray any character or characters featured in the book.

Special book excerpts or customized printings can also be created to fit specific needs. For details, write or phone the office of the Kensington Special Sales Manager:
Kensington Publishing Corp.
119 West 40th Street
New York, NY 10018
Attn. Special Sales Department. Phone: 1-800-221-2647.

Kensington and the K logo Reg. U.S. Pat. & TM Off.
LYRICAL PRESS Reg. U.S. Pat. & TM Off.
Lyrical Press and the L logo are trademarks of Kensington Publishing Corp.

First Electronic Edition: February 2016
eISBN-13: 978-1-60183-611-3
eISBN-10: 1-60183-611-2

First Print Edition: February 2016
ISBN-13: 978-1-60183-612-0
ISBN-10: 1-60183-612-0

Printed in the United States of America

For Gina and Diana

Acknowledgements

Very special thank you to the best CP in the universe.

Chapter 1

"My wife killed our daughter."

Nathan Gabriel strolled into the office and threw out the line as though he said things like that every day. For such a serious statement, he'd said it with no stuttering sense of urgency, no affect whatsoever. The sheen of sweat on his face and his pinhead sized pupils spoke to something underlying his serenity as he spoke.

"Your wife killed your daughter?" As a criminal attorney, I dealt with some big baddies, but never with someone who confessed so readily for his wife.

"They *think* she did." He twitched and scratched the side of his face. "She wants Rory Allden to defend her."

"But you said…" I shook it off. "Rory isn't here. I'm her partner, Grace Wade. I might be able to help you." I never offered services without knowing the actual client's name and never without a few more details than a statement condemning the person meant to be my client, but something about him…

He looked around, glanced back as though waiting for the door to open. His wife was suspected of murder, and he needed a lawyer. I fit that description. What was the hold up?

After a few long minutes, a couple of frustrated huffs and puffs of his chest, and more waiting, he nodded. "Fine. Let's go."

I jogged with him across the street to the police station armed with only his name and what I could remember of his words. His first damning statement spun around my mind.

It wasn't my usual mode of attack on a case, but I brushed my confusion aside and peppered questions at his back. He hurried faster than I could keep up in my pencil skirt and four inch heels.

Conveniently located in viewing distance from the new offices of Allden and Wade, Attorneys at Law, the police station looked more like a refurbished coffee house, with a picture window in front under a black awning with its edges flapping in the wind and a park bench on its wide sidewalk. The whole town had been designed right out of a Rockwell and the sheriff's department was no different.

I stepped inside a heavy glass door and breathed in the pungent smell of sweat and chilidogs. Pinching the bridge of my nose, I approached a counter marked Information in crooked gold lettering.

An officer behind the waist-high counter that doubled as a desk barely looked up from his *Bikes and Babes* magazine. "Can I help you?"

I curled my fingers in my palm to resist the urge to smack his feet off the cluttered Formica. "I'm Grace Wade, and I want to speak to my client."

"What client would that be?"

"I'm sorry. I didn't realize your town was so rife with crime that you could possibly be confused." *Well, more confused.* "Mrs. Quinn." I didn't even know her first name, for goodness sake.

He rolled his eyes and flipped a page. "Have a seat over there." He nodded to a semi-stained seating arrangement that I wouldn't risk my clothes to sit on. "I'll let the detective know you're here."

The magazine crinkled as he brought it closer to his face, investigating something on the inside. He'd missed a button when he dressed and more of his lunch dotted his shirt than could possibly have landed in his mouth.

He ignored the long, huffy breath that billowed between my lips. I counted down the ten more seconds I waited by drilling my fingers against the counter for each one that ticked off. *Enough.* I snatched the magazine from his fingers and shoved it behind my back as he reached for it.

"I can charge you with assaulting a police officer."

"Not until I smack you with it." I slammed the flimsy paperback down in front of me. "Listen, *Einstein.* If your detective is in there questioning her and she's asked for counsel, anything she says is going to get thrown right out of court, and who do you think is gonna get the blame? Hot shot detective or desk jockey?" I gave my most endearing and practiced grin as I mimicked his twang. "So, if I were you, I would get my big, lazy, too-many-biscuits-dipped-in-gravy ass out of that chair and let your detective know I'm here."

His white cowboy hat tilted as he shoved a phone receiver to his ear and punched a single digit into the phone. "I know that, Detective. Her attorney is here." He looked up at me. "Name?"

"Grace Wade."

"*Miss* Grace Wade." He took a pointed look at my ring finger, and I slid my hand off the counter to my side.

The sassy *miss* he added to my name was in an accent that drew out the syllables.

"I'll let her know." He took his time, polishing the receiver with his soiled shirt, then replaced it in its cradle. "She's in the interview room." After extricating all seven feet of his body from the chair, he made his way around a wall to stand beside me.

At five-foot-seven with another four inches of heel, I barely made it to his shoulder. "Right this way, *Miss* Wade." I didn't have to ask how he felt about single women.

His white T-shirt hung beneath the tail of his button down as I followed him down the hall. He stopped in front of an unmarked door and turned to me. "She's right in here."

I hid my mental eye roll with a wink and walked past him, noting his name for future avoidance. "Thank you for your hospitality, Deputy Wesley."

He grunted a reply and shut the door behind me, keeping her husband, Nathan Quinn, locked outside.

A plain clothes detective leaned across the table on his fists in front of a woman so shriveled I disguised my muttered "Whoa" with a cough.

He straightened, then looked me up and down, his eyebrows creeping up his forehead as his eyes made their way lower. A slow smile spread across his lips and he extended a hand. "I'm Detective Paul Roan, Texas State Police."

After the initial handshake, he continued to hold on. His slimy palm sweat slithered onto my skin. I yanked my arm back to my side and wiped my fingers down the outer seam of my skirt. "Grace Wade."

"You must be new in town. I'd remember such a pretty face."

You'll remember it now. "Detective, I know you weren't in here questioning my client after she asked for her lawyer."

He cocked his head to one side and crossed his arms over his chest. "No, ma'am. We were having a little chat is all."

"Of course, you were." I nodded to the woman. "Looks like she was enjoying it."

"She never asked me to stop."

His eyebrows issued a dare and I smiled in return. The quiet recesses of my mind came to life, and I started mentally counting the piles of money I would earn suing this police department.

"Well, Miss Wade, if you'll excuse me, I'm gonna go get my paperwork in order and call the prosecutor in charge of this case to let him know that we're booking your client on first degree murder." Honey didn't drip with such sweetness as his tone. He smacked his big, black hat on his head and grinned as though he'd won a war with his words.

I flipped a glance at the clock ticking loudly on the wall. Four o'clock, Friday afternoon. "Impeccable timing. I would expect nothing less."

He twisted the knob and tossed a wink over his shoulder. "See you soon, *Miss* Wade."

As soon as the latch clicked into place, I looked at the woman in the chair. "I'm Grace. Your husband hired me to be your attorney." She frowned. "Rory wasn't there, so I came instead. Right now, I want you to tell me everything that happened with your daughter, and I need you to do it as quickly as you can." She didn't move, didn't seem to breathe. I wanted to shake her, show her the urgency of her situation. Instead, I pulled a chair around the table and sat close enough to smell her coffee breath. "Listen, detective tall-hat is gonna be back in a minute to book you into the jail. They're going to fingerprint you, change your clothes, and put you in a cell. Because it's Friday, and this is Backwater U.S.A., you won't see a judge until at least Monday."

She didn't look up from the table.

When she continued to ignore me, my guilt-o-meter got confused. In my experience, guilty clients either gave me *the stare* or shouted too many details of their innocence like chirping fools. Catatonia was new, though. I had no expertise to call on to deal with that kind of response.

"Mrs. Quinn, I know this is awful, but I need you to focus on what I'm saying." I snapped my fingers in front of her. "What happened to your daughter?"

"My husband can tell you." Her voice wavered on the words.

"No." The sharpness of my tone caused her to look up while simultaneously becoming smaller. I softened my voice. "I need you to tell me."

"We went out to a movie and for a couple drinks with some friends. When we came back from Dallas, I checked on the kids while he drove the sitter home. Emily was already asleep, all tucked in, so I went to bed. When Nathan got home, he came up, and we went to sleep. Emily was fine." She broke into a sob.

"Okay. She was sleeping. Did you touch her or cover her or anything that told you she was okay at that moment?" I checked the clock as minutes sped past during her silence. She needed to move this along. "We don't have much time."

"No. I looked in and she was covered up. She liked to sleep with the blankets over her head. I could see her hair and I didn't want to take the chance of waking her up."

"What happened in the morning?"

"When I woke up on Sunday, I got our boy dressed and went in to take a bath." She twisted the fingers of one hand in the fisted grasp of the other. "I liked having some time before Emily woke up. She was difficult in the mornings and I thought if I could just get myself ready without her wanting me to hold her and… And I heard Nathan screaming. I ran down the hall, and he was holding Emily. She was dead." She shook her head and a wave of tears brimmed over her lashes. "So much blood."

"Okay. What happened to her?"

"Someone killed my baby." Her voice cracked, then shattered on a sob.

I ran a hand over hers, gave it a squeeze. I needed five more minutes of coherency. "Who could have stabbed your daughter?"

The withering continued. Mrs. Quinn slunk farther into her chair and fat, sloppy tears streamed down her cheeks. "I don't know." She mumbled the phrase three more times.

I covered her hand with mine. I didn't usually coddle my clients, but she needed contact, a sympathetic touch. "Okay. We're going to figure this out, but you have to listen to me. They're going to put you in a cell. Whatever you do, don't speak to them, at all. If anyone asks you anything, or tries to start a conversation, you ask for me. Do not say anything to them." I couldn't stress that enough. "To anyone. Especially if they put you in a cell with someone else." She continued to sob. "Do you understand?" Her body shook as she ignored my question. "Do you understand?"

"Yes."

"What's your first name?"

"Gabrielle. My husband calls me Gabby."

"Okay, Gabby, listen. Because of what they're charging you with, I probably can't get you out on bail, but I will do everything I can to make your stay here as short as possible."

A bubble of something I hoped was only gas formed in my stomach. In law school, it was drilled into us that asking the wrong questions limited our ability to defend our clients, but in this case, I had to know. Even if the answer meant I could never put her on the stand, a fire burned in me to get the answer. "Did you kill your daughter?"

She looked around the room, at the floor, the paint peeling from a far wall, the doorknob, a mirror that doubled as a window. Everywhere but at me.

"Gabby, did you kill your daughter?"

"No. Nathan didn't do it either. He's a wonderful father."

Oh, for him she was willing to spearhead a defense? In the words of William Shakespeare, *the lady doth protest too much.* I made a mental note to launch a little investigation into wonder daddy. I had a tingling feeling her case would live or die by whatever I discovered about him. Her shoulders slumped forward as she lifted her gaze to slide over me and finally land on a spot in the center of the table. She wouldn't meet my eyes, wouldn't look up again. That bubble in the pit of my stomach expanded.

"Okay." For the moment, I couldn't care about her husband or whether the world believed he did it. He wasn't the one holding down a chair in the interrogation room. I cared about this broken woman, thin and aged beyond her years. "Then let's figure out how to make sure a jury knows you didn't do it."

Chapter 2

Two hours later, she'd been charged and booked, then shoved into a cell to await an arraignment that wouldn't happen until the weekend passed. I hurried back across the street, my steps far more energized since I'd jogged behind her husband. In the far corner of my mind, I wondered where Mr. Quinn disappeared to. I'd walked out of the interrogation room to find him gone. A moment later, I stepped through the office door to find Rory Allden in high heels and a short skirt atop a metal receptionist desk. She strained, twisting and stretching, to change a light bulb in a fluorescent fixture. Her husband, Jack, ogled her from the ground, arms out as though prepared to catch a parachuter whose string wouldn't pull.

"Hey, Grace." She looked down at me, then went back to maneuvering the stubborn bulb into the fixture.

"What are you doing?" Seriously, no maintenance person in any building I'd ever worked in dressed quite like *that*. Even in college, she paraded around like a fashion model while the rest of us looked like we shopped in dollar stores.

Jack never took his eyes off her ass as he answered, "She's proving it only takes one lawyer to change a light bulb."

I tilted my head and shot Jack a squinty-eyed glare. "Lawyer joke. Original."

He chuckled and resumed gawking at his wife's exposed legs.

"He is totally looking up your skirt."

Rory gazed down at him and winked. "What a waste of perfectly good underwear." Her wide grin showed a set of straight, chemically whitened teeth. She pushed the plastic panel back into place with the flourish of a woman who'd implemented a plan for world peace, then reached a hand down and laid it on her husband's shoulder. He circled her waist with long, gentle fingers and lifted her down to the floor. "Where did you go? I thought you were going to unpack."

Miss OCD turned and motioned to the ten or so boxes stacked in the corner of the room. That morning, I'd promised to haul them into my office. In my world, cases came before good housekeeping. "A client came in."

One eyebrow shot up her forehead almost to her scalp. "A client? We aren't open yet."

At her curious stare, I realized Rory might not be nearly as eager about the case as I'd been. My excitement died, and my lips twisted toward my left ear. "Yeah, just a guy, um, he, uh"—oh crap—"came over while I was unpacking." I walked to the box on the highest pile and flipped open the lid.

In one smooth move, she stepped into her husband's arms. "I'll see you at home, hon." After an almost pornographic display of making out, he gave me a little wave and walked out the door.

"Grace."

I lifted my head out of the box I'd all but crawled into and quickly looked back down.

"What guy came in here looking for a lawyer?" The deadly calm of her voice said she had a guess, and her slightly opened mouth and flared nostrils said she didn't like it.

"He actually came looking for you, but you'd gone to the store…for whatever it is you went to the store for."

After what Rory had been through—ex-husband killing her son, former law firm selling her out on another case, almost being disbarred—maybe I should have known she would be angry if I took this case. But in our massive number of calls over the last weeks, she'd assured me she'd taken steps to deal with her residual depression, paranoia, and overall feelings of guilt.

She cocked her hip and leaned against the desk.

I twisted my hands in front of me, smoothed my skirt, then picked an imaginary piece of lint from the front. The words squeaked out as though something gripped the bass in my vocal chords. "Nathan Quinn."

Her eyes flashed and her cheeks turned a fiery shade of red. "Nathan Quinn?" *Oh, hell.* The ice in her tone chilled every bone in my body and I shivered.

"Yes." My voice lacked any sort of conviction, more squeaked from between my lips. "Nathan Quinn." I closed the box and walked around it, arms outstretched in surrender. "Rory, listen." I could do this without her, defend this client, and she could take her own cases.

Her blue eyes flashed fire. "No, *you* listen." She actually stamped her foot against the floor. "Do you have any idea what I went through? What these kinds of cases do to me?" All five-feet-two-inches of her blazed with rage bubbling below her surface, turning her skin a fiery shade of red. "You took the case of a baby killer?"

"What if she didn't do it?"

"What if she did? Do you know anything about it? Do you have any idea what happened to that little girl in that house?" Her voice reached a shrill that would have had a dog barking if one stood anywhere within earshot. "Someone killed her. Stabbed her over and over again. They didn't go after anyone else in the house. Whoever did this picked the most defenseless person they could. Random intruders don't do that, and they don't do it with that kind of rage. Fifty something stab wounds. Someone in that house did it." She stared at me, though the glassiness in her eyes said she saw more than my skirt and cardigan. "She was three, Grace. Three."

Fifty? Okay. I didn't have all the facts yet, and I didn't care much for learning them this way. "Rory, he came in and said his wife needed a lawyer." I shrugged. "I'm a lawyer. You were gone, so I went."

"Is that how you work? You snatch up any case off the street? Maybe we can dig up a few methheads and dealers you can put back out there so they can continue poisoning kids." She shook her head. "This isn't the law I want to practice anymore, Grace."

My own anger forged a path from my stomach heading north. "Then you should have told me that before you asked me to come here, because I'm not going to sit in an office all day and write wills and lease agreements. I want to practice law that matters. I didn't spend thousands of hours studying and working my ass off to sit behind a desk when I should be in a courtroom. I couldn't care less if old Billy Ray gets Granddad Bobby Joe's farmland." I spit the last words in the worst southern accent I could muster. "I came here to work, and if you don't want to do that, then I'll stop unpacking and head back to Illinois. Just say the damn word."

She turned, silent except for the stomp of her heels, and slammed her way out the front door.

Chapter 3

The thing with Rory… She'd always walked out on arguments, and though she had some sort of super genius brainpower, I never understood how she planned to be an attorney if she left all her verbal wars hanging in midair. We lived for verbal wars.

Instead of dwelling on it, I put my head down and unpacked, ignoring the rumbling in my stomach. I couldn't decide if the intense and almost painful growling in there stemmed from hunger or the fact that I was unpacking books that would require repacking if Rory and I couldn't work this out. I folded the last box, set it on the pile with the others, then strolled to the window.

Rory had decorated our offices in my absence and pulled out all the stops putting together a bunch of thrift store finds into a space that proved form and function could be cohesive and attractive. The black and white color scheme flowed from the reception area into our shared office. In the reception area, black and white guest chairs provided seating for the clients we would one day have, and a crystal chandelier gave off starbursts of light. Black lacquered desks with white wingback chairs provided the focal point in our offices. She'd put some time in painting and selecting the perfect photos for the walls. Still, it felt more like the waiting room in a dress shop than a lawyer's office.

I made my way around a settee between the bookshelves as my stomach, once again, roared. "All right already. I'll find a store."

Our office, convenient in its main street location, sat across from the police station, and in an inspired bit of humor by the town's planning commission, a donut shop. Down the street, lights glowed in the windows of the businesses that hadn't closed up shop for the night. From my spot, I could see a dress and hat shop, an antique store, a beauty shop, pharmacy, and bookstore. Hunting for a grocery store gave me the perfect opportunity to roam around and see what the town was all about.

I picked up the key taped to the inner side of the front door with the note "Our new home" attached and locked the office behind me before stepping onto the sidewalk. Park benches with quaint flowerpots on each end ate the space between gaslight lamps lining the bricked sidewalk. The streets, instead of concrete paving, wove an uneven path of cobblestones that turned around a curve toward my new apartment.

Leaving my car where it sat, I walked three store spaces—an old-fashioned ice cream soda shop, a craft store, and a photographer's studio—to the market.

A bell jingled over my head as I stepped back in time twenty or thirty years. Definitely not of the super-store, big box variety with bright fluorescent lights and large rolling baskets, this one was comprised of short, glass front freezers and skinny aisles. Refrigerators stretched down one wall, and boxed and canned goods lined shelves through the center.

Not blessed with any sort of culinary gifts, I passed the fresh meat section, veering instead to the frozen pizza cooler. I snatched up a small pepperoni and sausage, said a silent prayer of gratitude for the creator of such wares, then roamed until I had two arms full of food. Hunger shopping.

A metal can of coffee escaped from my tilted pyramid of future hours in the gym and rolled down the aisle in front of me. I secured my purchases with one hand, then reached out in front of me with the other, wishing I possessed the magical power to stop the can's forward motion with the will of my mind. Since I had no such skill, I chased the rolling Folgers until it came to a stop under the raised toe of a masculine and well-worn boot.

My gaze started at the boot, then ventured up a long leg, across a flat stomach and wide chest to the prettiest brown—no, chocolate colored—eyes I'd ever seen. I straightened up in a motion designed by the *Cosmopolitan* flirts of the world to be seductive, sexy even, but instead sent the rest of my groceries into a slow-motion cascade down my body. My arms flailed in a *Funniest Home Videos* attempt to save any item I could snatch from impending doom, but I ended up grabbing nothing more than air.

Heat raced along my nerve endings, probably singeing my hair as I death dropped to my knees to scoop up my purchases. He stooped next to me and gathered a bag of cookies and the package of condoms I'd picked up on a whim.

"Ribbed for my pleasure." My voice squeaked and my eyes closed as I tucked the small box tight against my chest. *Ribbed? For my pleasure? Oh, Lord.*

"I like a girl who plans ahead." He chuckled and took my elbow as we straightened. "You must be Grace."

I cocked my head to one side, then nodded. *Of course. Small town. Big gossip.*

"I've known Rory for years, and you're the only thing she has talked about all week."

Oh, the accent. Every sound curved as it fell from his lips. Perfect, kissable lips.

Brushing a city girl case of weird stalker fear aside, I stretched my fingers out from beneath my groceries, and the pile wobbled a little to the left before coming to rest neatly against my chest. Warmth traveled its way up my arm as his hand clasped mine. He held on a few seconds longer than necessary, ending with a little squeeze at the end of the simple touch. "And…and you're…?"

"Blane Chandler." In a motion so smooth I hardly realized it happened, he relieved me of my groceries, set them atop a line of boxed instant potatoes in a perfectly stable tower of junk food, then laced his fingers through mine. "Come with me."

"No." I wrenched free and reached for my stuff, unimpressed by the caveman act.

With the gentle touch of his hand on my arm, electricity tingled along my skin. "Come on. Take a chance. It's just dinner."

I must have made some sign of assent, because he tugged my hand, pulling me down the aisle and out the door behind him. If he'd picked me up and carried me, I wouldn't have been more helpless than I was at that moment. He tugged me across the street and up onto the curb before I dug my heels in and yanked away. What the hell was I doing? I'd let some random, and, okay, hot, stranger drag me behind him without once thinking he could be hauling me off to meet my death, and I hadn't even had a drink yet.

"Stop." I yanked my fingers out of his grasp and back to my side, squinting up at him. His raw beauty brought a flush of heat to my cheeks, and I reached down. "I have pepper spray in my purse." With shaking fingers, I patted the bag on my shoulder.

He shook his head and chuckled. "City girls." He waved a hand in a wide arc at the building in front of us. "I don't know how y'all season your food up there in Illinois, but here in Texas, we have shakers."

A diner? With the smells of home cooking wafting out the door? I took a deep breath and held it, savoring the aromas of cooked meats. "You brought me to a restaurant?"

He nodded. "Yeah."

"Wow." My mouth watered at the thought of a decent meal, and my neglected stomach started a happy dance in tune to the growling inside.

"I think the special today is open faced roast beef and potatoes." He held out his hand again. "Come on. I'll buy you dinner."

I looked him up and down. Six feet of tall, semi-dark, and drool-worthy handsome and the offer of roast beef—had I stepped out of the office into heaven?

"Okay." I slipped my palm against his and followed him inside. The box of ignored condoms at the market pushed all other thoughts right out of my head.

My heart hammered as he led me to a booth in the front corner of the building. I'd no more than slid in across from him when his carbon copy stepped up to the table. My mouth dropped open. The gene pool had opened up and provided the world two yummy specimens of perfection, and I, lucky traveler, sat gaping between them. "Two wins?"

"Hi." The standing twin barely glanced at me. Instead, he turned a wary pair of eyes on his brother. "Did you bring back bread?" His accent, an English lilt, delighted my ears as much as the drawl I'd all but swooned over moments earlier.

Blane looked down at the table, then back up with a grin that robbed me of the ability to breathe. "Oh, come on, Jamie. I brought a customer."

Jamie spun on his heel and stalked back to the counter, muttering as he went. "Bloody well forget it. I knew I should have sent Mum."

Blane shook his head and raised his eyebrows as his gaze searched my face. "I was distracted."

"All you have are excuses. You're not getting any food until I have bread. You can starve."

A woman, whose shade of blond matched my Miss Clairol number 001, and whose eyes mirrored those of the man opposite me, glided to the table and ran an adoring hand through Blane's hair. "Oh, my little lover boy." She pinched his cheek between her thumb and forefinger. "We can't have roast beef without bread."

"Sorry, Mom."

"You have to watch this one. He's a charmer." She shot me a wink over his head.

I'd never smiled this much in my life. "I'll keep that in mind."

"Charm is but one weapon in my arsenal."

Undoubtedly. He had the bad boy grin, the looks, the body—oh, the body—to woo women worldwide. "Maybe, if you play your cards right, we'll find out."

He nodded. "Maybe."

His mother frowned and tousled his hair. "Well, charmer, are you going to introduce me to your friend?"

"Mom, this is Grace Wade."

She clutched her chest. "Oh, it's such a pleasure. Rory has been singing your praises all over this town since you decided to move here. And she spent hours and hours shopping to get the perfect furniture for your office."

"She is quite the decorator." I couldn't help but agree. The place looked amazing.

"Maybe you could give me the tour." Blane's gaze caressed my face as he dropped his voice low enough I doubted his mother heard.

A warm feeling in the tiny space below my belly said he wanted more than a tour of the office. I twisted my hands together in my lap, a move normally accompanied by a mu-wah-ha-ha kind of laugh. "Anytime."

"I guess you're anxious to get to work?" His mother had a tinkling quality to her tone that brought an image of a bell to mind.

Blane raised an eyebrow. "I heard you had a busy afternoon."

"I did. My first client." Small town America. Some things never changed, no matter how far away from home I traveled. "The Quinns."

He tilted his head to one side, his eyes half lidded. "You're taking *that* case?"

Maybe because of Rory's reaction, or maybe because of the crime Quinn's wife was accused of, my stomach clenched and my voice escaped in a bare whisper. "Yes."

He nodded, but a new chill in the air sent a shiver across my arms. I rubbed my hands up and down the prickled skin. "And I can't talk you out of it?"

"Probably not." I lifted my chin a fraction higher and met his gaze.

"She's guilty, you know." His tone, and the sudden hostility dripping from it, rippled across my skin.

Blane's mother toyed with a cross hanging from a delicate silver chain as frown lines etched her forehead. "She killed her baby."

Oh, boy.

"Do you all have some inside information I don't know about? A hidden video, or maybe a witness hiding in the closet that's going to pop up in the eleventh hour?" I had virtually no details of the case, but I had a gut feeling about the broken woman I'd spoken to. More than my skills, and more than my education or knowledge of the law, I trusted my instincts.

Blane's mother turned without another word and the bell above the door jingled as she left. To calm my fury, I followed her with my gaze as she stalked past the window.

"Grace, what if she did it? Can you live with it if she goes free?"

"I've never had a problem sleeping at night before, and I can't see this case bringing on a rush of insomnia either." My peaceful sleep had nothing to do with the three or so glasses of wine I drank before bed. Probably.

The weight of a dozen angry gazes settled on me. People in booths who'd barely taken interest in my arrival now glared at me. I couldn't get a good read on Blane or his brother since neither would look at me.

Blowing out a breath, I lifted my head and drummed my fingers on the table. "If she did it, I have faith the system will handle it."

"And you won't interfere with that?"

What kind of question was that? Of course, I would. My job demanded I interfere using every resource in *my* arsenal. "You mean, will I hold back if I believe she's guilty?"

Without a word, he lifted his gaze to mine.

"That's not how the system works. I'm honor-bound to do my job completely or the whole idea of jurisprudence means nothing." I could have gone on forever about my beliefs in a system that had never let me down, but he dropped his mouth open as though my words offended him.

"Even if you know for a fact she did it? You'll stand up there and ask the jury to find her innocent of murdering a three-year-old?" He flopped back against the booth, crossed his arms, and shook his head.

"I'll never know for a fact she did it. I wasn't there and neither were any of you." I glanced from Blane to his brother, then around the room. Had it suddenly shrunk? All of these random diner customers seemed to be much closer than when we walked in. *Damn.* "Blane, thank you for offering to buy me dinner, but I think I'm going to take my chances with a frozen pizza and a bottle of cheap grocery store wine." At least in the safety of my apartment, I wouldn't be scowled to death.

"Grace."

I held up a hand. "No. It's okay. I've been in this spot before." Not that I'd enjoyed it. I slid out of the booth and stood, then stepped past his brother who'd come to stand at the edge of the table between us. His mouth gaped open as I leaned down. "See you around, Tex."

I stomped back to the grocery store, picked up the pile of stuff he'd set on the shelf and strode to the checkout counter. When the cashier picked up the box of condoms, I stared hard at the swirling silver font. "Never mind. I don't need those."

"Round here, we usually let the man take care of this kind of thing."

I narrowed my eyes. "How very nineteen eighties of you."

She shoved the box to the side, took my money, and bagged my purchases without another word.

Chapter 4

The ringing of my phone, along with the sunrise, woke me from a sound, dreamless sleep. I'd barely unpacked my pajamas before falling into bed. Why was the phone ringing at six a.m.? I glared with one open eye at the name on the screen. *Rory. Perfect.*

I slid the answer bar across and said, "Hello," waiting for the ding of round two's bell announcement.

"Grace, don't hang up on me. I'm sorry. I had no right to act that way."

No, she didn't, but my dad always said a little graciousness never hurt. I didn't always agree, but this time, in the interest of our working relationship and the renewal of our friendship, his words rang true. "It's okay, Rory. I should have consulted you before I took the case."

"That's not how this works, Grace. Five years ago, I would have hiked up my britches and jumped right on it myself." Her accent lacked the sexy slur in Blane's, but still softened every consonant. "I know this case isn't about me or my past."

If her past belonged to me, I would have been shredded. She'd come home to find her son dead. Maybe because she'd already lost too much, or maybe, because, in her grief, she believed every foul lie out of her ex-husband's mouth, successfully defended, then divorced the murderer when the truth came out.

A few years later, thinking she'd finally out-lived the pain of her past, she took a job with a big Dallas firm and was on her way to partnership. Her boss, whose judgment had been clouded by the promise of a judicial seat in exchange for her help with the case, set Rory up to relive her personal tragedy in defense of a guilty client. Risking her career, Rory exposed the truth to the prosecutor. Legal tabloid shows put her life on the screen every night for weeks. They dissected her behavior for a long time even after the case ended. Somehow, she survived, but I didn't have a clue how.

"I never thought about how this would affect you."

"And you shouldn't have to. You were right."

She had courage I could only dream of. "So you're okay with it? Me taking her case and defending her?"

Her sigh ghosted from satellite to satellite. After a few more seconds, she spoke. "Yes. I can deal with you working the case, if you can deal with me being bossy, overbearing, and not looking at one piece of paper attached to it."

"I can. If you can deal with me being insensitive and needy while I shove those papers under your nose every chance I get."

"Deal." She chuckled, though the sound hardly reflected mirth or good humor. After another pause—I could practically see her switching gears—she spoke again. "Now that it's all settled, did you bring a dress for tonight?"

I sat up in bed, marveling at her expectation that, without a drop of caffeine in my body, I should keep up. "A dress?"

"For the fundraiser at the country club. Mom sent you the invitation a month or so ago. Did you forget?"

Oh, shit. "Fundraiser for your mom's hospital charity thing. Nope." I sucked in a breath between clenched teeth. "Okay. I forgot."

She laughed. "That's not a problem. I'll pick you up at nine. I have to run into town and pick up Jack's tux anyway, and there's a great store over on Main Street by the office."

"Sounds good." Sleep and a nice, long cuddle with my pillow sounded better.

"I can call Margie and see if she'll open early. If we leave now, we'll have more time to find the perfect dress for your Texas debut."

Apparently, being a child prodigy genius meant Rory didn't require as much sleep as those of us with normal functioning brain cells. "No. Nine is perfect."

"Great. You can get ready at my place, and we can all ride together."

Rory always had a plan.

We hung up and at nine a.m. on the dot, she rang my doorbell, and let herself in. I'd fallen back to sleep after her call and barely made it to the shower before she arrived. The movers had been indiscriminant about how they tossed my belongings into the apartment, and I rooted through eight boxes before I finally got my hands on a towel. Her hair glistened in an up-do that highlighted my lack of style as well as my inability to locate my hairbrush in the packing boxes still stacked in my living room.

Once we finally made it to the store, she handed me several dresses to try on before she discovered *the one*. The long burgundy dress draped down my body in a single wave of perfection. Before I completed one spin, she shoved a pair of shoes at me and I fell in love. Red rhinestone accents wrapped around silver stiletto heels. The shoes were dyed the exact color of the dress.

"Oh my God. I think I'm having a shoe-gasm." I clutched them against my body, ready to attack anyone who threatened our new relationship.

"I can see that." Her dry smile belied her own love for stilettos and sling-backs.

The entire in-store excursion took about fifteen minutes, and she'd spent most of that time pulling dresses from the rack. "So, we're done here?"

She took the dresses from the room and returned them to their hangers.

I slipped back into my own clothes, smoothed a hand down the fabric, and walked to the counter with her. Margie, who I immediately liked better than most people I'd ever met, ran my credit card and handed me a pen. I paused, the tip inches from the signature line as I ogled the low price.

Margie laid a hand on my arm. "It's on sale," she gushed.

"Wow. That must be some sale."

She gave Rory a wink. "Well, little missy over there took care of a tax problem for me. Any friend of Rory's is a friend of mine. And in my store, she gets the friend and family discount."

"I guess we'll see you tonight at the club?" Rory pulled the dress bag and shoebox off the counter, then shoved them against my chest. I was thankful she didn't give Margie time to change her mind about the price.

"Of course. I wouldn't miss it. It's not often I can get Hank into a tuxedo. " She leaned closer to Rory. "Hank and I've been married so long I think he forgot a woman needs a night on the town every once in a while. I'm tired of seeing that man in the recliner in his underwear. You are a lucky girl to have a man like Jack. I would pay big money to have him sitting in my living room in nothing but his boxers." Rory chuckled and Margie jumped to a new subject. "Did you get that Marshall girl to sit for you tonight?"

All this marriage and family talk made my ovaries shrink back in shame, and I tuned them out as they discussed babysitters, then Rory's brother and his wife's pregnancy glow. I hadn't been in a serious relationship in years and didn't feel like I'd missed a thing. As I stood there half ignoring their conversation, it became clear to me the only thing that would ever make my skin glow was a good facial scrub.

 Melissa Shirley

* * * *

Rory whipped my hair into shape while her brother, Tyler, paced and complained in her living room and his wife, Krista, applied my makeup. As the clock chimed seven, we walked into a ballroom big enough to house the town square.

A beaded chandelier the size of my bed hung overhead and refracted shards of muted light around the room. Candles provided dancing shadows on the walls and red and white rose petals lined the centers of the round tables circling the room's perimeter. Arched windows emphasized by columns stretched up the walls and a domed glass ceiling let the moonlight shine through.

"Wow. This is beautiful."

"Jack and I got married here." She beamed a smile up at her husband. "Best night of my life."

He kissed her lightly, and Tyler elbowed her as a woman dressed in gold with Rory's hair and Tyler's eyes made her way across the room. "Straighten up. Mom's coming."

He adjusted his tie as I watched her glide her way across the floor. When she finally stood on the outer fringe of our little circle, she reached out to pat Tyler's lapel, smoothing it before he leaned in to lay a kiss on her cheek. "Don't you look handsome."

She hugged Krista, put a hand on her belly, welcomed me with an air kiss, then moved to speak with Rory. "Something's wrong. No one's dancing. I knew the orchestra was a bad idea. I should have gone with a band."

Rory stepped from under Jack's arm and took her mother by the shoulders. "Just breathe, Mom. It's early. People are mingling. They'll dance in a little while."

"Right." Her mother lifted her head, pushed out her chest, and shook her mass of sunny blond curls. "It's early." She looked out at the crowd, some seated, some standing, not a frown in the bunch. "Should I have gotten a band? I should have."

"Mom." At Rory's sharp tone, Mrs. Jordyn jerked her gaze back to meet her daughter's glare. "It's early."

I took the time during their exchange to study the room. Pricey gowns, designer shoes, and tuxedos fitted by the gods themselves, decorated every single body in viewing distance. It took me a few minutes, but when I found him, the breath sucked from my body—Blane in a tuxedo. I closed my eyes and said a silent prayer of thanks to God for creating the man who had the sheer and utter brilliance, and foresight, to design and market male formalwear. "Mrs. Jordyn, I have a sudden urge to dance. I think I can help you out."

"Grace, I wouldn't be able to thank you enough." She squinted at Rory as she spoke to me.

I strutted across the floor to the man whose gaze locked on to mine with my first step toward him. "I guess you're over being mad at me?" He stepped away from his friends. With the smallest whiff of his cologne, the slightest touch of his hand, he enchanted me, and I would have followed him anywhere he wanted.

I pulled a crystal flute off a passing waiter's tray and took a big gulp. *Much better.* "I decided you're allowed to have your opinion." I tilted my head and smiled. "Even if it's short-sighted and wrong."

He chuckled and the melody of it sent the first flutters of a thrill racing along my flesh. "I think I like you, Grace Wade."

"Enough to dance with me?" I set the glass down and held out a hand, palm up.

"No one else is dancing."

"In a minute, you won't care."

With a grin capable of melting cold steel, he clasped our fingers together and walked beside me to the center of the polished dance floor. He lifted his hand, sending me on a stroll around him, then wrapped one arm around my waist. We moved as one in an inappropriate waltz as he nudged my body a bit too close to his. Soon other couples floated out around us, and Blane drew me closer. The spicy scent of his cologne tickled my nose and the hand I'd previously rested on his shoulder crept up to trace a line down his neck. I smiled as his eyes closed at the touch. "Your accent is very different from your brother's."

He nodded, and for a moment, I believed it a mystery I'd have to solve on my own.

"Our parents split when we were born. Dad was from London and he wanted to go home. Momma couldn't leave her family behind. Jamie grew up with Dad in England and Mom kept me."

"They separated you guys?" Growing up without anyone of my sisters in my life would have changed me in ways I didn't want to contemplate. I pushed those thoughts away and smiled as I smoothed a silky curl at the back of his neck. "And nothing short of a chick flick, you all ended up back here?"

He nodded.

"Your dad gave up London for her." Some fairy tales had happy endings. I had hope.

"I spent a whole summer with Jamie and Dad in London. When it was time for me to leave, I didn't want to come home and be cheated out of all the things fifteen-year-old boys did with their dad and brother. I wanted to hang out and do more guy stuff, but I wanted to be with my mom too. Then, the good Lord stepped in and gave me appendicitis the day before my flight. She rushed over there. They fell in love over my hospital bed, and here we are."

His hand pressed more firmly into the small of my back, caressed the skin bared by the drop waist of the dress, and my heart fluttered. "Their own happily ever after?"

"It took a little while to work out the logistics of Jamie leaving all his friends and Dad getting a job over here, but they figured it out. By Christmas, Jamie and I were sharing a room, and Dad had a job at the auto plant." He brought our clasped hands up to his chest, fingers stroking soft and sure against mine. His heart thumped under the crisp white of his tuxedo shirt. "Do you have any brothers or sisters?"

I nodded. "Seven sisters." As I spoke, an unfamiliar pang of homesickness shot through my stomach. Homesick? Me? The little stab had to be something else.

"Seven?" His eyes widened, probably imagining seven females jostling for bathroom mirror space. Or maybe that was my own memory slipping in before I could stop it.

"It was a PMS nightmare."

He shook his head. "Your poor dad."

"He's a big tough guy. He handled it like a trouper." I'd just turned seventeen, and my youngest sister was three when Mom packed her bags and jumped on the next Harley rider out of town. It took Dad about six seconds to settle the waves left in her wake.

"Sounds brave."

"Well, I never found a monster under my bed."

"I guess that's all a girl can ask for."

We danced a few more minutes, his arms cradling me, his fingertips tracing the bones of my back in little circles. As the music ended, we stepped apart, him to return to his assigned seat and me to mine. Instead of letting me go, he held on to my hand. "Wanna get some air?"

I tossed a look over my shoulder to where Rory and Jack sat. Sit with people who would want to chat about auction items and dinner selections or take a stroll with tall, dark, and Texan? I nodded. "Sure."

The patio overlooked a golf course and stretched around the building on one side, ending on the other at a decorative pool lit by floating candles on plastic lily pads. Bistro tables with cast-iron chairs sat on the etched concrete. As soon as we stepped outside, Blane turned and leaned his forehead against mine, drawing me tighter, closer. The night air cooled my heated skin, and goose bumps rose on my flesh. *Yeah. Night air. That's it.* My heart pumped anticipation through my veins.

"I want to kiss you." The purr in his voice washed over me, and I almost sighed out loud.

"Are you asking my permission or telling me a plan?"

He grinned and lowered his head to brush his lips across mine. That simple touch morphed into a tangle of fingers and hair, bodies crushed together, skyrockets exploding in my mind. For however long it lasted, time meant nothing, exhilaration raced through me, and passion heated every square inch of my skin. His tongue danced with mine, heightening every sensation. He brushed his hands along my hips, up my ribs, and back down again.

I ignored the first soft "ahem," tuned out the slightly louder second, but the tap on my shoulder accompanying the third demanded attention. Sighing, I broke the kiss, eased back a hair's width, and glanced over my shoulder at the offender attached to the poking index finger. "What?"

Rory looked up at Blane. "I need a minute with Grace."

He smiled down at me, brushed a strand of hair behind my ear, and tickled my flesh with a whisper. "It was fun while it lasted."

With a wink to Rory, he strode back inside the ballroom, every step punctuated by a cool swagger absent of a single falter. I watched the shift of his back, the fit of his pants, and sway of his hips until he disappeared in the sea of dancers.

After snatching Rory's flute of champagne, I downed it in one long, smooth swallow. Handing her the crystal back, I smiled. "Thanks." She cocked one eyebrow, and I faked a glare. "You owe me. I was really getting into that." My heart pounded in my ears, the effect of the alcohol taking more time than usual to calm me.

"He's the state's attorney, Grace. He's prosecuting your client."

Of course he was. I turned without a word and walked away.

Chapter 5

After circling the building, kicking at imaginary stones, and muttering a few curse words, I came to a where Rory stood waiting with a fresh glass of champagne.

"Prosecuting my client?" I turned back toward the lush green grass off the patio. "I should have known."

Rory stood with her back against the railing. "I didn't know you knew Blane."

"I met him at the grocery store." And he liked me, dammit. "What would you do?"

She shook her head and held up a hand. "Oh, no. No. No. No. My *Dear Abby* days are over. I don't give love life advice."

The scent of his cologne arrived before he did, seeping into my senses, heating my body before he pressed close. His arm wrapped around my waist, offered a glass of some amber colored liquid. I took the drink and emptied the glass as he whispered, "I do, and I advise you to dance with me."

"I can't dance with you Blane. My client…"

He trailed his fingertip down my throat, and I forgot every single reason I shouldn't be in his arms, looking into his eyes, and pressing as close as I could get.

Rory shot me a one-eyebrow-cocked look, then left me to fend for myself. Where was the BFF support? The strength in numbers? "You're the prosecutor, Blane."

"Not tonight. Tonight, I'm a guy who wants to dance with the prettiest girl in the room. No clients, no office. Me and you. That's it." His voice, the cadence and come-get-me sexiness, could have heated hell.

The chatter of conversations and clinking of tableware said dinner started without us. "They stopped the music."

He pulled me tight against him. With one hand on my stomach and the other laced through mine at my hip, he swayed us side to side. Every cell and pore in my body burned with heat as he nuzzled the spot under my ear with his chin. The friction of his almost-beard against my sensation-heightened skin added a few extra beats per second to my pulse. "Tell me you don't want to dance."

I breathed in slowly instead of gulping in the rush of air I needed to stop the dizziness. "Blane, my client…" His lips replaced his chin on my neck, and again, I had no words to finish the thought.

"You're not going to compromise your case by dancing with me." The whisper of his breath zinged tiny fires over my skin.

I turned around in his arms, pressing as much of my body against his as I could manage, and closed my eyes to wish for a few less people and a lot less clothes. "We should go inside and eat." I didn't add the *so I don't embarrass myself.*

A moan rumbled deep in his chest. "I don't want to share you." He grinned and moved back a full body space. "Okay. Dinner."

With a hand pressed against the small of my back, he ushered me toward my table. "I'll be back as soon as dessert is cleared."

My breath caught on his whispered promise, and I took my seat.

Rory's smile disappeared as Blane walked away. When she leaned close enough, I could feel her breath. Our heads nearly bumped and I moved back. "What are you doing?" She hissed the words between clenched teeth.

I folded my napkin in my lap to hide the trembling of my hands and pasted on a bright smile. "Eating dinner."

Well into the third course, my body still burned from his touch even under the intensity of Rory's random glares.

As a waiter behind me plopped a dollop of gelato from a crystal serving dish into the silver bowl in front of me, a voice from behind me interrupted the conversation I'd been ignoring. "Well, well, well. If it isn't *Miss* Wade."

If there was anything that could ruin this dreamy night, it was that voice…the deputy I'd threatened with the magazine.

Drawing in a calming breath, I put on my most practiced, fake smile, and turned to face him. "Deputy Wesley."

He looked around the table. Rory sat to my left, Jack next to her, her brother next to him, then his wife, and Rory's parents. "We were wondering…" He motioned to the bar and a group of men, a couple of whom mockingly saluted with raised glasses.

I leaned my cheek into the open palm of my hand, my arm braced against the table. "I can't wait to hear. What were you wondering?"

He looked me up and down, from cleavage to crossed legs, and my skin prickled. For the first time ever, I wanted to cover up in shame, or anger, under a man's attention. "Do you really think dressing like a whore and shaking your pretty little ass in front of Blane is gonna make that woman any less guilty, or make him take it any easier on your client in court?"

Jack and Tyler each stood to defend my honor, but handling men was one of my finer tuned skills. I looked over my shoulder and reassured them with a smile. Neither man sat, but neither advanced.

I swept my gaze over Wesley's overly ripe form. "Listen, Deputy Dawg, I don't know how long it took you to drink enough courage to come over here, but I'm guessing you're about six or seven drinks in." I stood, tilted my head, and ran a finger under his long tie. As I advanced, he retreated. "And I'm also guessing you have a collection of complaints in your personnel file. I could probably dig up a bunch of plaintiffs who'd be lining up to sue your ass until a card box underneath an overpass would be too rich for your blood. So, I recommend you don't screw with what you don't know about. And make no mistake, you don't know about me."

"That bitch is guilty as hell."

Blood pounded in my ears, but I shrugged a careless shoulder. "Prove it."

"People in this town ain't gonna take well to some big city *lawyer* coming here to defend a baby killer. I'd watch my back if I were you." He spit the words as though they tasted bad in his mouth.

"Is that your pathetic version of a threat, officer?"

He shook his head and smiled, holding up his hands and backing away. "Just a friendly warning, sweetheart." He tipped his Stetson toward the table. "Y'all have a nice evening."

I rolled my eyes at his slurred term of anything but endearment. My heart performed a cowardly somersault, betraying the courage I'd spouted. I waited for him to walk away before I turned to Rory and pursed my lips. "Wow. You folks sure know how to make a girl feel welcome around here."

"You make friends quickly, don't you?" Jack, because Rory still wasn't speaking to me, chuckled as he spoke the words.

"I'm a work in progress where social skills are concerned."

Tyler snickered into his napkin. "What the hell was that?"

I toyed with the stem of my water glass. "I'm guessing it was the low budget version of the welcome wagon."

Rory cocked her head to the side. "Grace took Gabrielle Quinn's case."

As though time shifted to a stop, silence enveloped our table. Six gazes rested on me. I lifted my chin a notch higher and willed the flush of heat to remain buried in my chest.

"She killed her daughter."

It didn't matter who said it, and at that moment, I couldn't have pointed a finger at who uttered the words, but anger pulsed hard in my veins. Had no one in the great state of Texas ever heard of the United States Constitution? Did innocent until proven guilty not apply here?

I picked up my bag, pushed my chair back, then turned to Mrs. Jordyn. "Thank you for inviting me. I've had a wonderful time." I hadn't seen Rory since we graduated college and vowed to remain best friends. I'd only talked to her a few times before she called to propose this partnership, but I'd assumed bringing me here and inviting me back into her life implied friendship. Yet, she hadn't stood to defend me against the deputy, and now she had turned our table into a hostile environment.

"Grace, don't go."

Her soft voice and small measure of pleading came a little bit too late to calm my anger. I shook off the hand Rory put on my arm. "I need to get home and unpack. My place is a wreck." I formulated the excuse despite the strong urge to call her out on her less than friendly behavior. It took a full ten seconds for my frustration to clear enough for me to remember I'd ridden with Rory and Jack. "I'll call a cab. You guys enjoy your evening."

When I turned to try to fish my cell out of my bag, I slammed forehead first into Blane's chest. I bounced off, jostling my chair against the edge of the table. His hands caught my waist and held me upright. "Leaving so soon?"

"Yes." I stepped around him, gathered the hem of my dress into my fist, and almost jogged to the door. With no ticket to hand the valet, I made my way down the circle drive toward the street. A sharp grip wrapped tightly around my elbow and tugged, stopping my progress. Inhaling a gasp, I jerked free, but didn't move to get farther away.

"Let me take you home." The curved sounds of his words softened the demand in his voice.

I shook my head. "Why? Nothing can come of this. You're the prosecutor, and I'm some kind of social pariah for doing my job. Run away while you still can."

"I don't run from anything." He stepped back. "I'm only sorry you do."

"What do you want from me, Blane? You want me to give up and walk away from this woman because her crime is too horrible for you? If it's not me, it'll be somebody else. You're still going to have to fight the same fight."

"But I won't have to fight you." His voice dropped to a slow, seductive vibration as he stepped closer.

"Does it really matter?"

"It does to me." He ducked his head for a second as though his words embarrassed him. "Come on. Let me take you home. We can work the rest out later." He blinked twice. "Come on."

As though Mother Nature planted her feet on his side of the ride debate, a loud clap of thunder rolled overhead. "It's hard to make a good exit scene here." I didn't have an umbrella, and the shoes, while one of the prettiest pairs I owned, pinched my toes and squeezed most of the blood flow from my feet. Taking the ride made sense. Lightning split the sky. "A ride sounds great."

He smiled, held out his hand, and led me back to the valet station. After a moment, a small foreign car with a shiny paintjob and a convertible top pulled up.

Blane helped me in and leaned down, feathering a soft kiss against my cheek. Then, he straightened and walked around the front. In seconds, we were off, zooming around curves, over hills and down straight-aways toward my apartment. He pulled up in front, and I glanced from my building to him.

I crinkled my brow, then offered a smile. "How do you know where I live?"

He shut off the ignition. "I made it my business to know about you."

I couldn't decide if that fell in the good or creepy category of potential boyfriends. I hoped for good and ignored the burning in the pit of my stomach that usually signaled something amiss. "Thanks for the ride, Blane."

He nodded and shifted his weight to the elbow rest on the console. His face hovered close enough I smelled the wine on his breath. "Invite me in, Grace." His lips grazed my cheek, moved down to my throat, and I tilted my head back.

I'd left home and everything I knew to turn over a new leaf, to change my wicked ways, but something about this guy plunged all my good intentions into a holding pattern. He claimed my mouth, used his tongue to part my lips and hand to cup the back of my neck, urging me closer.

"Blane, there's a light on in my apartment. Will you come in and check it out?" Each word was punctuated with a kiss after. That morning, I'd switched a light on anticipating a late, and probably tipsy, return. It never occurred to me I would be bringing someone home.

He smiled against my lips. "Sure." As he walked around the car to open my door, I breathed in slowly and exhaled in a whoosh of window-fogging air. His arm around my waist as we walked to my front door did nothing to calm my nerves. Instead, it sent a rush of shivers along my skin.

With trembling fingers, I fit the key in the lock and pushed the door open as Blane spun me in his arms and laid a breath-stealing kiss on me. My vision blurred and my knees weakened. His arms around me stopped me from melting to the floor in a full-on swoon. I backed in the door with his lips still attached to mine, heartbeat throbbing, hands groping the lapels of his tuxedo. Before the lock clicked into place, I pushed his jacket off his shoulders.

"Grace, you're not alone."

In a move inspired by too many viewings of *Poltergeist*, I spun my head toward the interrupting voice. "Hope! What the hell are you doing here?"

I held the front of my dress in place as Blane fumbled with the clasp of the halter top.

"I came to stay with you. I thought you might be homesick or lonely since you're new in town. And I unpacked for you." My youngest sister, at nineteen, took after our mother with her impetuous nature and sneak attack visits.

I glanced around the apartment. She hadn't unpacked. Unpacking implied putting things away. She'd rooted through boxes and found whatever item she wanted to borrow, then left the boxes opened with the flaps in disarray. "Hope, you can't stay here. What about school? Or work? What about Dad?"

"Quit school. I'll get a job here, and Dad is killing me." She frowned, puffed out her cheeks, lowered her voice and said, "What time will you be home? Who are you going out with? Where are you going?" She twirled a lock of hair around her finger. "He's suffocating me. I'm almost twenty years old for God's sake, and I wasn't allowed to go to Mexico for spring break."

"So you quit school? Way to show him." I pumped a fist in the air before dropping it to my side, still clenched.

"Don't send me back, Gracie. Please? I can't live with him anymore." When I looked at her, I didn't see the almost adult woman she'd grown into, but the three-year-old who crawled into my bed every night as she cried for our mother.

"Does he know where you are?" The words squeaked out as Blane's finger trailed down my spine. "I mean, go in my room and call him."

She pasted on her most endearing smile and took a full inventory of Blane from shiny black shoes to loosened tie, to those sinful brown eyes. "Aren't you going to introduce me to your friend?"

"No. Go call Dad."

"If you guys wanna have sex, you can have the bedroom."

Heat flooded my cheeks. I wasn't a prude by any means, but hauling a guy I just met into my bedroom while my baby sister occupied couch space in the next room landed in no-no territory. Even for me.

"Go. Call. Dad." *I love my sister.* I repeated it over and over again until I could look at her without clenched fists and gritted teeth. She flounced down the hallway, and I turned to Blane.

He leaned his forehead against mine and smiled. "We could go to my place."

Usually, when I went head to head with temptation, especially temptation dressed in Armani with a body like a superhero, temptation won. Images of peeling away his jacket, tossing his tie over my back, ripping the buttons off his shirt, and rolling around on a bed with him— no. "I can't, Blane. I wish I could." He leaned in for a kiss I cut short. "You're not gonna make this easy, are you?"

"I live ten blocks away. We could be there in two minutes."

Ten blocks? I blew out a sigh. "Rain check?"

He leaned down slow and brushed his lips across mine, then moved them to my ear. "I'm counting on it." Everywhere south of his whisper caught on fire. "Can I see you tomorrow?"

I gulped in as much air as I could. At this rate, he would think I had lung problems. "Oh, yeah. I'm counting on it, Tex."

With one last kiss, one that curled my toes and had me rethinking the entire concept of clothing, he turned and left. I watched him walked down the sidewalk. He leaned both arms against the roof of his car, looked up at me, and waved. As he pulled away, I shut the door and turned to find my sister close enough I could smell the pizza she'd ate for supper.

"Who's that guy?"

"A friend."

"Yeah." She smirked. "Whatever."

I stepped around her, shucking my shoes as I walked down the hallway to my room.

She followed like a shadow on a summer's day. "Where did you meet him?"

"Eight-Eight-Eight-Buy-a-Date. Now go away."

"He's cute for somebody your age." At nineteen, her tastes hit all ends of the spectrum. One week she dated a garage band guitar player. The next she loved a philosophy major who quoted Socrates and the Dalai Lama on the same breath he ordered a cheeseburger.

"Hope, I have to get up early tomorrow. I have a case to go over."

Her smile faded to a frown. "Already? I thought we could hang out, do some shopping, maybe sightsee. You know, sister stuff." She puffed out her lip and shot me the pout I'd perfected as a teenager. "We used to spend time together. I miss you, Gracie."

Only she got away with calling me that. Ever. I shook my head, examining the fuzzy tan carpet under my toes. "If you get up early, maybe we can find somewhere to run, then we can shop for a little while." I didn't add the word grocery or I knew she'd sleep till noon. "But I need to get work done at some point."

She grinned and threw her arms around me in a squishy hug that reminded me of her childhood. "Deal."

* * * *

My dreams that night flashed images I'd run across that day and every horrible memory I had of myself—Blane in a mirror wearing a tuxedo, Deputy Wesley with his crooked shirt and ten gallon hat, a ballroom filled with a hundred pairs of eyes staring at me as I strolled in wearing my coke-bottle glasses, high school hoodie, and a bad case of acne. By two in the morning, I had no intention of attempting more shut-eye.

I padded out to the kitchen, started a pot of coffee, and opened the file I'd retrieved from the police station.

With a sigh, I pulled out the crime scene photos. An eight by ten black and white showed an overall view of the bedroom. A white twin canopy bed sat in the middle of one wall, a closet to the left, and a dresser with a mirror on the right. Long gauzy curtains shielded a window behind the bed. The body, blankets, and sheets had all been removed before the camera captured the image.

I put it aside and moved to the next. At the following photo, I sucked in a breath, turned it on to its face, then closed my eyes. *Holy God.* I could only imagine what she'd gone through, the pain, the suffering. Flipping the picture up, I recited a prayer under my breath. It took a full minute to breathe through my nausea. After one last calming inhale, I lowered my gaze to take in as much detail of the image as I could.

Her almost transparent skin contrasted heavily with the blood pooled at various incisions on her body. Dark eyelashes rested against her paled cheeks. Long, blond hair matted against her head, and her body lay tucked on its side, one arm against her hip the other bent toward her face. She could have fallen asleep peacefully if not for the blood and cuts. Dots and stains of red colored the blanket pushed down to her feet.

Bile worked its way up my throat, and I stood, leaned over the sink, and pulled in deep drafts of air. The splash of water against my face cooled my heated cheeks and, after a moment, my dizziness subsided. "Shit." If I couldn't get through a single photo without the urge to throw up, the odds of making it through court slimmed.

I sat back down and pushed the pictures to the side in favor of the autopsy and police reports. The photos could wait.

Deputy Wesley, the first officer on the scene, documented every detail, and his report stretched on for nineteen neatly typed pages. For a socially inept human being, he'd proven his attention to fact and supposition.

I scanned for the high points, ignored his opinions, and jotted notes on a tablet of Post-its.

Date night. Babysitter—Jenny Walker. Home by eleven. Checked on kids. Emily covered completely, only hair showing. Male child asleep on sofa. Back gate open. No forced entry. House in reasonable state of cleanliness. Heavy odor of bleach. Four people in the home. Two adults, two children. Body found in bed. Empty trash can.

By the time I finished, notes covered the entire surface of my kitchen table and ran up the wall separating the kitchen from the rest of the apartment.

A while after the first rays of sunlight streaked through the blinds and left swirling patterns of dust in the air, Hope hobbled into the kitchen rubbing her eyes, her mouth open in a big yawn. "You redecorating already?"

She picked up a Post-it, read it, and smoothed it onto the front of her shirt.

"Put it back, Hope. I need these in the order I wrote them."

She rolled her eyes and slapped the yellow sticky note back into place. "You got coffee?"

I nodded to the counter and handed her my cup.

"It's empty." She picked up the glass pot and stared at it as though she could telepathically make more appear.

I pushed back from the table, snatched it out of her hand, and began the process I'd already repeated twice. As the water ran into the carafe, I turned away from the sink. "Hope, do you know if the girls have anything going on at home right now?"

She pulled out a chair and plopped down before pulling her knees to her chest. "No. Why?"

I sighed and finished making the coffee before I turned to answer. "I might need Charity"—a forensic investigator—"or Joy"—a criminal psychologist—"to help me out a little with my case."

I stared at my notes, a nagging feeling in the pit of my stomach churning with the gallons of coffee I'd consumed. My gaze ventured from one yellow paper to another, but always strayed back to one hanging on the wall. *Emily completely covered—only hair showing.*

I snatched the page off the wall. Didn't mothers worry about suffocation? With the note still clutched in my hand, I looked from Hope to the door and back again. "I need a mom."

She scoffed and rested her head on her knees. "Don't we all?"

I shook my head. "No. Not for me. I need to ask a mom a question." The gnawing in my belly burned for an answer.

"Doesn't Rory have a kid?"

"Yes." But the last thing I wanted to do was drag her into this. We'd reached a tenuous truce, and the question I wanted an answer to held the potential to start a world war between us.

"Go ask her."

I shook my head and tapped a finger against my lips. Who else could I bother with this? I took a mental inventory of the people I knew in this town—the hot prosecutor, Tyler, his wife, Rory's parents, an angry deputy, Jack, and Rory. Because my question involved the pertinent details of a case, and I was bound by attorney-client privilege, I didn't see another choice. "I guess I'm gonna have to."

Chapter 6

Because I'd been raised to bring gifts when visiting, and not because I needed to butter her up, I stood outside Rory's door with a box of donuts and a bundle of flowers I'd picked up on a whim from a stand outside the bakery. With the file stuffed in my bag and a practiced smile on my lips, I knocked and held out the bouquet in front of me when she opened the door.

"Grace? What are you doing here?"

I held up the pastries and stepped past her. "I brought food."

"Jack makes breakfast on Sundays."

I shrugged. "Okay, I brought me some food." Thrusting the flowers under her nose, I added, "And daisies."

She smiled and closed the door. "Is your new place a little lonely, Grace?"

I shook my head and followed her into the kitchen. "Actually, Hope showed up last night." I didn't mention the bad timing, but went with the headline. "She quit school."

"So your new place is crowded, and you came here seeking the peace and quiet of a house with a four-year-old?" She tilted her head, and her eyebrows formed a single line across her forehead.

"No." I hedged around the table. "I came here looking for the experience of a mother of a four-year-old."

She glanced over her shoulder at Jack who stared daggers at me. "Experience?"

I blew out a breath. *Might as well go all in.* "Not the experience of losing a child." I held up a hand and shook my head. "Not experience at all, I don't think. Maybe instinct is the better word."

"In that case, Grace,"—Jack whirled back to the stove—"can I make you some pancakes to go with your murder and mayhem?" He held up a spatula and a bowl of batter.

Rory roller her eyes at me, her back to him. "We're just going to go in the office for a few minutes."

He looked over his shoulder and frowned. "It's Sunday, Ror."

"We'll only be a few minutes, honey."

"I've heard that before."

She ignored the bite to his tone and motioned for me to follow her down the hallway. At the end, she popped open the door to a room decorated in every shade of blue she could have possibly located. Electric blue throw pillows leaned in the corners of the navy colored couch and a pale blue wingback sat behind a dusty blue painted desk.

"Don't mind Jack. Sunday is family day." She air-quoted family day. "He doesn't work, I'm not supposed to work." She curled up on one end of the sofa. "Sit." She waited a beat while I stood chewing my bottom lip. "Grace, it's a sofa."

Even in college, faced with her brilliance, I never trembled at speaking to her. Now, I had a case of the shakes mimicking withdrawal. With a nervous chuckle, I sat at the other end. Facing her, I blew out a big breath, and looked away. Gathering my last smidgeon of courage, I turned back to her. "I know you don't want to be a part of this case, and I completely understand, but if I had a question, not a legal question, but a question about parenting, would you answer?"

She tilted her head to the side, her eyebrows drawn to the center. "It's not that I don't want to be a part of your case. It's more I don't think I can."

I discounted her lack of faith in herself with a wave of my hand. "Rory…"

She pulled a pillow from behind her back and hugged it to her chest. "Your question?"

I clamped my fingers in my lap. There was only one way to do this. I pulled in a lungful of air and breathed it out with my words. "I read the statements Gabby Quinn made to the police. They went to the movies that night and came home right afterward. Nathan took the sitter home, and Gabby checked on the kids. I think she said the boy was asleep on the couch, maybe, but the little girl was in bed." My teeth swiped at my lips as my courage waned. "And this is the part I'm stuck on. She said the little girl was in bed with the covers up over her head so only a patch of her hair stuck out."

"And?"

"Well, when I read it, I couldn't imagine leaving her there with her head covered. Don't you parents worry about air intake?" I settled back against the arm of the sofa as Rory twisted her mouth from left to right considering the question.

"I don't know, Grace. I do, but Jack doesn't. He is more laid back with it all and says I'm uptight because of Kyle." At the mention of his name, a dark cloud passed over her eyes. "The truth is she might have relaxed a bit more after her little girl was born. With first babies, it's all antibacterial soap and not letting them get dirty. With the second kid, it's more a case of as long as they pick the worms out first, go ahead and let them eat the mud they're sitting in." She shook her head. "I would have moved the blanket down and checked on her."

"But you don't consider yourself a normal mom?" To me, her house looked normal, her life seemed as close to perfect as anyone who wished for that life could imagine, even taking into account her past. She had the white picket fence, dreamboat husband, and gorgeous child along with a career that left her time at home with them.

"I would wrap Haley in bubble tape if I could get by with it…if Jack would let me and I could get her to hold still long enough." She chuckled, but it lacked any mirth. "I wish I could be more help, but I don't think I'm the parent you should measure her reactions by." She shook her head. "I'm sorry."

I couldn't read whether her apology came sincerely and decided to take her at her word even though the ball in my stomach protested. I stood and shook my head, reached down to pat her shoulder. "It's fine. I'm sorry I interrupted family day."

She rose to her full height of five feet and led me to the door. "Don't worry about it." She studied me—workout pants, T-shirt gnarled by too many washes in a machine hell-bent on the destruction of my favorite garments. "What are you doing today?"

"I'm going for a run with Hope, then maybe a little shopping in town."

"We can go over her statement tomorrow. Have you talked to Blane about it?" She cocked one eyebrow, and I measured her disapproval in degrees as it took over her face.

"No. I'm planning on making a visit to his office tomorrow. I want to see what he'll give up without waiting for a discovery motion."

She chuckled and took in my outfit, seeming to dismiss the importance of the *Mork-from-Ork* logo on my shirt. "I'd go with a tiny skirt and something low-cut."

I rolled my eyes. "You don't think he'll respect my legal skills more than my fake boobs?"

"It never hurts to use what you have going for you."

"I'll keep that in mind." Not that I hadn't used my surgically enhanced beach body and the wardrobe that highlighted it before. I seldom needed dirty tricks pointed out for me.

* * * *

When I returned to the apartment, Hope had commandeered my bed and snored loudly while drooling onto my pillow. I shook her twice before pulling my hair back and heading out for a thinking run. Some of my best contemplating happened with Bon Jovi pounding in my ears and my feet smacking against pavement in time to the beat.

I drove my car out to the lake at the far edge of town and took off on the path that circled the water's perimeter. The place was mostly deserted, and I made my second lap before another jogger joined me.

Jamie.

Blane had that cool, dangerous glint, a swagger missing from Jamie's confident, not cocky gait.

I popped out an ear bud as I sprinted to catch up, then bumped him with my shoulder. "Hey, Jamie."

"Well. Grace Wade." He stopped and I turned, jogging in place. "How did you know it was me?"

I smiled and stopped. "I don't know. I think I just picture Blane on a treadmill in a gym."

"You're very observant." He grinned and the world became a tiny bit brighter. "There are marked trails in the woods if you get tired of lapping the lake."

Trails? Into the woods? "That's a little too scary movie for me."

"I'd have thought you fearless."

I laughed and stopped moving my feet. "Not so much. Spiders, snakes, darkness. Pick a phobia." His chuckle vibrated through my body. "I guess you're not afraid of anything?"

"Fear is just a prelude to courage."

"You should stitch that on a pillow." And if he could stitch it with that accent attached, I would decorate my apartment with them.

Sweaty, with my hair plastered to my forehead, I walked away toward the grass at the edge of the path and sat down, wishing for a towel and something to make me a bit more presentable. After a big gulp of water from my bottle, I patted the ground at my side. He shook his head and wagged his finger at me. "Come on, pretty. I think we should run."

"I'm already two laps up on you. You run. I'll relax." I flopped backward, the plush lawn tickling my neck.

He eased down next to me and pulled up a handful of grass, then tossed it out one blade at a time.

"Something on your mind?" I leaned up on my palms and nudged him with my shoulder.

He shook his head and continued mutilating the lawn while he stared straight ahead. "Are you dating Blane?"

Dating? One dance. A few minutes, okay, a few glorious minutes, of making out in my apartment. "I don't know that I'd call it that exactly."

I followed his gaze across the water. Though looking at him provided infinitely more entertainment. "But it's what you want?"

Awkward. Only a moment earlier, I'd hoped to look better at bachelor number two. "Um…" In true lawyer fashion, I steered the conversation away from anything I didn't have an explanation for. "This is a pretty deep chat for a morning run. It's more an over coffee discussion." I shrugged.

"Why did you take Gabby Quinn's case?" Instead of looking at me, he began a careful investigation on the handful of grass he still held.

"Do you have some quota for the number of questions you ask in a day?" He didn't look up but pulled his lip between perfectly straight, glowing white teeth. I pushed down a burst of attraction, bit back a moan. Was I attracted to him because he looked like Blane, or because he looked like Blane but seemed more interested in my thoughts than my body?

A question for another time I supposed as I looked into his waiting eyes. "Okay. Why did I take the case?" I'd asked myself that same question a hundred times. "Her husband came in and asked for Rory…" Jealousy when Quinn asked for Rory? Maybe, but in truth, I'd only known he'd needed a lawyer and I fit that description. "I just did."

"What if she did it?"

Gee. I hadn't heard *that* before. At least, not in such a lilting accent. "I suppose you have an opinion?"

"I'm trying to keep an open mind, but Blane took it to a grand jury."

I'd faced this argument before and had a reply at the ready. So, I breathed out a whooshing breath and launched into it. "They only hear one side, and this is a case where people want the easy answer so they don't have to consider the alternative."

"Which is?"

I shrugged and took a big drink of water to stall for an answer. "I don't know, a boogey man preying on their kids, or a passer through who fixated on a three-year-old." He shook his head. "Those things happen, Jamie. Accusing Mom, believing she could do it, let's people sleep better at night. It's horrible, but it's true."

"And when Mum actually is that awful?"

I tilted my head and gazed out at the path, considering his question more than any other. "When that happens, we have to hope justice prevails. We have to hope the prosecutor is as good as he thinks he is." I smiled. "And that maybe I have an off day."

"You're confident."

"I don't have any reason not to be."

He nodded for a full ten seconds before he stood and held out a hand to me. "Shall we?"

I did a full body just-woke-up stretch, then stood. While we ran, he gave me a little local history and a few murmurs of encouragement. He told a few jokes, slowed when I did, and sprinted to the end one step behind me when I raced to beat him.

When we walked back to the car, he smiled a smile that would have melted hell. "I run every morning." He toyed with the lid to a water bottle he'd reached in through an open window and retrieved from his car. "If you want company." His cheeks colored and I swallowed a smile.

I gave him one last, thorough go over before I nodded. "Around seven good for you?" Who wanted to run alone anyway?

Chapter 7

Driving home, I passed all the points of interest Jamie mentioned in his history lesson while we ran. A former bank, closed after a robbery in the 1950s, turned business offices on the upper floor and a boutique clothing store on the main floor, an ice-cream shop, the first business built in town, a drive-in, one of the last of its kind that played movies from dusk till dawn all through the week.

I pulled up outside my apartment to find Hope on the front steps reading my case file. "What are you doing?"

"Seeing what you've gotten yourself into this time." She handed me a slip of paper. "Someone rubber-banded this to a rock and threw it through the window of your apartment."

I opened the crumpled paper and rolled my eyes.

Go home, bitch.

I nodded. "Jesus. The welcome wagon here needs a good heads up on exactly what welcome means."

I scanned the street. A little, old lady walking her dog and a couple of middle-schoolers riding bikes were unlikely candidates for vandals. I jogged up the steps and into the building with Hope close enough she stepped on the back of my heel.

"Aren't you going to call the police?"

"No, Hope. I'm going to take a shower. After I'm finished, I'll call the super and have him come fix the window, then I'm calling Charity to talk to her about this case."

Her grin faltered as I puffed out my chest. "You should at least report it, Gracie."

"It's a nasty little letter and a broken window. Did you see the person who threw the rock?"

She shook her head.

"Right. There's nothing they can do." I slipped my arm through hers. "Come on."

She breathed in, wrinkled her nose, then turned away. "Good Lord, Grace. Did you roll around in a pool of sweat? You stink."

"I went for a run." I smiled in memory and wiped my forehead on her shoulder as I walked.

"Eww." She jerked away. "You're disgusting."

"You'd be disgusting too if you held up your end of the sister day plan. Remember? A run, then shopping."

"You went to Rory's and never came back."

"And you went back to bed." A faint pink blush stained her cheeks. "I knew it."

"Go take a shower. You still stink."

It took two hours before the super, a seventy year old Santa Claus wanna-be, arrived and another hour and a half before he decided to board the window and wait until the hardware store opened on Monday to replace the glass.

"You'll have to pay for that." He slammed his little black toolbox shut and stood. "I'll be back in the morning to finish the job."

I nodded and followed him to the door. "Thanks."

"In the meantime, if you have any more problems with vandals, give me a call." He winked and wiggled his furry, white eyebrows as he adjusted one strap of his overalls. "I got me a prescription for them Viagra pills you see on the TV." He leaned in. "I'd be happy to let you give 'em a test drive."

I glanced at Hope who nudged me. "I'll keep that in mind."

We followed him out the door.

My stomach had been growling for a good half hour. I could have almost eaten the dirt out of the potted flowers on the front walk.

I followed Hope into the diner. She stopped and stared at the empty room as I came to stand beside her.

"Grace, if the food is supposed to be so good, where are all the customers?"

I couldn't deny her logic. The only sound other than her voice was the loose bell still jingling over the door. "I never said it had good food. I said it had food."

"The sign on the front said best food in town."

I hadn't noticed anything about the exterior beyond the door. I shrugged. "Well, I guess if the sign says it, it must be true."

She rolled her eyes and turned a full spin. "Where do you want to sit?"

"I don't care. You pick." A picture on the wall of the diner as the building once looked caught my eye, and I stayed put to investigate while she wandered over to a red leather coated booth.

The photo wasn't dated but showed the destruction of the diner and the two buildings attached to it. A fourth building, the bank Jamie had spoken of, remained untouched.

I pretended to be engrossed even as Blane bounded through a swinging door ,then stopped mid-step. After allowing his gaze to rake up and down my body, he came around the counter and walked toward me with a wolfish smile. In three easy strides, he invaded every inch of my personal space. With his chest pressed against my back, he used his chin to nudge my hair back. "Say you're free tonight."

A shiver skittered over my skin. I tilted my head and turned, leaning back against the wall. "I have my little sister here."

He flipped a glance her way, then moved closer, aligning our bodies. "She looks old enough to babysit herself."

I shook my head. "I don't know. She's good at finding trouble wherever it lurks."

With a hand on each of my hips, he tugged me closer. "Family trait? Something in your DNA?"

"You can see why I feel the almost constant need to watch over her." My fingers, without any communication from the last two brain cells working for me, crept up his chest to rest on his shoulders.

He batted a pair of eyelashes that I would have been happy to have. "Live a little, counselor. Let her live a little too."

I did my fair share of that before arriving in Texas, but tilted my head and shot him my come-get-me smile. "Suppose I say yes. What's your plan? I mean, it would have to be pretty good to convince me to leave Hope home alone." Oh, who was I kidding? He could have planned to take me to a state execution. As long as he wore that cologne and nuzzled into my body, I would be there.

With his lips touching my ear and a voice designed to seduce, he said, "Oh, I promise. It'll be the kind of good that ruins you for other men."

"What about my client?" I wanted to smack the Good Grace right out of me as she used my mouth to speak. I ended the sentence on a frown.

He chuckled. "Well, bringing her along would be kind of awkward, since I'm prosecuting her, but if you insist and it's the only way I can get a date, I guess she can ride in the back."

I glanced from his smile to my sister. Blane's mother stood at the edge of the booth, her back to us, chatting with Hope. "I suppose if she doesn't mind going it alone tonight, I could skip out for a few hours."

He grinned and my heart palpitated. My skin tingled where his breath brushed against it. "I'll pick you up at eight." He lowered his head once more, and this time, instead of a fleeting taste of my lips, he went in full force, tangling his tongue with mine, holding the back of my head, grinding into my hips. He pulled away, leaned his forehead against mine, and smiled. "You better get back to your sister before my mom tries to adopt her."

I forced my breath to come in a normal slow pull in, easy push out rhythm, but my heart pounded in my ears, out of control. The man could kiss like a god and I staggered through the mish-mash of table placement to the booth Hope parked us in.

She shot me a knowing glance.

Blane's mother looked at me, a mixture of surprise and something I couldn't define written in her wide gaze and the thin line of her lips. She turned back to Hope and said, "I'll see you tonight then? At six?"

Hope grinned. "Thank you so much."

My little sister's smile beamed off her face in a ray of joy so bright my own lips turned up as I waited for her to share her news. "I got a job."

I patted her hand. "Aw, Hope. I'm proud of you."

"Now, you can't send me home." She sipped from a tall glass of lemonade.

"I wasn't going to send you home." At least, not unless Daddy commanded it.

"I was thinking. Maybe I could register for a couple of classes here." Excitement bubbled up in her voice and erupted in an inspired teenaged squeak.

"That's a good plan."

She yammered on and on until I tuned her out in favor of staring at Blane behind the counter. He looked up and I pretended to be engrossed in reading the carvings on the table. Initials, sayings, love poems scarred the wood surface and a thick coating of sealer protected the professions of undying commitment. After a moment, I sat captivated, reading them one after another. *VC+BS=4EVER... DAVE LOVES TARA... BE MINE KENDRA*

"Did you hear me, Grace?" Hope reached across the table to snap her fingers in front of my face.

I blinked twice and looked up. "What?"

"I said we should order."

"Yeah." Blane stood at the edge of our booth, pen poised over a waiter's pad.

"Just a salad." My stomach rumbled. "And a burger with everything." Another low grumble shook me from the inside out. "And chili cheese fries with extra cheese." He chuckled and I finished with a weak, "And a strawberry shake."

Hope ordered a chicken wrap and Blane walked away, shaking his head.

* * * *

When I turned fourteen, Dad sat me down and warned me about the dangers of riding in cars with boys. Ten minutes after I'd convinced him of my finely honed listening skills, my sister, Charity, guarded the bedroom door while I snuck out the window, crossed the street, and hopped into Carson O'Hara's Firebird.

Now, sitting in Blane's convertible, the wind in my hair and his hand on my knee, Dad's words came rushing back. Keeping true to history, I tuned it out with a grin at Blane.

"Where are we going?"

All I'd managed to get out of him, as far as details, was what I should wear. *Comfortable.* Since I doubted he'd be as attracted to me in my old sweats and Bon Jovi T-shirt, I chose a loose skirt and a silky, sleeveless blouse.

"Movie." He pulled into the drive-in, wheeled around the rows to the back of the lot, and parked, leaving lines and lines of empty space in front of us.

I cocked my head to the side as he tuned the radio and sound, matching the action on the screen warbled through his radio speakers. "A drive in?" With a popcorn box dancing alongside a soda cup on the screen.

He grinned. "We can chat without disturbing anyone, and if we have one of those awkward silent moments, we can pretend the movie caught our attention." He pushed a button on the dash and the top fit itself back into place. "And now, we have privacy we wouldn't have in a theater."

"And why do we need that kind of privacy? Feeling lucky?"

He leaned in close enough his breath warmed my skin as he cupped my cheek, then drew me even closer. "I hope so." His lips brushed mine, soft, slow, the kind of kiss filled with promises of sex, before he drew back and grinned. "I like you, Grace Wade." He tangled his fingers in my hair, anchoring me to him. My heart pounded. All thought of anything but Blane, his hands, his mouth, the low groan rumbling in his chest, left me.

After a few intense minutes, he pulled away, slid his seat back, and lifted me sideways onto his lap with my knees bent over the console. I didn't have time to consider how quick this was moving or that his hand had crept fully up my skirt to stroke my hip. Instead, I concentrated on the sensations of his skin caressing me, his tongue teasing mine.

He slid his fingers across my stomach, then fanned them across the tops of my thighs, nudging them apart as he moved to nip at my neck. Powerless to do more than moan, I leaned into his touch and spread my legs, silently begging him to go farther.

As he moved my panties to the side, his phone rang through his car speakers. "Shit. Ignore it." He captured my mouth with his once more as he used his fingers to work magic on my body. Desire pooled in my stomach and I pressed closer.

He slid his other hand from my hair down my spine and up the back of my shirt to unhook my bra. Without breaking contact, he reclined the seat until it lay flat.

"Take those off," he commanded, half panting as he unfastened his jeans, then rolled on a condom. With my back against the door, I shimmied out of my panties, the sheer naughtiness of the moment hurrying me along.

"Come here." He lifted me into position so I hovered above him. With a handful of each side of my shirt, he yanked, sending the plastic buttons clinking against the window and console. He pushed the fabric away and tossed my bra to the backseat.

"Get it in there, baby." He sat up, his teeth closing around my nipple. A bolt of pleasure/pain rushed through me as I slid down the hard length of him.

He tore his mouth away before scooting up the backrest. With a hand in the center of my chest, he pushed me against the steering wheel. "Oh my God," he moaned as I lifted myself, then moved down again.

I'd only repeated the move a few times, was just getting into the groove, when he threw his head back and cried out. His hips bucked twice, then he threw an arm over his eyes.

With a chuckle, he sat up and hugged me close. "That was"—*over too quick*—"amazing, but I'm kind of cramped here, babe."

I snapped my gaping mouth shut, snatched my bra off the backseat headrest, and climbed over to my own side. His phone rang again, and this time he answered while I fumbled with the clasp, then shrugged into my shirt.

"Well, what's he gonna find?" His voice low, he turned toward the window, then snapped his jeans and turned to me. "I'll be right back." He stepped out of the car and headed off to the concession stand.

After twenty-five minutes, leaving me alone to fume with a destroyed blouse and a cartoon movie playing in front of me, he returned. "Hey, babe, I have to cut our date short."

"Date? That's a generous description, *babe.*" Didn't date mean more than a quickie in his car?

He jerked his wide-eyed gaze to me. "Are you upset?" My cheek tingled as he trailed his finger down it. "I'll make it up to you. Tomorrow night is all about you. I'll leave my phone at home."

I cocked my head to the side, feeling more than a little used. And a lot disappointed. "What if I have plans?"

"You'll break them." *Smug. Arrogant...sexy, hot.* The car purred to life and he maneuvered to the exit.

"You think so?" I couldn't control the angry bite to the words, so I didn't bother trying to soften the question. Something in his playful gaze, the smile on his lips, and the finger pushing my hair back from my face melted my frustration.

"For a full body massage and a happy ending that will ruin you for all other men." He nodded. "Yeah. I think so."

If tonight's performance was the yardstick by which I should measure his promise, I highly doubted other men had anything to worry about. Of course, I was the one sitting in the seat, rethinking the speed with which we'd moved. After all these years, what had I learned? *Not much.*

And the mental berating began. Was I so desperate to be accepted in a town that already hated me I would sleep with an almost stranger who seemed to accept me, no questions asked? I shuddered at the thought. Aside from being as handsome as he was in need of a little blue pill, the town seemed to love him. Maybe, somewhere in my sub-conscious, I thought if they liked him and he picked me, they would like me too.

I turned to the window, unable to look at him while I mentally dissected my own behavior.

"I know you're disappointed we have to end our night this soon. I am too, and I *will* make it up to you. I promise." He twined his fingers through mine and gave a little squeeze. "Give me another chance. I think this thing between us is worth checking out, and I mean it. Tomorrow night is all about you. No phone. No distractions." His voice ended on a soft note that could have been sincerity. "I mean it. No phone."

Phone? He'd said it twice. Never mind leaving me hanging after getting my motor revved up, then letting me idle while he zipped across the finish line. And, in a cocky move that should have me kicking his ass, he'd brought me to a kiddie movie. Instead of noticing more than how good he looked, how perfect he smelled, I'd jumped on top of him like I pro-rated by the hour. But I'd jumped on without so much as an ounce of force. Half the blame belonged on my shoulders. *Shit.*

I turned to face him. "You owe me a shirt." But I smiled, unsure as to why I'd given in other than to appease my own sluttiness. Shame rolled around in my stomach. At some point, a lucky therapist would get her hands on me and force me to examine all my motives and behaviors. That would have to wait, though. At this moment, all I cared about was the smile half lighting his face.

"I'll buy you ten shirts." He puffed out his lower lip. "Forgive me? Please?"

"Okay, but I'd like to get to know you before I jump back into your bed. Or car seat." It was a small compromise to ease my conscience. I liked most of what I'd seen in him and had a moderate amount of time invested already. Giving him another chance made sense.

He chuckled and pressed a kiss against the back of my hand before drawing the tip of my index finger into his mouth. "I have no secrets, beautiful. I'll tell you anything you want to know. All you have to do is ask."

Thousands of dollars of expensive education and years of training to ask the right question blew to pieces as he nibbled the pad of my index finger. I couldn't form a single word. "Mmm."

"Is that a question?"

"I'm gonna go in and make a list."

He pulled up in front of my building. "Whatever makes you happiest."

I popped the door open and held my shirt closed as I stepped onto the sidewalk, not sure I could handle any more hormonal ups and downs. Before I could turn to wave, he zoomed away.

Chapter 8

After a night spent punching my pillow into submission and tossing and knotting my blankets into a tangle, I trudged out to the kitchen at dawn to make a pot of coffee.

Hope had strolled in after my second cold shower last night and fell right to sleep on the couch. Now she turned over groggily, eyeing me through her one open eye as I tapped my cup against the counter. "What's your problem, Grace?"

Replaying the previous night's events, I shook my head. "Remember when Daddy said boys were bad?"

She nodded.

"He's right."

Of course, he was right. He was always right. Had it not been a hair later than five a.m., I would have picked up the phone and apologized for not listening to him.

Hope padded across the floor and yanked out a chair. "Pour me a cup, would ya?"

I rolled my eyes. "By all means. Let me serve you."

"God. You're in a crappy mood. Don't take it out on me."

Her drink sloshed over the side of the cup, burning the side of my hand. Guilt washed over me as I considered her observation. "Sorry. How was work?"

She brightened as though she'd been up for hours dying to share her news. "It was great even though I messed up a lot of orders and spilled enough drinks that Jamie ended up carrying most of them out for me." She slanted a glance at me. "He's super nice. And that accent is dreamy, isn't it?"

I nodded, a bad feeling settling in my stomach, warring with my lack of sleep and too strong coffee.

"Did you know he works all day, then helps his mom at the diner in the evening?"

I plopped into a chair, cradling my steaming mug as though it held precious, life-saving medicine. "He's too old for you, Hope." I sounded more like our dad every day and, dammit, it added to my frustration.

She shrugged a shoulder. "Not for you." She almost succeeded in hiding her grin behind a sip of coffee.

I shook my head and tapped my finger on the table. "Thanks, but one Sheperd man in my life is quite enough." The bitter taste puckering my lips had nothing to do with my coffee.

"Bad night with bachelor number one?"

I took a big swig to keep from spilling all the details to a sister too young to be a confidante. "Something like that."

"Well, those hickeys on your neck say otherwise." She clucked her tongue. "What would daddy say?"

Hickeys? Seriously? Heat trailed to my cheeks and out the ends of my hair. I ran to the bathroom and checked the mirror. Sure enough. Three dark red blotches colored the left side of my throat. "Son of a bitch." I rubbed at the marks, wishing my hands were some sort of magic eraser.

"Why are you so freaked out? No one's going to yell at you. You're not a kid anymore."

"That's the point, Hope. I'm not some reckless teenager who can walk around with love bites winking at people from my neck. I'm a professional, grown-ass woman."

"With a couple hickeys. It's not the end of the world."

I pushed her out of the bathroom and slammed the door.

* * * *

"Hot date with my brother?" Jamie asked as I stretched a leg behind my back. He reached out and touched one of the bruises on my neck, a soft, slow trace over my skin, the caress lasting longer than necessary. The whisper of his fingers warmed me deep inside, comforting licks of a flame that promised sweeter things. "He's rather like a dog marking his territory, isn't he?"

Well, dog fits the description in more ways than one. Okay. Maybe my thoughts were still angry.

"Lucky you're not a fire hydrant."

"Did you come to chat or to run?" I snapped the words out a second before I took off sprinting around the lake. The heat in my cheeks didn't come from the sprint but from the burning desire to get away from his words. My hands clenched tight as I pushed myself further, the blotchy dots at the corners of my vision brought on by his words.

What was wrong with me? Jamie's teasing tone took any sting that might be perceived from his words. I wanted to hit something, hard. I… I wanted him to touch me again.

Pushing it all from my mind, I concentrated on the running. After the second curve and the first long straight away, he caught up and grabbed me by the arm. "Hey. I was only kidding."

His hand was a warm brand, and even after I shook him off, the heat lingered. I couldn't keep looking at him and looked off into the woods. A trail ran off to the side, and instead of answering, I jogged down the marked path, under a canopy of trees and beside a bubbling creek. The temperature difference between the lake path and here cooled the sweat I'd accumulated trying to outrun Jamie's astute observations about his brother.

He caught up easily as I slowed to take in the beauty of nature.

"Are you mad at me?" His voice washed over me, slow as though the answer mattered to him.

I'd never been a real outdoorsy girl before, but now, I stood enraptured by the peaceful solitude of it all. A squirrel skittered by, chasing a nut that continued to roll away as soon as he touched it. I smiled over my shoulder at Jamie. "No."

"Liar."

I risked a look at him. His slight smile, the way he looked at his shoes when he said it, the flush of color in his cheeks… Lord, help me. I whipped my head back to study Mother Nature's handiwork.

"It's okay…to be mad. I mean… I overstepped."

I ignored the rush of heat that sparked through me. "It's pretty here." This time I looked at him, measured the moment with that one glance. I couldn't stand out here and decide anything while he took the time to care if I was mad, said all the right things and looked so damn hot I needed one of those hand fans.

I'd broken the magic of the moment. He straightened and smiled. "You don't go into the woods much, I guess."

"I'm not really a wilderness walk kind of girl."

"Come here. I want to show you something." He led me a few yards into the trees, then stopped, looked around for a second, and set off again. "It's through here." We walked on until we came to a fallen tree almost as tall as my car. He climbed up easily as I stared at the obstacle. "Come on." He jumped off to the other side.

I gripped a branch and pulled myself up to stand atop the trunk. "I always wondered about the view tall people have."

He chuckled. "I don't know anyone that tall."

"In a town this small you don't know that Amazon deputy?" I looked down. The idea of jumping off the log sent fear racing through my veins. I shook my head. No matter which side I went down on, jumping was my only option. I choked back a gasp.

"Come on. I won't let you fall. I promise."

"No way." I looked both ways down the fallen tree. Neither end tapered to a shorter height. I was stuck.

His voice, the cadence and soothing vibration, comforted me, made me want to trust him to catch me if I fell.

He held out his arms and waved his fingers at me. "Come on. Don't be a princess."

I narrowed my eyes at the challenge, held a deep breath, and jumped. True to his word, he caught me in the air, and I powered into his chest, knocking us both down, me on top. His eyelids fluttered shut and panic welled up in my throat.

"Oh my God. Did I kill you?" I sat up, straddling his lap, ignoring the irony of straddling a second Sheperd in two days. Trembling, I ran my hand over his chest, looking for an injury I wouldn't be able to find with a road map if it existed. "Jamie? Oh, please be okay." I cupped the back of his head with my palm and lifted gently, feeling for cuts or abrasions.

As I leaned down and pressed my ear against his mouth, feeling for breath, he whispered, "You smell like flowers."

I scrambled off him and stood, brushing the leaves from my legs, adrenaline pulsing through me. Was I angry or relieved? I wanted to be mad, but my mind wouldn't let go of the feeling of his body, solid and warm, beneath mine. My knees quivered a little as I remembered the strength in his legs as they'd tangled with mine.

"I thought I killed you."

He sat up and grinned, dusting a twig from his hair. "I'm a pretty strong guy."

I took in the mischief in his eyes and the smudge of dirt left on his cheek. Pressing my lips together, I was determined not to smile or laugh and tried to frown. With a hand on my hip, I stared at him. "Really? Because I just knocked you down."

He bound to his feet, then took a step closer.

I backed away, imagining danger in the glint in his eyes.

He leaned in. "I think you should start running now."

"And why's that?"

He chuckled. "Because if I catch you, I'm going to throw you in that lake." He pointed to a spot in the distance. A waterfall from the stream ran into the bright blue water of a lake smaller than the one we ran around.

I giggled like a school girl and ran toward the clearing. When I stopped in front of the water, Jamie came to stand beside me. I smiled up at him. "How about a swim?" Sweat dripped down my back and patches of dirt darkened my legs. A dip in the sparkling pond sounded heavenly to me. I shucked my shirt, tossed it onto the grass at my feet, then yanked down my shorts until I stood in only my sports bra and semi-sensible underwear.

Without waiting for his reply, I ran to the water and jumped in. I swam out, then turned back and treaded water while I watched him stand there, mouth open. "Too scared?"

He scowled and moved to kick off his shoes and yank his shirt over his head.

I swam to the bank and waited for him to test the water with a toe. "You coming in?"

Even his laugh sent tingles to places that should have cooled in the freezing water. Everything about him counteracted the chill of the lake—the laugh, the rippled stomach, that grin, and oh, the accent.

"You bet." He dove head first into the water, staying under long enough I whirled to look around. After a few moments, he surfaced farther out. Water sprayed around him as he shook his head. "Wanna race?" He took off for the far bank, leaving a wide wake behind his kicking feet.

Twenty or so strokes in, a searing pain twisted my leg muscles. I cried out and stopped kicking. The throbbing pain hunched me over and towed me in a slow weighted fall toward the bottom. Lungs burning for oxygen, I flailed my arms to the surface. In a mad struggle to stay afloat, I took in big gulps of air immediately followed by large swallows of pond.

The tightening in my legs worsened, and I started to go under again. My mind flashed on my dad, my sisters, their faces blurring as I sank beneath the surface. In the face of sheer exhaustion, the thrashing and panic receded. Before I reached unconsciousness, and before my lungs exploded into shards of bronchial tissues, I became weightless, floating toward the light at the surface.

Was this death—sluicing through the water toward the heavens? Strong arms pulled me against a hard chest as we broke the surface. We bobbed in one motion as Jamie kicked his feet to keep us suspended in the brightness of the day and the gentle waves his movements created.

In the face of my impending death with his body wrapped around me, I forgot about the pain in my leg until he braced an arm around my chest and hauled me toward the shore. After a few swings of his arms, he anchored me against him again and cradled me to the small patch of sand on this side of the pond. I flopped back onto the grass and grasped my burning calf muscle. It throbbed in perfect time with my heart rate, and I squeezed my eyes shut.

With gentle fingers, he massaged my leg, brushing his fingers over my skin until relaxation washed over me. My pain ebbed and a new awareness battled for mind space. With every tender touch of his hands, my breath hitched.

"Are you okay?" His voice rasped as though having his hands on me affected him as deeply as it did me.

"Mmm-hmm. I think so. I feel like an idiot." Jamie's hands on my body had me contemplating how alone we truly were. Wasn't it Blane I was attracted to? And if that was truly the case, why was my heart trying to make itself a path out through my ribcage?

I bit my lip, and he bent my knee in, then straightened it back out. His gaze held mine captive.

"Did you forget to wait for an hour after you ate?" He knelt facing me with a half grin and his hand still resting below my knee. His thumb drew slow circles unlike any massage I'd ever had. Warmth spread through me from the caress.

"Old wives' tale," I said, voice scratchy.

Oh my. Maybe I had a case of hero worship because he'd saved me, or maybe I was simply attracted to him in the same measure as Blane, whatever the reason, my skin flushed. His hand skimmed across my thigh and my eyelids fluttered shut, the sensation blazing through my nerve endings, from collarbone to kneecap.

"Jamie." I had nothing more. Only a whisper of his name.

He inched closer and cradled my cheek with his palm. Heat smoldered in his eyes, and a low thrumming electricity crackled on the air between us. I couldn't breathe.

"You're dating my brother."

Damn. My desire went to war with my good sense of right and wrong. I couldn't sleep with Blane one day and kiss Jamie the next. Of course, my heart pounded and my palms itched to run through his thick hair. Sexual confusion, nothing more. They looked exactly the same. Being attracted to both of them had nothing to do with anything more than a surface issue. But, oh my, their surfaces appealed to me. Jamie… I wanted to swoon

    Melissa Shirley

into him. He said the right things, made me want to tell him stuff I never said. But I'd met Blane first…oh, hell. Why was this so hard?

I scooted away, and he dropped his hand. "We can't do this, Jamie."

He hung his head.

I missed his touch. Damn, what was wrong with me? "I didn't mean to lead you on."

He stood and paced two steps before coming right back to stand in front of me. I had a vision of long legs and loose running shorts and battled the urge to twist my head to have a quick peak up one leg hole. Instead, I focused on his face.

"He's not what you think."

I shook my head. "No one ever is."

As though summoned by Jamie's words, Blane jogged up the path from the other side. "Hey, beautiful." His grin for me morphed to a grimace when he turned to his brother. "Jamie. What are you guys doing out here?" He looked from me to Jamie, then did a slow circle with his arms outstretched. "Alone?"

Jamie stood, brushed past him, and moved to lean one shoulder against a tree. His gaze never wavered from mine as he crossed his arms. While his pose said this was no big deal, his face spoke of something else altogether. Lines formed brackets around his mouth in an intense scowl he aimed at Blane.

Blane offered his hand, clasping mine in a tight grip as he helped me up.

I shook off my embarrassment as I wiped sand from my backside. "Um, we went for a run this morning and a swim." At Blane's frown, I continued in a rush. "I almost drowned. He saved my life." Blane ran his hands over my shoulders.

"My brother took you skinny dipping?"

I looked down. Wasn't skinny dipping a naked kind of event? I still had on clothes. "Just a swim, Blane, with more coverage than my swimming suit."

He glared at Jamie.

"And I got a cramp."

He ignored me and took two steps toward his brother. "And as always, Jamie to the rescue." He kicked at a rock half buried in the sand, then turned to face me. "He's good with damsels in distress. Except what was her name?" He tapped his chin with a finger, looking every bit the tough courtroom prosecutor, and Jamie puffed out his chest, squared his shoulders, looking more rugged by the second.

The air around us grew heavy, and I moved to stand between them in case something needed broken up quickly.

Blane nodded, eyes on his brother. "That cracked out hooker you brought home? Was it Sheila or Sarah? What was her name?"

Jamie's hands clenched at his side, and I moved closer to Blane. I cupped his cheek and gently pressured him to focus on me. "Hey. Um, I need to get home. I have to work today, and I don't think I can walk back. Could you give me a lift?"

Blane continued to stare at Jamie as he pulled me close and kissed me, long and deep. I pulled away, reeling less from the power and intensity behind it, and more from embarrassment and confusion. "Sure. I'll take you anywhere you want to go."

He propelled me away from Jamie. "Hey, gather her things and bring them to Mom's. I'll make sure she gets 'em back." His tone held enough command that I snapped my head up to gaze at him. Fire blazed in his eyes.

Blane moved us down the path, stepping around to stand in front of me as soon as we came to a clearing. In a move I would normally find sexy, he ripped his shirt over his head and scowled. "Put this on." He shoved the shirt at me, then crossed his arms, blocking my way out. "What were you doing with Jamie?"

"I already explained." Venom burned through my tone. One date, not a good one, did not a boyfriend make. I didn't owe him an explanation.

"Let me get this clear…last night you're banging me, and today you're in your underwear making goo-goo-eyes at my brother? My twin brother? That's kind of fucked up, Grace."

I shoved my arms through the sleeve of his shirt and shot him a glare as I edged past him. "Go to hell, Blane." I didn't need to be reminded of my bad behavior the night before, and I didn't need his jealousy.

He grabbed my elbow and spun me back to face him. "Don't walk away." I jerked free and crossed my arms as he dropped his hand, closed his eyes, and sighed. "I'm sorry. You're the most incredible woman I've ever met, and I know last night didn't go the way you wanted."

I cocked an eyebrow and drummed my fingers against my bicep.

"I… I like you, and Jamie always goes after what I have. He's not satisfied with his own life, so he's pissing all over mine." He reached out a hand and rested it against my crossed arms.

"I don't need some jealous guy I went out with once acting all Tarzan over something innocent and… It was innocent."

He shook his head and looked down at his feet. "You're right. I was jealous because you're the kind of girl I could see myself building a forever with, and I don't want anything to ruin that." He wrapped his fingers around my forearm and tugged me closer.

I took one grudging step closer and he tugged again.

"Come here, baby." He lowered his head and brushed his lips across my cheek. My hands crept up his bare chest, and he grinned down at me. "I want you in my life, Grace."

He laid a kiss on me that robbed me of the ability to breathe or think. Anger? What anger?

"Let's get you home, because if you stand here much longer wearing my shirt with so little on underneath, I'm not gonna be responsible for my actions."

Halfway to his car, he swung me over his shoulder and patted my bottom as he walked. When he reached the passenger side, he slid me down his body, pinning me between him and the car.

"You are beautiful." He brushed my hair behind my ears, his fingers stroked over the sensitive flesh there, and I sucked in a gasp. "I couldn't sleep last night for thinking about you."

I grinned. "Stalker."

He winked and opened the door.

Chapter 9

Hope snored quietly as I walked into the apartment. She didn't so much as stir as I strode to the bathroom to wash the pond water off. As I blow-dried my hair and put on makeup, I tried not to think on the morning's interlude. Not twenty-four hours after fooling around—okay, having sex with Blane—I lusted for a kiss from his brother. I scowled at my reflection in the mirror.

What had I done? I'd stripped to my underwear, flaunted my body in front of Jamie, and worse, let Blane treat me like property while I left Jamie in the woods.

Something about the Texas air must have affected me. It had to be that. I couldn't tolerate any other explanation.

An hour later, I strolled into my office, case file in hand, and picked up the phone to call my sister. Charity had insight like no other. I'd called on her expertise to win more than one case. The check from the Quinns sat on my desk, allowing me the security of knowing I would be able to afford her plane ticket.

"Hello?"

I looked at the receiver in my hand. "Daddy?" Had I dialed wrong?

"It's my amazing Grace. How's Texas?" His voice, the medicine to cure all my ailments, boomed through the phone straight to my heart.

"I have a new case."

"And that's why you called Charity?"

So, I hadn't dialed wrong. "Yeah. Why do you have her phone?"

He chuckled. "I won it playing poker with her last night. Got her car too."

I'd lost a new watch before, but never played for anything more expensive than what could be replaced at the local Wal-Mart. "Must have been a hell of a game."

"You know Charity. Always raising the stakes." He chuckled. "Tell me about this case."

"I think I might be in a little bit over my head."

My dad was the perfect mixture of Ward Cleaver, Danny Tanner, and *Father Knows Best* all rolled into one handsome, barely aging Anthony Hopkins look alike. I trusted no one else to give me advice. Ever. I told him about Rory's reaction to the case, the way the town seemed so sure, and how everyone hated me for choosing the wrong side even though my nagging gut instinct said otherwise.

"Well, it's about time."

"Excuse me?"

"Do you have any idea how much money I spent on law school?"

I assumed it a rhetorical question and remained silent, even though I had a reasonably close ballpark figure in mind based on the statements I'd seen.

"I'm glad you're finally going to use all that education."

"What are you talking about? I've been a lawyer for a long time."

"Grace, you are the brightest star I have, and I sat here watching you take case after case you could have won in your sleep. I was beginning to think all those nights we stayed up studying for the bar exam were wasted. Now, finally, you get to use that big, beautiful brain. Don't be afraid of it, honey."

"Won in my sleep?" I worked my ass off to win all those cases, and it pissed me off that he was reducing my career to a matter of trivia.

"Oh, don't get kerfluffled." Daddy spoke his own language. "You did a great job, and I'm not saying otherwise, but all those other opponents were too easy for you. You need a challenge, a worthy adversary. And now, you have one."

"Are you trying to say I was lazy?" I'd lost sleep, boyfriends, and friends because I threw myself into making sure my clients won their cases. There wasn't one damn lazy thing about it. I clenched the phone tighter, ready to slam it down if he took this much further.

He laughed. "Not at all, cranky pants. You picked a safe zone and stayed in it. I'm coming to Texas to watch you in court. I want to see my girl battle it out."

I leaned back in the chair. He'd spent too many nights studying with me and later helping me read case law for it to be believable that he thought I was lazy. Then what was bothering me?

"What if I lose?" There it was. I couldn't stand the thought of disappointing him, and my voice wavered. "What if someone who doesn't deserve to go to jail, goes to jail? Amazing Grace won't be so amazing if she loses, right Dad?"

"Oh, honey. You will always be amazing and wonderful, some of my best work." He chuckled, then after a moment sobered. "You fight so hard and you win because if you believe it, you make sure everyone else does too. Remember Brett Hawkings?" Of course I did. He'd been my first real case, a DUI. "We all know he was drunk as a skunk, and by the time you were finished, he practically got an award from the mayor. You're the best of the best, baby. Don't you doubt yourself."

Nothing like a little flattery to renew my happy outlook on life. I'd spent all my teenage years, and the better part of my adult life, running from advice I should have listened to way sooner. Life would have been much easier.

"Okay."

"Now, you get off the phone and prove your client didn't do it. Then you call me, so I can say I told you so."

"Thanks, Dad. I love you."

"I love you. Call soon. Tell Hope to go back to school."

Rory burst through my door at the exact moment I put the receiver in the cradle. She thrust a newspaper under my nose.

Quinn fails Polygraph. A full half page spread included pictures of the Quinns, their house, and Emily alive and happy—all photos that had been included in the police file.

I stood and snatched the paper from her hand, then paced, skimming the article. A source inside the police department? Bastards.

I read a few more paragraphs, looked up at Rory, and back down at the paper to continue.

Authorities have concluded with no forced entry and the amount of rage involved in the murder of four-year-old Emily, Gabrielle Quinn will be spending the rest of her life in prison. The prosecutor, Blane Sheperd, stated he will not seek the death penalty. He prefers the defendant spend the rest of her life facing the horrors of prison as she is forced to remember the sweet smile of the beautiful little girl, and the way she extinguished the life that once grew inside her.

I spun and faced Rory, shaking the paper at her. "Who writes this shit? Some wannabe novelist?" I stomped to the front door, paper still in hand.

"Where are you going?"

"To break a date and maybe a leg."

* * * *

I strode across the street and straight into Blane's office. His secretary didn't stand quickly enough to stop me. I flung his door open. "What the hell do you think you're doing?"

"Well, good morning, again." A wry grin said he might have sensed this visit had nothing to do with kisses under a canopy of tree branches in the morning sun.

"Don't good morning me. You sent pictures to the press? You gave an interview that's prejudicial and it's"—I sputtered for words—"bullshit."

"Quite the mouth you have, Grace."

"And quite the cheater you are."

His skin paled. Maybe I'd struck a nerve there and wonder-boy wasn't wonderful after all.

After a moment, a slow smile spread over his lips. "I don't have to cheat to win, baby. I have the evidence and the facts."

"Evidence? Really? Where's your smoking gun? Your bloody glove? You have shit. Nothing." No murder weapon had been found. The newspaper source said they'd taken every sharp object and blade they could find and tested them all. Not a single item had been positively identified as the weapon used. Of course, Blane explained that away. He told the reporter he believed the parents had disposed of it before calling the authorities.

Bastard. I threw the newspaper on his floor and turned to go prove my client innocent.

Before I reached the door, he moved between me and the exit. "Whoa. Whoa. Whoa." He put a hand up in the universal sign for stop. I drew back in the Grace Wade sign for get the hell out of my way or I'll hurt you. "I have evidence, Grace, and maybe it's time we sit down and talk about it."

I crossed my arms and glared up at him. "Okay, smart guy. Show me the evidence. Prove you don't need to cheat to win."

"All right. But let's have a seat." When I cocked my head to the side and shot him my best go-to-hell glare, he smiled. "We aren't enemies, Grace. I promise. Just sit down."

I shook my head. "No. I don't want to *sit down* and have a leisurely chat. I want to know what makes you so damn sure you have the right person. Why her?"

"I'm not going to tell you my whole case, Grace." He ran a finger over my jaw.

I jerked my head out of his reach. "Then what do you want to chat about? The weather in godforsaken Texas? The feeling of all this down-home southern hospitality? I'm not interested."

"Grace, come on."

My breath broke as he drew his lips from my ear to my chin. "Show me the evidence I would get with a discovery motion." I stifled a moan as he dug his fingertips into my hip, pulling me closer. "Um, I want in that house, and I, uh… I want to see what you think is your big piece of ah-ha." I lifted my hands, waved them in spirit fingers reminiscent of twelfth grade cheer camp.

He moved back a step, then smiled and rocked back on his heels. "I have her confession."

"No, you don't." I shook my head and smirked. "Confession? Unrecorded. Out of context." I ticked the words off on my fingers. "Did I mention unrecorded? And she never signed a confession."

"Three officers heard it."

"Three officers who didn't think to turn on a tape recorder or a video camera? Three officers who dropped the ball. I'll make them look like incompetent rookies. Go ahead. Put 'em on the stand. I dare you."

"I have a little girl with fifty-seven stab wounds on a three foot body. Seen the pictures yet?" A small crowd gathered outside his office, their whispers and unintelligible murmurs floated on the air.

"And not one of Gabrielle Quinn with any blood on her clothes, hands, or body."

He pursed his lips and shook his head. "You want in the house?" He snatched his Armani jacket that perfectly matched his custom fitted Armani pants from a coat tree and shoved his arms into the sleeves. "Let's go."

I followed him to the street where he'd parked his flashy car in front of the building. As I popped his car door open, he grasped my shoulder. "How many cases have you lost, Grace?"

Not to brag, but… "None. And I don't intend to start now."

Chapter 10

I watched out the window as he drove. The houses, all two-story cookie cutters, had garages facing the front. A group of boys, maybe middle school age, played ball in the street, and two little girls sat in the grass having a tea party picnic.

"Tell me about the family." I had nothing to lose by asking.

Blane pulled into the driveway and shut off the car. "Nathan works in shipping at the factory. Gabrielle is a stay at home mom, usual money problems for a family with two kids, credit cards, car payments, a house they overpaid for. Their little boy is an average seven-year-old with video games and T-ball on Tuesdays."

"So, they're living the American dream?"

He shrugged a shoulder. "I don't know that the American dream includes murdering your daughter."

"Well, I don't know that *they* did."

"You're right. I meant *she*." He turned to me and raised his eyebrows while a smirk turned his lips heavenward. "Grace, the police did a canvas. No one heard anything or saw anyone out of the ordinary. No random dogs barked. No security lights popped on. Whoever did this lived in the house. I guarantee it isn't dad, and the boy is a normal little kid. That leaves a slightly off center mother who had problems dealing with a difficult little girl."

Difficult? This was the first I'd heard of that. "You don't even have the murder weapon."

"I will. It's just a matter of time."

I laughed and looked at the house. A police sticker still attached to the front door proclaimed it off-limits, but only a few small pieces of crime tape attached to a couple of bushes blew in the breeze. For eight months, the house had been sealed, abandoned by its owners.

I chewed on the inside of my cheek. What made this the magic week he arrested Gabrielle? The thoughts spinning through my head didn't make me like him better.

"You brought Gabrielle in now because Rory and I opened a law office and you were scared she'd take the case." The words came slowly, first with no conviction, then with a big *gotcha* flourish at the finish.

"I'm not afraid of Rory. She said months ago she wasn't taking the case. I arrested Gabrielle Quinn because it was time." As though he needed to reinforce the notion, he repeated, "I'm not afraid of Rory."

"I would be. She doesn't lose."

"Neither do you, and still, I'm not over here thinking of dropping the charges." He held out a hand, palm up. "Steady as a rock."

I gave him five and smiled. "You should be shaking. You have nothing. I specialize in making prosecutors who have nothing look stupid. It's a skill."

"Grace, I'll get her confession in before the jury, and there's nothing you can do about it."

"I'm not worried about that confession. My little sister hasn't had a day of law school and she could shred it."

I stepped from the car and walked up the twisting sidewalk past a Barbie car that had withstood sunlight and heat to gleam a bright pink in the front yard. On the porch, three dead ferns dripped leaves onto the wooden platform, and a baseball bat sat ignored against the doorframe.

"Evidence collection. Tsk. Tsk. Tsk. I would have had them collect everything in the house. Every toy, piece of furniture… This house would be empty about now." I brushed past him onto the porch and kicked at a loose board.

He hurried up the steps after me. "Do you not care that she did it?"

I spun around and spoke quickly, the thoughts in my mind racing off my tongue. "What if she didn't? What if there *is* someone out there preying on little kids, and you can't see it because you're convinced that Gabrielle Quinn is a murderer? What ifs are everywhere, Blane."

"Not in my world."

"Well, your world is a little narrow then."

"She was three, Grace."

"And it's a tragedy that her life was cut so short, but you are only making it worse by putting the wrong person on trial." He opened the door, and I pulled it shut not quite ready to go inside. "How do you know it isn't him?"

"It's not."

"Prove it."

"He loved the little girl."

"And she didn't?" I'd looked into the saddest eyes I'd ever seen when Gabrielle lifted her head that first time we met.

"Grace, have you ever been around a three-year-old who is allergic to almost every single thing you can feed her? Who still wets the bed every night and who shrieks at dogs barking down the street? Who wakes her mom up at all hours because she heard a clock tick and it scared her?"

I shrugged. "Loud clock."

He shook his head, waved a hand out in front him. "Beside the point. Difficult three-year-olds cause moms to snap all the time."

"And that description fits Emily?" His words weren't nearly as important as the meaning behind them. "If you think Gabby went around the bend, then why first degree? Why not second? Heat of the moment?"

"You don't cover up heat of the moment to the point the police can't even find a murder weapon."

I shook my head. He'd been in cowpoke country a little too long if he honestly believed what he said, but I wasn't about to play that card until we were in front of a jury of Gabrielle's peers. "What if the killer took it with him?"

"There is no other killer." He pulled a key from the little black mailbox attached to the brick and opened the door. "And I'll prove it. Come on. Let's start in Mom's room, give her story the thorough investigation it deserves."

I wrinkled my nose at the musty smell of a house abandoned and followed him up the stairs. Twelve steps from main floor to the second floor, another nine footsteps down to the parents' bedroom. I wrote that on a mental Post-it. The bed, still unmade, extended from the far wall to about halfway to the middle of the room and faced a television on top of a chest of drawers to the left of the door. One of the two windows had been boarded up—probably necessitated by the town rock thrower. Blane headed to one of the two doors on a near wall. "The bathroom."

It needed a good cleaning, but only because it had been ignored for more than half a year. Otherwise, it was a normal, lived-in house.

"Gabrielle Quinn called the police at seven forty-seven a.m." He knew the facts without the aid of the unopened file clutched in his hand. "It took four minutes for the first officers to arrive. The first thing they did after phoning the coroner was check the bathtub and showers. There was no evidence that any had been used."

"Did Gabby have any blood on her?"

He shook his head. "No."

I already knew there was no blood on my client, but wanted him to get into the habit of admitting it. I investigated the polish on one of my nails as though savoring the victory, but instead focused my thoughts on his other statements. Why would he think a dry shower and tub damned Gabby, especially if she came away blood free? Didn't that mean she couldn't have taken a shower to wash the blood off?

But more than that, why wasn't she covered in blood? Surely, a mother would go to her child in grief. Take the small body in her arms, hold it to her. Blood wouldn't necessarily have meant she'd killed her kid. To my way of thinking, the lack of blood was even more damning. She should have been covered in it. Of course, her husband may have held her back. Right then, I didn't know, but made it a priority to find out.

I slid a long look at Blane. What was his story, other than wanting to win? Something beneath the surface, something about him and his words that I couldn't quite pin down, irked me.

I filed everything away for later. Now wasn't the time. Instead, I'd go along with what he said, not voice my deep ringing worries over it all. Give them nothing, take everything. That was my motto.

I placed a hand on my hip.

"If the shower had been wet, you would have found that just as damning because then it would mean she cleaned up before you got here. The dry shower and or lack of water in the tub means nothing." By the time I got finished, it wouldn't anyway.

He pursed his lips. "Moving on then." He stomped to the hamper and flipped the lid open in a move designed by some academy award-winning director of the most dramatic movie ever taped. With raised eyebrows and a thin line for lips, he turned to face me. "We asked for her pajamas." He walked to a dresser between the two doors. "She didn't take them out of here. Your girl took them from the dresser. And the coroner put time of death around midnight. That's plenty of time to commit a murder, do a little laundry, give the house a good scrub, then phone it in."

That was the ace up his sleeve? I mentally scoffed. "Or it could have been the babysitter, or someone she let in the house."

"The neighbors said no one came or went." He frowned. "I know you think we're all a bunch of hicks, but the police checked. They canvassed and went door to door in the whole neighborhood. No one saw anything."

What did these people do? Stare out their windows all night long? "I've done my share of babysitting, and let me tell you, the neighbors of the people I sat for never knew when I was sneaking my boyfriend in. There are backdoors and sliding windows. Easy peasy."

"That's reaching."

I rolled my eyes. "Well, all you have are folded PJs, a dry bathtub, and a confession that will never see the light of day. That's reaching." But it would look bad in front of a jury, especially with the time of death versus time of emergency call issue.

"Maybe singularly, but if you put all that with the handful of hair the little girl was holding, it's pretty powerful."

"Handful of hair?" A knot in my stomach churned to life. I had examined and studied my Post-it notes. Either I was slipping or there was no mention in any report about a handful of anything.

"Consistent with Gabrielle Quinn's."

I shrugged. Consistent meant nothing in a world where DNA ruled the day. "This is the twenty-first century and technology is our friend. What did the report say?"

He looked down at his shoes, toed the carpeting, then smoothed it back into place. "The hair is lost, but we'll find it. It was mislabeled or packaged incorrectly or something, but don't worry. We have it somewhere."

My eyes widened and my mouth dropped. "You are out of your ever-loving-tobacco-chewing-red-neck-mind if you think that's getting anywhere near a courtroom."

"We have pictures."

"Try getting them past me." There had to be more. Something that definitively pointed to Mrs. rather than Mr. Quinn. "Why not dad? You can't tell me you're just relying on his undying love for the little girl to save his skin and put Gabrielle away."

"I've known him my entire life."

"So what? Just because he was your kindergarten BFF doesn't mean he didn't grow up bad. If she was driving mom batty, what's to say dad didn't jump over the edge?" I walked my index and middle finger over my other palm and "jumped" them off while emitting a low whistle.

"She went to a counselor, parenting classes, was treated for postpartum depression." He wiped his hands back and forth against one another as he wiggled his head quickly from one side to the other. His lips twitched from side to side.

"When?"

"What?" He narrowed his eyes and moved closer to me.

"When was she treated for depression?"

"Right after Emily was born." The cocky prosecutor, convinced of his own invincibility, disappeared and a slightly confused, less than confident first year lawyer stood in his place.

"Three years before her daughter's death she was depressed, which happens to one in four women." I might have exaggerated my knowledge of that particular statistic, but I would have the correct numbers researched, committed to memory, and testified to if I needed it. "Come on, Blane. You have absolutely nothing."

He nodded. "That's right. I don't have forced entry. I also don't have any evidence that anyone except this woman killed the girl."

"You don't have evidence that she did either." I left him in the bathroom and walked across the hallway to the first door, closest to the parents' room. Expecting it to be the little girl's room, my thoughts screeched to a halt when I found it heavy with video games. Sports memorabilia hung on the walls and bright colored paint glared in the green and brown of a baseball diamond. I stepped inside and picked up a photo of the little boy with his arms wrapped around his parents' waists. The picture, recent because of his size and approximate age, showed three fourths of a happy smiling family. At the bottom, the hand of the fourth member was visible as she clawed up her father's leg.

I tucked the picture close to my chest and made my way to a desk where a notebook sat open. Spelling words written over and over. I flipped a few pages and found a drawing. It was easy to pick out mommy and daddy. They towered over the little boy in the picture. I turned another page, then another, and five more. Each picture was the boy with his parents, but the sixth picture included the little girl. The whole family had dark red Xs for eyes. Gone were the sunshine and flowers he had drawn on the others. This one had a scribbled black background.

"Blane!" I shouted louder than necessary and jumped when I turned to find him leaning against the doorframe. "Is this still a crime scene?"

He shook his head. "No."

I nodded. "Good. My client asked me to bring her a couple things." The lie rolled right off my tongue as I tucked the notebook in with the picture and lifted my head. More important than what I decided to take, I could come and go as I pleased. "I want to see the little girl's room."

I backed away from the desk, then shuffled some of the clothes inside an open closet as he walked away. Nothing extraordinary jumped out at me, but something niggled, something I should see that I couldn't put my finger on.

"Are you coming?" His voice echoed from the hallway.

I took a quick glance at the door, whipped out my cell, and snapped a photo of the closet. Something about it…

A moment later, I stood behind Blane in the little girl's room—about half a size smaller than her brother's. Nothing had changed from the crime scene photos, but I dropped to my knees and looked under the bed. *Damn.* It wasn't like I expected to find the murder weapon, or a glaring sign flashing the killer's name in bright red neon, or even dull blue Crayola, but it would have been nice. I looked up at Blane and shrugged as I sat back on my heels. "Is this the only room where they found blood?"

He nodded. "There wasn't so much as a drip anywhere else in the house. Not the basement, garage, cars, or anywhere else."

"Did you check her shower drain?"

He nodded. "Nothing."

"So again, why her mother?"

He raked his fingers through his hair. "I don't have to explain it to you, Grace."

"I know." I stood up and walked to the closet. The door was open, a simple sliding wooden panel on a metal frame, revealing more lacy dresses and shoes than any other little girl's closet I'd ever seen. I pulled a couple out and examined the price tags still attached. "Wow. For not liking her, they bought her some fancy stuff."

"Hello?" Rory's voice floated up the stairs a couple of seconds before she appeared in the doorway.

Chapter 11

Rory frowned, the grim set of her lips betraying the strength in her voice. Being here, in this house, couldn't be easy for her. "I went to your office, Blane. We had a meeting scheduled for that city council thing. Your secretary said you were here with Grace."

He checked his watch. "Damn, Rory. I forgot. Grace wanted to see the crime scene."

"And we all know how important it is to give your opponent the guided tour." Rory didn't smile, instead her brow creased and she pressed her lips together. "Well, I'm here now. I'm sure the county has more important things for you to concentrate on. I'll give Grace a ride back."

She put her body between ours, and suddenly the room became crowded.

He nodded once, shot me a squinted look, and left.

With the click of the front door latch, she wheeled to face me. "Grace, what are you doing?"

"I just spent the last hour hearing his case, and he doesn't have one."

She shook her head. "He has one, some ace up his sleeve he isn't going to play until the jury is watching. This"—she waved an arm around the room—"is about illusions and misdirection, smoke and mirrors. Whatever you think he gave you is bullshit. He doesn't play fair."

I shrugged. Neither did I. "I'll keep it in mind."

"So what are we doing here?"

"Looking around."

"And?"

"I don't know. Something isn't right. What do you know about Nathan Quinn?"

She shook her head and walked to lean against the dresser. "Regular guy. Works in a factory. Goes to church on Sundays." She crossed her arms. "He's lived here since he was a kid and everybody knows him."

 Melissa Shirley

"Do people like him? Is he trustworthy?"

"I don't know. I've never seen anything to indicate otherwise."

Something about the man gave me a bad feeling in my stomach. "I really want to know why her and not him. He has no alibi either, and he found the body, or claimed to. He arrived home at the same time she did." I gauged Rory's reaction. "And I found this." I opened the boy's notebook to the page with the drawing that had me take the book, then snapped it shut. I couldn't decide if it meant anything or not and there was no point in drawing her further in until I knew for sure. "Never mind. Let's get out of here. I've seen enough for now, and I want to go over the crime scene reports."

She looked at the picture in my hands. "You taking that to Gabrielle?"

I nodded. "Yes. I thought she might need a little something. She couldn't come back here after...." Plus the picture bothered me on some level that had me staring at it as I followed Rory downstairs and out the front door.

We left the house in the same condition as Blane and I found it, minus the items I'd taken from the boy's room. On the drive back, Rory kept one eye on the road and one on me. She pulled up in front of the office and gasped. "Holy shit. What the hell?"

"What?"

I followed the direction of her gaze to my car. Flat tires. Every window busted. *Burn in Hell* spray-painted on the side. And right across the street from the police station.

"For the love of God!" My shriek bounced around the interior of her car and back at me with piercing clarity.

I bounded out of her SUV and over to my poor Nissan.

"Grace? You okay?"

I ignored her, stomped across the street, and flung the door open. It crashed against the brick front and rattled, but the glass stayed intact. The young man behind the information sign pulled his feet off the desk and sat up straight. "Can I help you, miss?"

"Yeah. You can tell me how my car, sitting on the street right across from you, could be vandalized." I picked up the community copy of *Bikes and Babes* and flung it behind me. "Who the frick is the sheriff around here?"

Jamie walked around the corner, all dressed in black from his T-shirt to his cargo pants, and I sucked in a breath.

"That would be me."

"You're kidding, right?" He shook his head, and I aimed a serious stink-eye at him. "You're the sheriff?"

He raised his eyebrows and nodded.

"And it didn't occur to you to mention it?"

"Does it matter?"

"Actually, it does now." I grabbed his arm and dragged him outside. Three steps toward my car, my equilibrium jolted and I stumbled. He reached out and caught me around the waist. My stomach tingled where his fingertips burned through my shirt. As soon as my breathing leveled out, I jabbed a finger toward the opposite side of the street. "That's my freaking car. And this morning, someone threw a rock through my apartment window."

The vandals in this town had no fear—probably no reason for it, since an arrest wouldn't likely result from the damage. "What the hell kind of sheriff are you if this can happen right under your nose?" I'd reached my limit for patience.

"Wait here." He turned and left me gaping at the broken glass and spray-painted driver's side. I knew enough not to touch the car, but whipped out my cell and took a couple pictures.

Rory walked inside the building and came out a second later, tears streaming down her face. "Our office is trashed. They destroyed everything."

"Shit."

She had her ear pressed against her phone as she sobbed into it.

I walked with a semi-calm fury to the office, flung the door open, and walked inside. "Oh."

No wonder Rory was devastated. Stuffing bits from every piece of furniture we owned lay about the room in piles of what looked like snow dotting the surfaces. Thousands of dollars worth of legal volumes laid in ruins, their spines torn apart, pages littering the floor. Papers and file folders covered every available space inside the office. I shut the door with a quiet click of the latch and walked back outside to stand next to a still sobbing Rory.

Leaning against the trunk of my car, I waited for Jamie to return and Rory to get off the phone, or someone to pass by and throw a rotten tomato or two in my direction. Instead, passersby merely stopped passing and stood gawking.

Blane, still in Armani, raced out of the front door of the police station and pulled me into his arms. "I'm sorry, Grace." When I struggled to break free of his possessive and public grasp, he forced my head against his chest. "Don't look."

"It's not a dead body, Blane. It's just a car." And fortunately not one I loved.

I'd left that one in a garage back in Illinois. This time, I extracted myself from his arms with more force than necessary at the same moment he loosened his hold and I stumbled backward. My heels hit the curb, and I landed in a cement plant holder. I sat down on the begonias, squashing them completely. Unfortunately, someone had recently watered them and wet mud soaked through my clothes to my ass. "Perfect."

I stood and brushed my hand across my backside, coming away with a handful of black potting soil. "Oh, enough already. I'm going home." I turned and stalked my way through the growing crowd.

"What about your car?" Blane called after me.

"You can have it."

Ten minutes later, I slammed my apartment door behind me and headed straight for the shower. I wanted to start the entire day over again.

After I ran the hot water cold, I stepped out and looked into the mirror. "Okay. So, Blane has something. Something big." Not only did I not like to lose, I often talked to myself to make sure it didn't happen. So far, so good. "What could it be?" I checked off the possibilities. "Is he hiding the murder weapon?" I shook my head. "No. Not enough shock value, but he's definitely keeping something from me." I smiled at my reflection through the fog on the mirror. "Okay, big boy. I do want a happy ending. Just not the one you have planned."

By the time the doorbell rang, I'd changed and torn all my Post-its off the wall. Holding the pile in my hand, I opened the door to find Jamie, still in uniform, on the other side. I narrowed my eyes and willed my traitorous heart to slow, my hands not to tremble, and my stomach to calm down. "What do you want?"

"I came here to take a statement about the broken window and to let you know Blane made arrangements to get your car towed."

I left the door open and walked away.

"I thought you were the save the damsel guy."

"He has his moments."

I shrugged and plopped down onto the sofa. "Well, there's the window." I pointed behind me, then handed him the note I'd left folded on the coffee table. "And here's what was wrapped around the rock that broke it. I have nothing more to say about it."

He stood back. "Are you angry at me?" His eyes darkened and I looked away, concentrating on the peeling of my nail polish.

"Well, *sheriff,* you seem a bit like a liar to me."

"I didn't lie to you. I just didn't tell you. That's different."

Every syllable curved, and my heart pounded in my chest. *Stop it. You're mad at him.*

"To a liar, maybe. To me, it's the same." I shook the cobwebs out of my head and hardened my resolve to remain as pissy with him as I could. "Listen, Jamie, you have what you came for. Now shut the door on your way out, okay?"

He nodded and almost made it to the door when he turned back to face me. "I didn't lie to you, Grace. I wouldn't lie to you."

He walked out, and I sat on the sofa for a full ten minutes before I moved again. Brothers, both on the wrong side of my fence. Not that I would substitute one for the other, but what were the odds? I had a sudden hankering to Google identical twins. I wanted to see if anyone had ever thought to do a study to determine if their attractions to women mirrored one another as much as their looks, or if this thing with me had more to do with the underlying rivalry between these specific brothers. My attraction made perfect sense. They were identical.

I shook off the thoughts and grabbed my purse. If the inner offices were as destroyed as the reception area, Rory would need help cleaning it up. I couldn't spy on Blane until later, so I headed down the street to pitch in.

She sat in the middle of the floor surrounded by file folders and crumpled papers. A thick binder full of untouched papers sat open in her lap. Not a single piece inside had been threatened, shredded, or marked in any way. "What's that?"

She shrugged and slapped the lid closed. "A file I put together on Kyle's case and on the McCaferty case. I was on my game then, and I thought maybe if I read through this, reread it, I'd be able to figure out how I missed all those clues in the beginning, how they pulled such an elaborate scheme on me."

"Rory." I sat beside her and took the binder, then flipped through a couple of pages. Intimidated by her absolute legal prowess, I shut the book and looked over at her.

"Grace, five years ago, I was a good lawyer. I had faith in what I did and who I was."

I nodded, unwilling to break eye contact until she'd gotten this all out. I would wait to tell her that skills like hers didn't fade or go away. She'd simply lost confidence in them.

"Today, I wanted on Gabby's case so bad. I came in here and this binder"—she took back the five inches of legal pleadings and evidence photos, along with details and hand-written notes about the McCafferty case—"sat waiting for me. You know where it was?"

I shook my head.

"On my desk. Undisturbed." She smoothed a hand over the cover. "Just like this." She stood and paced. "They wanted me to find it, Grace, to remind me nothing good can come from fighting for this woman. And you know what? That pisses me off."

"So, what now?" I bit my lip. The Rory spark danced in her eyes as she regained some of what her ex-husband's case and the one mentioned in the binder had taken from her.

"I think we go see your client. Something's going on here that's bigger than Gabrielle Quinn." She bent down, picked up a bunch of papers, then tossed them onto the desk. "Let's figure out what it is."

Chapter 12

When we arrived, Nathan Quinn sat across from his wife at a visitor's table. His fists were clenched atop the table, and he spoke quietly but through gritted teeth. I couldn't make out the words, but his anger glowed through his posture and the glare he directed at her. He jerked his gaze toward us when we approached, and I took a seat next to Gabrielle. Rory remained standing at the edge of the table. Gabrielle looked up, her eyes rimmed in red, her nose running.

"You okay?"

She flicked her eyes at her husband, then back down. "Yes."

Nathan rose to his feet and stalked to the exit. I patted Gabby on the back and raced to follow him out. He had a stride I couldn't match, and I jogged to catch up.

"Nathan, wait."

He whirled and almost knocked me down with a waving arm. I ducked out of the way, then straightened to my full height. Good Lord. All the men in this town towered over me. Maybe everything was bigger in Texas after all.

"What?"

"I need to ask you what happened the night Emily died." I kept my voice measured, calm, hid the tremors of my hands by clasping them together in front of me. Something about this guy gave me the creeps and I shivered.

His eyes narrowed and he crossed his arms. "Why me? I don't know what happened. You should be asking her." He nodded his head in his wife's direction.

I tilted my chin, heard the meaning behind what he hadn't said. "You think she did it?"

"Well, I sure as hell didn't do it."

"What happened that night?" Maybe hearing it from his perspective would enlighten me to some of the things Gabby hadn't said, bring out a discrepancy I'd been unable to nail down so far. Or, more unlikely, maybe it would reinforce her story.

He glared at me, a sneer turning his somewhat handsome face angry. "My daughter died, and I have suffered in ways no one understands. I lost my baby girl, my wife, my job, my house. I have nothing left." The muscle in his jaw ticked as he shook his head. "I have a son I need to try and explain this to. His whole life's been torn apart by a…a…mistake he doesn't understand. Excuse me."

I stood there for a full minute watching the door he'd stomped through. He suffered? No. His daughter suffered, and now his wife was suffering. This tantrum seemed a bit over the top, since he wasn't the one sitting in jail. What had he said? A mistake he didn't understand? I'd heard murder described as a mistake before, usually by the client I defended, but the way he'd said it, softened his voice, that meant something. I just had to figure out what.

With my mental notes piling up, I turned away from the door and made my way back to the table. Rory had an arm around Gabby's shoulders as she spoke quietly to the woman.

I plopped down across from them, chewing the corner of my lip. While Nathan's words bit, something behind them gnawed at me, something he hadn't said. The venom in his tone, the poor-me-I-lost-I-suffered attitude while his wife sat behind bars… But the contempt etched into every line on his face, it said more than any syllable he'd uttered. *A mistake he doesn't understand?* Unfortunately, I was a little rusty on my guilt speak, having convinced myself of every single one of my clients' innocence.

"Gabrielle, what was your marriage like before Emily's death?" I didn't know where the question came from, but I wanted the answer.

She looked up. The tears on her face dried before she answered. "It was fine. We were happy. Nathan got a promotion at work, and we had more money coming in. Emily was starting preschool in the fall, and Adam was doing so well. He had tee-ball games and piano lessons. We were happy."

I shook my head and drilled my fingers on the table. "I don't think so. No. How was Nathan's relationship with the kids?"

She closed her eyes. "He's a busy man. The kids were my responsibility."

"Yours alone? That must have taken a toll. You had a sickly daughter and a seven-year-old boy to manage by yourself while Nathan was busy. Did he get angry a lot? Maybe when Emily cried?" I knew the chance I was taking in trying to get her to implicate her husband, but I believed in her innocence. "Did Nathan get angry with Emily? With you?"

Rory's eyebrows shot up her forehead as though controlled by strings in the ceiling.

"No." Strength, coupled with anger, burst out in Gabby's voice. "Never. He didn't even raise his voice."

"He did, didn't he? And he took it out on you, and you took it out on her."

"No!" A guard stepped forward, and Rory waved him back. "He's a good husband and a wonderful father. This is not our fault."

"Really? Because even if neither of you did it, someone walked into your house and killed your daughter on your watch. How is that not your fault?"

"That's enough, Grace." Rory put an arm around Gabby and shot me a fierce, squint-eyed glare.

I didn't know if we were playing good cop/bad cop or if she was honestly trying to stop me from uncovering the truth, but I didn't care. Until an hour ago, this case was all mine and no damn way could I let her stop me from doing my job.

"No, it isn't, Rory. Someone killed a little girl, and I want to know who. In the absence of an obvious truth, hard questions are all we have, and you'd better start thinking up the answers to go with them." I spouted the platitude as though it was a personal belief rather than something I made up on the fly, then whipped my head back toward Gabrielle. "Answer me. Who killed Emily?"

"Are you my lawyer or some cop they sent in here?" Gabrielle stood, her fists clenched but still bound by handcuffs to a ring attached to the center of the table. Fire flamed behind her eyes.

Suddenly, she had strength enough to start a stare-down.

"I'm your lawyer, and until you tell me exactly what happened in your house that night and every night before it, my only choice is to defend you in the best way I know how. If that means you have to answer hard questions, then you better buck up, sister, and answer them. If it means I have to accuse your husband, neighbor, or your parish priest, you better sit back and let me. If you don't, Emily's blood is as much on your hands as the person who killed her."

"Gabby"—Rory's soft voice broke through the tension, preventing my badgering from continuing—"tell us about your marriage. Let's start there. Just talk to us so we can help you, okay?"

For the smallest fraction of a second, Rory's eyes narrowed and her lips compressed into a fine line of perfect pink gloss. She swallowed hard and turned to face Gabrielle who returned to her seat as a guard shot her a pointed look. "A few years ago, I was a good lawyer. I had an amazing career, a beautiful son, and a husband I adored. My little family meant more to me than anything in the world. One day I was at work thinking how absolutely perfect I'd planned my life. Then, the call came in. Something happened to our boy. I raced home. I don't even remember getting in my car or driving there. I was just so desperate to make sure he was okay."

She closed her eyes. "My husband was a drug addict and he admitted it, got treatment, then came home. He'd lost his job, so he was staying home with our boy while I worked. I trusted him to stay clean, but he didn't, and I came home to find my son broken and dead. Michael was a mess, a big mess. He said he owed a lot of money to someone bad and because he so readily admitted to his addiction, the one I'd never seen, I believed he was completely honest about what happened to our son. He told me he'd had to watch them torture our boy, and he'd been powerless to stop it." She covered Gabby's hand with her own. "He told me the drug dealer had someone murder our boy to show him that he'd better pay up."

I'd heard bits and pieces of this story, but never straight from Rory and never with such emotion.

A tear slipped down her cheek. "When I walked into court I was certain what little evidence they had against my husband was wrong, because he hadn't told me the truth yet. I went in believing his innocence. I argued for him, fought with everything I had, because I loved him and we'd already lost so much. We hadn't even had time to grieve. He was arrested right away." She nodded twice, then looked down at the chipped paint on the concrete floor.

All other noise in the visitors' room faded to the background of my mind. I no longer heard the child playing at the next table as her mother, handcuffed and shackled, cooed next to her, or the smacking of lips at another table as a woman made out with her boyfriend. It all dulled as Gabby and I hung on Rory's words.

She lifted her head and faced Gabby. "My husband killed our boy and I set him free. My son never got justice, and that's my fault. I want you to get justice for Emily. I want her killer behind bars, and I want you to go home to your son."

I blew out a breath as Gabby dissolved into tears.

"I can't do it." The sounds in the room resumed in my mind and all but drowned out Gabby's whisper.

Rory nodded. "Think about it Gabrielle. You don't have to spend your life in prison for something you didn't do. There's no reason to protect anyone."

She stood and patted Gabrielle's shoulder before she turned and walked to the door. I stared from her to Gabby and back until she cocked her head to the side. "Let's go."

When we'd stepped out of the jail into the sunlight, she breathed out a long sigh. "If that doesn't bring her around, nothing will." She left me standing in the street, staring after her as she climbed in her car and drove off.

* * * *

I walked home, cell phone in hand, waiting for a call, a text, or something that said Blane hadn't forgotten about our date that evening. He'd made big promises. My stomach churned and my skin heated in all the best places as I imagined how he would keep them. As a bonus, maybe I could wheedle a bit more information about the case out of him.

As soon as I walked in the door, I distracted myself with digesting all I'd learned that day. I tried to concentrate on raising a defense for my client. After glaring at the file in front of me until the words blurred, I spoke aloud, trying to piece together the undisputed facts of the case. My eyes were drawn repeatedly to the dormant android cell phone sitting next to me on the sofa.

By mid afternoon, I'd all but given up and changed into a sensible ensemble of pajama pants and a T-shirt. A dying doorbell's tinkle did nothing to wipe away my bad mood, and I flung the door open.

The scent of roses hit me full in the face. A second delivery boy huffed and puffed a...ninth vase up the steps.

"Grace Wade?"

"Uh, yeah." I eyed the flowers with moderate interest and scanned each of the bouquets for a card.

"These are for you." The second delivery boy shoved a card and a clipboard at me before he leaped off the porch to retrieve yet another armful of roses. I signed the delivery receipt and waited while the first kid crumpled the copy, trying to tear it apart. Instead of watching his struggle, I shoved the card into my pocket, then bent down to pick up a vase and inhaled deeply before counting its identical friends on my stoop. Twenty vases. Two dozen flowers in each.

I broke a sweat as we worked together to cover every single surface in my apartment, including the yet unpacked boxes we rearranged to accommodate the extravagant gift. As soon as the delivery boys had been tipped and sent on their way, I shut the door, leaned against it, and stared into my apartment.

At a knock behind me, I turned, so as not to disturb the vase on the small table next to the door, and tugged gently on the knob. This time, on the ground at my feet, sat a small gift box wrapped in delicate silver paper with a glitter-sparkled deep blue bow. Still not having read the card for the flowers, I snatched the one off the gift box as though the secrets to happiness and success would be found in the printed words inside. I don't know what I expected, but it weighed heavy in my hand and almost toppled to the ground before I quick snatched it out of the air.

Stepping around my earlier gifts, I made my way to the couch and tore open the card. "So that you can see the beauty I see in you." No signature.

I carefully untied the bow, set it aside and removed the lid. "Oh." Made of some sort of silver and designed with elegant swirls along the back, an antique hand mirror sat nestled inside the gauzy tissue paper.

Deliveries came every half hour for the rest of the afternoon. A first edition book of poetry "because only the great ones have the right words to express the emotions" I inspired. Next came a dress of spun silk and Italian lace, because "only the finest fabrics should touch skin so pure." Then a diamond necklace and earrings that "pale in comparison to the vibrance of my beauty" arrived. Finally, a bottle of expensive champagne along with wildflower scented lotion and bubble bath so that I could "prepare for a night that would make all his dreams come true" came wrapped in a silver, metal basket.

I got tired of answering the door and left it open. Hope strolled in and stopped barely inside the entrance. "Did you die?"

"I think I'm being romanced." It hadn't happened in such grand fashion before, so I couldn't be sure.

"Well, it looks like a funeral parlor in here." She maneuvered her way around to the sofa and plopped next to me. It took one full minute of breathing before the sneezing started. Her eyes, a normal electric blue, disappeared behind puffed up eyelids, which left barely a slit for her to see through.

Apparently, we'd both forgotten she was allergic to flowers. Honestly, in the excitement of my package receiving day, I'd forgotten she'd even come to town to live with me. I shoved her into the bathroom, turned on the hot water, and told her to stay there and breathe until I could get the flowers outside. Moving with the speed of the Flash and the strength of the Hulk, I hauled and carted, pushed and shoved until my front steps looked like a garden had sprouted through the concrete.

Once back inside, I settled her into my bed with a cold compress for her eyes and a couple allergy tablets.

"I'm sorry, Hope. I forgot."

She shook her head. "It's okay."

"No, it's not." I checked the clock. Seven-thirty. With a sad heart and slow fingers, I picked up my phone to send a break-the-date text.

ME: Can't make it tonight. My sister had an allergy attack, and I don't want to leave her alone.

I hit send, then pulled the covers up to her chin. "Do you need anything?"

Her breathing had returned to almost normal, with only the occasional wheeze to indicate she'd suffered any sort of reaction after returning home to find the apartment covered in pollen and fragrance.

"No."

The beep of a text shrilled in my hand. Ignoring it, I fussed with her pillows, recovered her as she kicked the blanket away, poured her water, anything to not have to read his disappointment.

"Grace?" Her whisper stilled my tucking her in fingers.

"Do you need something?"

"Yes. I need you to go away."

"Okay." I stood at the doorway watching her. Guilt slouched my stance as I leaned my head against the wall. "I'm sorry, Hope."

She sat up, flung her pillow at me. "Get out, Grace." Flopping back against the mattress, she sighed. "I'm the one who came to sit next to you in a room doing a bad impression of a flower shop. Don't you have a date or something?"

"I can't leave you here like this. What if you relapse?"

"Then I'll die in your bed, and you'll have to buy a new one." She flung her forearm over her eyes.

"That's not funny, Hope."

She peeked out and said, "You're making me miss Dad. Now, go on your date and don't you dare call me."

She flopped onto her side, tucked her hands under her cheek, and within a few minutes happily snored her way through whatever dreams had her smiling into my pillow.

Chapter 13

An hour later, I'd showered, perfumed myself in the lotion Blane sent, and dressed in the silver satin gown.

He stopped a foot inside the open door, and a slow smile spread across his lips. "You look beautiful."

Oh, he was one to talk. From the gelled hair to the tailored suit with a pair of silver studded cuff links, I could only manage a single, "Wow." He took my hand in his, brought it to his lips to press a gentle kiss against the pulse point in my wrist.

His heart hammered underneath my palm when he placed my hand on his chest. "See what you do to me?"

Oh my.

He lowered his head, smiled softly. "If I don't kiss you right now, I'm not going to be able to breathe."

I took a step closer.

"But if I do, I won't be able to stop with one." He leaned in and brushed his lips against my cheek.

Magic. He'd wrapped me in a perfect moment with beautiful words, a touch of his skin against mine, the smell of his cologne. A haze surrounded my consciousness, fading everything but Blane to a blackness that didn't matter.

Before I could catch my breath, he'd propelled me into his car and whisked us off. He pulled up in front of the country club and a valet took my hand to help me out of my seat.

Once inside, I gulped my first glass of wine, hoping it would calm my nerves. Along with the gifts, seeing him was powerful and my body trembled.

I looked up to meet a steamy gaze. "What? I was thirsty."

He ordered for both of us, then reached across the table, his thumb swirling little circles in my palm. "How do you not belong to someone?"

"I have a few too many short skirts to be a good candidate for wife. I'm more a Friday night fling than a meet the parents' kind of girl." He tilted his head to the side and I sighed. "The same personality that makes me seem like I'm fun is the one that scares men away. I don't suffer from a big lack of self-esteem and sometimes it's intimidating."

"That's one of the things I love about you. Your confidence. Your walk. Your smile. You have a walk that makes men stop to stare and a smile that should have its own patent. You're beautiful and smart. I will keep you for as long as you let me."

Wow.

His eyes burned with desire and my breath caught somewhere between my lungs and throat. And he wasn't through quite yet.

"I ne'er was struck before that hour
With love so sudden and so sweet.
Her face it bloomed like a sweet flower
And stole my heart away complete."

I had no defenses for a man who quoted John Clare. I didn't know if this was part of his normal dating ritual or if the half smile and color in his cheeks spoke to sincerity, but I didn't care either. For that moment, I chose to believe he meant it only about me. He slipped his fingers over my palm, back and forth with a friction that sparked heat through every cell in my body.

"Blane…"

Before I had the chance to throw him onto the table and have my wicked way with him, he stood and held out his hand. "Dance with me. Let me hold you."

Soft jazz music I hadn't noticed until that moment played from speakers strategically hidden in potted plants and fixtures in the ceiling. I looked left at the dance floor, slid from my seat, and tried to breathe normally. He spun me into his arms, cradled me with soft pressure at the small of my back, and nuzzled my hair with his chin. My pulse pounded in my ears, and I stepped on his foot. A low rumble of a chuckle sounded in his chest. With his forefinger under my chin, he tilted my head up to look at him. "Just breathe."

Easy for him to say. I hadn't taken a full breath since he started quoting poetry and looking at me with enough fire in his eyes to start an inferno.

He swayed us back and forth, moved us around the floor in a sensual haze. Finally, he lowered his head and captured my mouth with his. He brushed his tongue over my lips until I opened my mouth and let him in.

My heart raced, my steps faltered, and when he pulled back, the stars in my eyes clouded my vision of everything but him.

"I'm falling for you, Grace."

A mewl escaped my throat. The music stopped, yet we stood on the dance floor, clinging to the moment. "We should"—I pointed over his shoulder at our table—"um, go back."

He hauled in a deep lungful of air and nodded. "Right."

Our food arrived a second after we were seated, and I pushed mine around my plate, the butterflies in my stomach not leaving room for anything else.

We stuck to safe subjects—our families, hometowns, my days as homecoming queen, college—until finally dessert was served. A little cup of ice cream smothered in chocolate and sprinkled with nuts melted in front of me. Blane lifted his spoon, reached across the table, and fed me a bite. "You're a daddy's girl?"

"I guess."

"I could see how, even with that many sisters, you'd be the chosen one."

He made me sound like some kind of super hero daughter, and I smiled as he fed me another bite. I shrugged, unable to come up with an explanation for the phenomenon that had become my relationship with dad.

"What about your mom?"

I shook my head. "When I was seventeen, she just got up one morning, packed a bag, and walked away."

"That must have been hard."

I nodded. "I think it was harder on the younger girls. And on Dad." I had my demons, but nothing suitable for an over ice cream chat and nothing I wanted to chance ruining such a perfect date.

He leaned back in his chair and finished off the ice cream with a flick of his tongue against the spoon.

I clamped my mouth shut to quiet a moan.

"I could never leave my kid."

I shrugged. "She said she fell out of love with my dad, and it wasn't fair to expect her to stay because of us." The forgiving words tasted sour, and I helped myself to his half-full wineglass.

"I would think it was the only fair thing, for a mother to stay with her girls."

I finished the glass and set it next to mine, toying with the stems. "We all had each other, and Dad made it feel normal. He cooked, cleaned, and cured our broken hearts with pizza and best friend chatter. We did okay."

"I would never let you go, Grace." He said all the best things, and said them with such sincerity reflecting in his eyes I had no choice but to hang on his every syllable. The waiter took Blane's credit card and returned as we gaze at one another. "Are you ready?"

I nodded and slipped my hand into his. Together, we waited for the valet to pull his car around.

"Why aren't you and the homecoming king happily married with a couple kids, a mini-van, and a white picket fence?" My heart did a double thump as he took a part of our earlier conversation and brought it back out for further discussion. This man paid attention.

"It's a long story, and I don't exactly come off as the heroine." I hoped he'd let it go at that.

"Oh, you can't say something like that, then leave me hanging. Come on. What happened?"

Saved by the valet. He pulled Blane's convertible up and stepped out. Our frown inspiring story-hour resumed as Blane pulled away.

"Did you break his heart?"

"This is not a good date conversation."

He glanced away from the road for a second to look at me, the full pout on his lips as sexy as any smile I'd seen.

"I cheated on him. Then I told him and he dumped me." Funny, it wasn't such a long story after all.

"Poor guy."

"He was the guy every boy wanted to be and all the girls wanted to date. It took him about five minutes to get over me."

"I bet they were five very difficult minutes."

I smiled as he reached out and ran a finger down my cheek. "You're very kind."

"My heart would still be shattered. I'd be alone, unable to look at other women, ruined by the loss."

"Well, it all worked out. We're friends now." We'd reconnected after college, had a couple beers, and chatted over old times.

"Being friends with you is enough?" His voice dropped low, injected with a bit of flattering disbelief.

"I think his wife prefers it that way." She'd been the exact opposite of me, and he seemed to love that about her. He'd glowed as he hauled out baby pictures of their daughter, showed me a wedding photo he carried in his wallet. Jackson Teller had no problem getting over me.

"He doesn't know what he's missing." After our third left turn, he pulled into a space in front of the grocery store, still a block from my house. "I'm driving around in circles because I don't want this night to end, Grace."

From the way he said my name to the way his fingers caressed my hand, I couldn't find one imperfect thing about him or this night. The date faded the drive-in debacle to the same realm as every other forgotten memory I'd ever let slip from my mind.

"We could go for drinks. It's still early." The digital time on his dashboard said barely nine o'clock.

"We could. Or"—he bit his lip in that adorable kid way—"we could go to my place."

"Your place?" *Oh, Grace. What are you thinking?* I mentally berated myself for even considering sleeping with the man, again, who was prosecuting my client, for allowing lust to cloud my better judgment, and for contemplating carrying on with this relationship. But I had a mirror to see how beautiful I was and a book of poetry because only the great ones had the words to describe how he felt about me.

"No pressure. No hidden agenda except not letting such a perfect night end. I don't want to share you with a bar full of people. I want to talk to you and get to know all the things inside that beautiful mind…learn what makes you happy and sad, and what song makes you get up and dance because you can't stop yourself. I want to know your dreams and the secret wishes you make when you blow out your birthday candles. I want to know *you*."

When this guy made a speech, he went all in. I had to wonder about that night at the drive-in and the change in him from then to now. My emotions jumbled inside me, twisted in a state of flux, and no ready decision came, so I smiled over at him. "You're going to be tough to beat in court with arguments like that."

He grinned, brushed the hair back from my face. "Let's not talk work."

"Okay." My voiced squeaked higher than a cartoon mouse.

His smile evaporated and his tongue brushed across his lower lip. "What do you say? Let me have my chance to know you?"

I blew out a short breath and nodded, words more than I could manage while he batted those deep, chocolaty eyes rimmed in long, silky lashes at me.

He grinned and pulled away from the curb. We wound through town until he reached the outskirts, then turned onto a country road that ran alongside the riverbed.

As though I needed a tour guide, he introduced me to the river and shared the names of the occupants of two farms. After enough inane chatter to fill a volume of books, he pulled into a long drive that curved and bent its way up to a beautiful, two-story brick house. It had more windows than his closest neighbors' houses combined. "This is nice."

The porch, a wrap around with rocking chairs and a swing, spanned enough square footage half the townsfolk could stand comfortably along it if lined up. He struggled with the lock, a number pad that required the right combination to move the tumblers. When the latch clicked, he looked over his shoulder, grinned, and pushed the door open. With a flourish of one arm and a slight bend at the waist, he stood back to let me take the lead, then reached around me to flip on a light.

As I stood gaping at the enormous chandelier overhead, he walked past me making a left into what I could only assume was a living room. An expensive arrangement of flowers sat on a marble-topped table against the wall and artwork of various design—two landscapes and one abstract that all looked pricey—hung on either side of the foyer. I shut my mouth and stepped into the room he'd entered. He had two candles lit and a long lighter held over a third as I walked in.

Either the man had feminine tastes, or someone, a high paid designer probably, had helped with the décor. Floral chairs flanked a cream colored sofa with matching throw pillows. A grand piano gleamed a brilliant polished finish in the corner, and tables of the same polished white held crystal lamps at the ends of the couch atop a plush ivory rug. Blane had obviously done well for himself before surrendering it all to become a public servant.

He leaned back against a white marble fireplace tucked into a stone wall and smiled. "Nothing has to happen here tonight, Grace." He shoved one hand into his pocket as his opposite shoulder tried to dig through the wall as if to get away.

I crossed to him and placed a hand on each lapel of his jacket, pressuring him on one side and pulling on the other until he faced me. My body made decisions before my brain had time to catch up. "Are you trying *not* to sleep with me?"

"I want it to be special if that's what you decide you want."

Something about that statement rubbed me the wrong way, and I dropped my hands, smoothed my skirt, then stepped back. Maybe my better instincts were trying to tell me something. "So, what was the drive-in? Satisfying a need?"

He closed his eyes. "The drive-in. Right." When he opened them again, something changed. He pushed off the wall and headed for a cart with bottles of alcohol atop its gleaming metal surface. "How about a drink?"

I held up a hand. "I'm good." Jack Daniels or whatever other expensive liquor he had on that table would not help me figure out what just happened. "Blane, what's wrong?"

He took a big swallow from his glass and refilled it before looking up at me. "I don't want you to base your decisions on that night." He looked at me, drained the glass again, then slammed it against the table in a crash of metal and shifting bottles. "Shit. I can't do this, Grace."

The southern from his accent faded, and I stepped back until my back hit the wall he'd been standing against. "Jamie?"

"Blane is married. Technically, they're separated, but she's back in town and he didn't have time to break this date with you. I was just supposed to call and reschedule. It was wrong and I know it, but..." He turned to the window.

How dare they? "Is this something you do for him regularly?" *Oh, Lord.* "And you were going to sleep with me and let me believe it was him?"

He shook his head. "No. I wouldn't have slept with you." He shoved his fingers through his hair and spun to face me. "Not if I could help it."

"And the gifts?" Oh, what a tangled freaking web...

"Blane gave me his credit card and cell phone." He pushed his hands into his pockets again and began a thorough investigation of his shoes. "I got carried away."

"You lied to me, and he lied to me. I would shove all those flowers and the mirror and all that other stuff right up your ass if I could." I whirled away, considered flinging the expensive vase on the table at him, then clenched my fists at my side to keep from hurling it across the room.

Anger boiled in my veins and my eyes clouded with a batch of tears, inspired not by sadness, but rage. "You son of a bitch. Take me home. I would walk to keep from being in a car with you, but I have no idea where I am and I have no one to call for a ride. But if you try to talk to me, I swear to God I'll jump out. You will have to explain my cold dead body and how it ended up on the side of the road in this Podunk, weed-infested town to seven angry Wade girls and one over-protective father with a collection of shotguns that have never missed anything he aimed at. I'm nothing compared to them."

His whisper barely reached my ears. "I think you're everything."

I ignored his words and took a minute to tread through the deception and get to the headline I'd somehow overlooked. "Blane's married?"

He nodded.

"Why didn't he break the date?"

"He had to leave early this morning. He wanted to get her out of town before you got an eyeful of her." His toe-curling English lilt had returned. "He couldn't exactly say, 'Hey Grace, I can't go out tonight. My wife wants a chat.' So, he told me to break the date."

Another lie? Hadn't he said Blane didn't want to break the date, and he'd offered to pretend to be his brother?

"Why didn't he do it himself?" I shook my head. "Or why the hell didn't you let me break the date when I tried?"

I'd never even read his reply to the text, but he showed up anyway. I couldn't say much because I'd been dressed and ready to go. But still…

He scrubbed his face with his hand. "Because I wanted to see you."

I choked on a scoff stuck in my throat but battled through. "Well, you've seen me. Did this do it for you? Because let me tell you something, pal, *this* is not the happy ending I was promised." I clicked my tongue against my teeth. "Oh, wait. That was ass-face brother number one. What were *you* hoping to get out of this night?"

"Time." He didn't look at me, didn't lift his eyes from the spot they fixed on, but the man knew how to use words in a way I doubted I ever would.

Still, anger pulsed through me. "Well, your time's up and thanks for playing. Take me home, Jamie."

He nodded, then finally brought his gaze to meet mine. "But I want to say something first."

I crossed my arms and glared, but didn't move to stop him.

"Tonight, the man I was when I was with you is the man I really am. This thing with Blane was wrong, and I'm sorry. I wanted to be… I guess I wanted to be him. To have you look at me the way you looked at him at the lake."

My head wobbled back and forth for a minute as though I had a big decision to weigh. "Well, the joke's on you, pal. Because that day at the lake, when you saved me, I wanted you to kiss me. And you know what else? If tonight is the guy you really are, I would have chosen you."

"And that's done?"

I nodded. "Oh, yeah. Both of you can go straight to hell. Play your games with someone else. Now, take me home." I turned and stomped out to the foyer.

Chapter 14

On the way from Blane's house to my apartment, Jamie opened his mouth, and as soon as the tiniest of sounds escaped, I curled my fingers around the door handle. "I swear to God, I'll jump."

I wouldn't have, but I couldn't bear to hear another lie come off his lips. I'd heard enough already. Blane seemed to make it his personal mission to deceive me, and now Jamie had played along. Added to my own confusion, I could barely breathe from the weight of the pain in my chest.

When he pulled next to the curb in front of my apartment, I moved to open the door. He reached out a hand, then laid it on my shoulder. I ignored the traitorous zing of desire that raced from that spot straight south.

"Please, I'll go away, but I never meant to hurt you. I only wanted to know you."

I nodded. "Then you shouldn't have lied to me."

"I will always wish I hadn't."

I need a drink. "Me too."

"If it matters, I'm sorry."

My jaw clenched with effort as I held it shut so as not to dole out forgiveness. Heat rolled in waves along my skin, and my heart thudded against my ribs. I wanted to forgive him, he'd quoted poetry, for goodness sake, but I stepped out of the car and walked between a dozen vases up the steps to my apartment before I could change my mind and throw myself at him. At the door, I made the awful decision to glance back. His forehead rested against the steering wheel. "Aww, crap."

I turned to go back to the car.

No. I will not be that girl.

I spun away, then reached down to right a vase I'd disturbed. As I breathed in the floral scent of the gift he'd picked out, my brain battled my aching heart to see which one could make me act first.

He told me the truth. That has to count for something.

I yo-yoed between running back to him and heading inside until the car's motor purred behind me. My lower brain connected quickly with my feet, bypassing the higher and more rational brain functions, and I ran down the stairs and popped the door open as he pushed the shifter into gear.

"Wait." I slipped into the seat and covered his hand with mine. "I want to be very clear about something. I'm only in this car because"—I swallowed hard—"tonight was the best date of my life."

A smile flirted with his lips. "Grace…"

I shook my head. "I'm not finished, Jamie." I pushed away the nagging doubts about him and concentrated on the minutes before he'd informed me of his deception. "We're not square yet, and I have no intention of making a habit of taking my clothes off for the Sheperd boys. In short, this evening will remain one of those suitable for the Cartoon Network, a rated-G kind of night." I'd drank enough wine to be able to find my compassion, but not so much I was ready to fall into bed with him. "Just saying."

"Okay."

I nodded twice, two quick stutters of my head. "Was that your house?"

"No. It's his."

Tucking my legs into the floorboard, I slammed the door to Blane's car shut and said, "I wanna see where you live."

He flipped the key backward, opened his door, and walked around to open mine. "I live above the grocery store." Since it was only half a block down from me, there was no need to move the car to another spot

"Oh."

My heels clicked on the concrete and the echo bounced off the walls of the building as we made our way around the side into an alley to a set of stairs attached to the brick exterior.

Before he opened the door, he turned to me on my step, three below the landing. "I'm kind of a slob."

I shrugged. "I still have packing boxes stacked in my living room. I won't judge."

Lightening split the sky into three pieces, and right behind it thunder roared, shaking the ground close enough to hurry me off the metal staircase and in behind him.

He hadn't lied. Sty would have been a generous description. Clothes in a pile occupied two-thirds of his couch, pizza boxes formed a tower on his countertop, and beer bottles littered every table. "You're a slob."

"I thought you weren't going to judge."

"I'm not judging. I'm merely agreeing with your earlier assessment."

He smiled and gathered an armful of laundry to toss into what I assumed was a bedroom. I ignored him as he cleared away the trash and instead sank into a well-worn, uber comfy recliner.

"TV on," he said and the ridiculously large screen, probably seventy inches of television hanging on the wall in front of me, came to life.

"Impressive. If you can get the refrigerator to bring me a beer, that would knock me right out of my shoes."

He smiled and went off to the galley kitchen to fetch drinks. I nosed around his table. A girl could learn a lot about a man by what he kept within easy reach of his favorite sitting spot. An iPad, a notebook with a scribbled top page, my address, my phone number, and a copy of the police file on Gabrielle Quinn. Well, I already knew my vital stats, so the exposed papers didn't interest me, but I wanted to see what notes he'd jotted into a private file he kept on my client.

"You, my friend, have very girlie handwriting." I took a big swig of the beer he handed me and traced a finger over the swirling script in the margins of the official police report open in my lap. "Did you work on this case?"

He nodded and sat in the chair beside the table next to mine. "The place was too clean. I think that's what bothered me the most about it. Not that there weren't toys laying about and dirty laundry in the hamper, but no dust, no footprints on the floor, or smudges on anything at all."

"You think she killed her kid, then gave the place a royal scrubbing?" I scanned down farther. "And hid the murder weapon?"

"How would you explain it?"

"Maybe the house isn't the crime scene. Maybe she was killed somewhere else."

Straws. I'd begun grasping at them as a lifeline for anything I couldn't explain since I took the case. I didn't see a reason to stop now.

"Then the killer brought her home and tucked her in?"

Okay. His argument had merit. Not one I could refute in that moment. I closed the file and grabbed the one marked confidential underneath it. Before I could open it, he snatched it away.

"Did you come here to snoop through my stuff?"

I shrugged. "Maybe." I nodded toward the folder he tucked under his arm. "What's that one?"

"It's an open investigation."

"Hmm. Someone need a lawyer?"

"Taking up ambulance chasing?" But he said it with a grin.

"I don't see any swirling lights. Come on. What is it?"

He shook his head and tucked the file under his sofa cushion, then plopped down on top of it. "I can't talk about it, Grace."

"So a relationship with you is all secrets and lies. Good to know." I cocked one eyebrow and stared at him as I fought to hang on to the anger dissipating in the face of his beauty.

He shook his head, rose to his full height, then crouched in front of me, one hand on each arm of the chair. "No. A relationship with me will be whatever you want it to be."

I leaned back to escape the intoxicating scent of his cologne, the sincerity in his gaze. My anger dissolved to a puddle of confusion and disappointment. "How would I ever know it's you and not him?"

His mouth twisted from one side to the other. "We could work out a secret code that only we know so you'll never be confused again."

I shook my head. "And you could tell him anytime you want or not use it when you're pretending to be him."

"I'll get a tattoo." At my frown he took my hand in his, kissed my knuckles, then continued holding it. "I won't make that mistake a second time." Oh, those eyes. Jamie had a depth in his missing from Blane's. He gazed at me with longing, desire, sincerity, and hope all mingling together as he spoke. Like a sappy teenager lost in a world of poetry and romance, I imagined I saw his soul reflected in his eyes.

I shook it off and clicked my tongue against my teeth. "Too little, too late, lover boy. You should have broken the date for him, then showed up and asked me out as yourself."

He nodded and stood, raked both hands through his hair before clasping them at the back of his neck. "I think you're lying to both of us." He eyed me up and down. "You wouldn't be here if you weren't attracted to me and didn't want to give me another chance."

At this rate, my eyes would see more of the inside of my head than the world outside it. "You're easy to be attracted to. My sister's been singing your praises like you pay her to do it. You have a pretty face, a nice smile, an accent that inspires swooning, and you get to carry a gun. That's hot, but having men take advantage of my trusting nature is on my no-no list. Sorry. Doesn't matter if you're a Burberry model with a heart as big as the moon and eyes I could drown in, I'm not the chick who's going to be making you breakfast in the morning." As an afterthought, I added, "Or any morning."

He nodded, the hint of a new smile playing with the corners of his lips. "Okay. I'll make breakfast."

"I think you might not have taken that in the manner to which I intended." I hid a half-sigh behind a chug of beer.

He sobered and turned away. "So, you're looking for that forever guy, the one who quotes you poetry and can't stand sleeping without you, wakes up with a smile because you're there, and hangs on every word you say, even if it's ridiculous, simply because you said it?" He turned back before I could respond. "I'm that man, Grace."

I didn't want to be drawn in and should have walked into my apartment, ignored his moping, and shut the door. Instead, I sat there in his space, ready to fall at his feet over some lovely words spoken in perfect Queen's English. I had no shield or cape to protect myself from the magic in his sentences. I called on whatever wits I had left. "You secretly have a stash of romance novels around here, don't you?"

He watched me, mouth open, eyes wide, as I brushed past him to the bookshelf. "You know. Half naked cover models, perfect sentiments touted by some hard-bodied hero designed by the writer to convince women that the perfect man is out there, somewhere, waiting for her. I mean, if it can happen in two hundred pages, despite the slight imperfections of said hero and seemingly insurmountable problems stacked against the couple, then by God, that man must exist for one and for all." Shakespeare, Poe, Asimov, a Bronte collection. Mark Twain. Not a single shirtless male model on any cover.

I spun around and faced him. "Where they at?"

"I don't own romance novels."

"Really? Because no real guy talks like you do, and I know somewhere a woman writer is calling her attorney over your plagiarism."

He chuckled. "Well, Miss Big-time-I-never-lose-a-case lawyer, I would have to write and print it for it to be plagiarism. Where'd you go to school again?"

My smile slipped, and I couldn't stop the words before they fell out of my mouth. "Why did you have to lie to me?" I didn't fight the longing in my voice, the regrettable whisper that heightened the emotion behind the statement.

When he closed the distance between us, I didn't pull away or move as he brushed the hair back from my forehead. "I would sell my soul to take it back."

He lowered his gaze, fixed it on my mouth, and sucked in a sharp breath when I licked my lips. My eyelids fluttered shut. Anticipation warred with apprehension in my belly. When his lips touched mine, I pushed all thought away and sank into the moment, plunged my fingers through his silky hair, and lost myself in the caress of his tongue against mine. He tasted like the finest whiskey soaked in maple syrup, and I let all sense of right and wrong fall away. My heart did a slow roll while my stomach fluttered. I wrapped one hand around his neck and laced my other into his.

Tugging me closer, he deepened the kiss while clutching the fabric of my dress in his fist, pulling it tighter, stealing any breath I didn't already share with him. Somehow, my fingers tangled in the silk of his hair and I held on, afraid the kiss would end, more afraid I wouldn't be able to stop it.

After a moment of passion-fueled insanity, I opened my eyes, broke the contact, slid my hands down to his chest, and pulled my lips between my teeth, savoring the taste and sensation of his kiss still tingling there. "I need to go, Jamie. It's wrong to be here like this and know that nothing is ever going to work out between us."

"But it could. We just have to give it a chance." I had to be a fool to resist everything he had going on, but I didn't have a choice. The hurt from this heartbreak would cripple me. I shook my head, took three steps backward into the bookshelf. "I can't. I'll never be able to trust you."

He shoved his hands into his pockets and looked down at me. "Friends, at least?"

Oh, how I wished I had the strength to keep my hands off him. I couldn't promise to be his friend, since he posed such a worthy temptation, nor could I speak the words that would end our association. Unable to manage enough breath to accomplish speech, I shook my head.

I couldn't look at him for another moment and turned and walked to the door. Every snap of my heels against his scarred linoleum sounded with a purpose.

Before I could give the knob a life-saving twist, he caught my elbow and propelled me into his arms. "If I only have this one minute, I'm not going to let it pass by."

His kiss seared my insides. My knees liquefied and I sagged against him, my hands gripping his biceps, clinging to his body as though I had a choice. His tongue traced the line of my lips, urging them apart, slipping between to dance with mine. And I was lost.

He cradled me, then increased the pressure, melded my body to his in a way that hid none of the urgency behind the kiss. No amount of resistance I could summon would be powerful enough to get me out the door, to the sidewalk, and on my way home when he pulled my bottom lip between his teeth.

Instead of coming on full-force, he backed off enough to leave me craving more—more of his taste, his touch—I was ready to beg for it. His gentle kiss captivated my senses, held me a willing prisoner, but when he went all in, my world lit up in a shower of skyrockets and star bursts. He pressed my hips against his, our hearts aligned, leaving no space between our bodies as he continued to tease me with his tongue, pulling it back when I wanted more.

As he trailed his mouth along my cheek down to my throat, I tilted my head, denying him nothing, ready to give every part of myself to him in any way he asked.

"Tomorrow, Grace. Tomorrow we can start not being friends. Not tonight." He nipped at my earlobe as his whisper heated every spot below it. "Stay with me, tonight."

Without a sound other than the harsh puffs of my breath, I loosened his tie, slipped it free of his collar, then worked the buttons of his shirt, one by one, scraping my pinky nail along the bare skin underneath. I looked up, blinded for a minute by the intensity of his gaze. "Tomorrow, I'm going to chalk this up to being drunk."

"You didn't drink that much."

"But I'm going to tell myself and anyone else who asks about my goofy smile that I did."

The shiny white of his teeth gleamed at me through his grin. "Deal."

My fingers trailed over his chest as I pushed the shirt off his shoulders. The muscle definition in his stomach took my breath away and I faltered. He tugged me in and closed his eyes as I swirled my tongue in the hollow of his throat.

Ignoring the nagging thoughts of all my past mistakes—well, not all, but the men I'd fallen into bed with without a second thought—I went into full-on attack mode. I walked him backward to the chair, nudged him down without breaking contact with his lips, then hiked up my skirt and straddled his lap. The low timber of his moan as I ground us together spurred me on. I inhaled a sharp gasp and wrapped my legs around his waist as he carried me into his bedroom.

With one arm at my waist, he used the other to clear the bed of the laundry he'd tossed in earlier, then gently lowered me to the mattress. Stretched out beside me and leaning on one elbow, he ran his finger along my jaw. I could only stare up at him, mesmerized by his gaze, entranced by his touch, enthralled by the electricity sparking in the air around us.

While more desperate than ever to feel his skin against mine, I also felt safe, wrapped in our own bubble of passion and desire. There was nothing frenzied or desperate in his moves. Every practiced dip of his head, every slow glide of his hand, burned into me, and emotions I'd never experienced slicked over me, pulling me deeper and deeper into him.

"I want to be man enough to give you the choice to walk away, but I'm afraid if I do, you'll take it and it will break me."

I rose up on my elbows to lay a kiss over his heart. His breath caught, and he sucked in a quick gasp. I looked up at him. "Do you want me to leave?"

He shook his head, a ghost of a smile on his lips.

I quivered at the thought of those lips on my skin.

"No."

"I don't know what's going to happen tomorrow, but tonight, I want you. This." In emphasis, I wrapped my fingers around the back of his neck, pressured his head down, and captured whatever words he'd been about to say with my mouth.

My eyelids fluttered shut, and I gave into a world of sensation coursing through my veins. While I wanted more skin-to-skin contact, and did everything I could think of to encourage it, he kept our interlude in PG-13 land. I wanted to taste every inch of him, feel whatever he could give. He left his hand resting on the curve of my hip. I shifted closer, a slow move of my body against his, then trailed my fingers up and down his smooth skin, hoping he would inch his upward to my aching breasts or down and inward.

When he changed the fiery heat of the kiss to a sweet warmth, I pulled back. "Jamie? Is everything okay?"

He shook his head, sat up with his back to me.

"I can't make love with you while you're marked by another man. My brother, for God's sake."

I bit back a retort. The hickeys hadn't magically appeared. They'd been there all night, and he hadn't seemed to care. What happened to breaking him if I left? Another lie. This one to get me into bed? Shamefully, I didn't care. He could have told me he was king of America or any other huge impossible lie, and I wouldn't have been able to summon an emotion strong enough to overpower the lust.

Every awakened nerve and live-wired cell in my body screamed for him to end the ache between my legs, to shut up and take what I wanted to give him. Instead, he ran his hands through his hair, then brought them down to his sides.

I closed my eyes, willed my heart to slow and my brain to resume its normal function. It was impossible to formulate an answer that didn't involve begging him to ignore the bites Blane left as evidence makeup still wouldn't cover.

Heat crept into my cheeks, and I hid behind my hands. "I should go." I scooted off the other edge of the bed and stood, smoothing the fabric of my dress with fingers shaking from my own embarrassment.

With the slightest shake of his head, he looked away. "I don't want that either."

"You have to tell me what you want, Jamie, because I don't know what to do." I walked around to his side and sat on the mattress next to him. He continued staring at the wall in front of us. "I can't help what's already happened."

"Do you want him?"

"I want the guy who quoted poetry and who wants to know what I wish when I blow out my birthday candles. I want the guy who sent me a mirror so I could see how beautiful I am."

"But you wanted it to be him."

Oh, God. "No, Jamie. I *thought* it was him because you led me down that road by lying about who you were by faking his accent and wearing his clothes and cologne and driving his car. I was disappointed when I found out you lied to me, but *only* because you lied to me, *not* because it was you."

Still he stared at whatever crack or line he'd found more interesting than me. Anger, maybe at being ignored or at being duped, then blamed for it, pulsed through my veins and ate away any leftover lust.

"Okay, I slept with your brother. It was a moment of weakness I would gladly take back. I wasn't drunk or anything more than horny, and I'm sorry for it in a way I can't even explain. It doesn't change the fact you lied to me about who you were. You let me believe Blane was the perfect date tonight, and *that* is your fault."

I knew the rules of dating and too much honesty up front about other men was a no-no that topped the list, but I couldn't help myself, couldn't quell the rush of words.

Finally, he turned to me. "I'll take you home."

I rolled my eyes and stood. "It's a block. I can get myself home."

With nothing left to say and no reason to wait, since he obviously wouldn't be begging me to stay, I stormed out of his apartment and down the metal steps to the street. Ignoring the darkness, I stalked through my apartment and straight to my room, then flung my shoes and the damned dress into a corner before I slipped under my cold, lonely sheets.

Chapter 15

Sleep came slowly, in fitful bursts of unconsciousness disturbed by every sound and creak in my apartment. The refrigerator hummed. A clock ticked. Some wayward branch scraped against the outside of my window. Every single noise jarred me awake. Yet, I remained in bed with the blankets tucked to my chin. More than once, I punched my pillow into a more comfortable shape until dawn broke outside and sun streamed through my curtains.

Catching my reflection in the mirror on my dresser, I pulled my skin back toward my ears, smoothing the bags under my eyes that immediately reappeared when I let go. There wasn't enough makeup in the world to hide the damage caused by lack of sleep.

"Damn." I pulled on my robe and hunchbacked my way out to the kitchen. My phone on the counter blinked with a dozen unread texts and voicemails. My finger hovered for a second over the message envelope. What now? The first message opened.

CHARITY: Dad had a heart attack. Call me as soon as you get this.

My stomach flipped, caused a shooting stab inside of me.

Instead of wasting time to open any more messages, I tried to phone my sister. I couldn't control my trembling enough to dial while I held it and had to set the phone down onto the counter to dial her number.

"Hello? Gracie?"

"Char?" Oh no. My brain screamed the words a second before she told me.

"He's gone, Gracie. Last night. You need to come home, now." I didn't have to see her to know tears streamed in big droplets down her face.

"Where's Hope?" I'd left my baby sister home to deal with this on her own? Guilt, grief, more guilt slammed into me from all sides.

"She tried to call you last night, and when she couldn't get you, she flew home on her own. She's here."

Stupidly, all the little details flooded into my head. I had no car to drive home, no way to get to the airport. I wasn't even wearing underwear, just a bathrobe with a torn pocket. *And my dad died.* I slid down the wall and sat with knees tucked to my chest, the sound of Charity talking in my ears drowned out by the pounding of my heart.

"Can you hear me?" When I didn't answer, couldn't speak around the lump of anguish in my throat, she shouted through the speaker. "Answer me, dammit. Grace."

"What?"

"Can you get home?"

"Yeah. I'll be there as soon as I can."

I sat there trying to clear my mind enough to formulate a plan. Making a mental list, I dialed Jamie's number. "Hello? Is anyone there?"

"Hey, babe. Sorry about last night. Did you get my gift?"

Blane? Had I dialed wrong? I focused on the smooth sound of his voice, smothered a sob behind my hand. "My dad died."

"Oh my God, honey. I'm sorry."

"I have to get dressed and find a flight home and—"

"I'm on my way, babe. You hang in there. I'll take care of everything."

A quiet click introduced silence into my ears, and I remained seated on the floor in my kitchen until he burst in, calling my name. I turned my head to the side as he crouched beside me, wrapped his arms around my shoulders and brought me against his chest.

"What can I do to help you, sweetheart?" I shook my head, words still too much to form. "Never mind. I'll take care of everything." With one arm still cradling me, he pulled his phone out of his pocket, typed a command with his thumb, and held the phone to his ear.

I blocked the sound of his voice from my head and focused on the things I could control. A breath in. A breath out.

"Okay, sweetheart, we have two hours before we have to be at the airport. Let's get you ready."

I didn't answer. He lifted me into his arms and carried me to the bathroom. Propping me against his body, he reached into the shower. Steam clouded the air, and I breathed deep, trying to pull myself together.

"I'm okay." I shoved him back as he tugged the belt of my robe.

"All right. You take a shower, and I'll pack you a bag."

The spray of hot water washed away the tears I set free. I cried until the water ran cold, then stepped out and wrapped a towel Blane set on the sink around me. He'd also deposited a pair of jeans and a T-shirt along with a bra and underwear.

With the moves of a robot in need of a good oiling, I dressed and pulled my hair back. I ignored the mirror, the ringing phone on the vanity, and the knock at the door.

Blane poked his head in and took me by the elbow. He led me to the sofa and sat me down. "I wasn't sure what to pack, so I brought a black dress and a pants suit I found. I also got you…"

I tuned out his words and closed my eyes, leaning back. My thoughts wouldn't form, and I couldn't organize the words floating through my mind into anything that resembled a command from my brain to my body. I was helpless.

My dad died.

* * * *

The hustle and bustle of the airport, the voices announcing boarding for flights, and the passing of travelers as Blane led me to the terminal didn't shake me, or so much as inspire a sound to escape from my lips. It wasn't until the flight attendant asked me if I wanted a drink that I found the strength to speak. "Jack and Coke."

From the aisle seat next to me, Blane handed the woman his credit card, and a minute later, I had a cold drink in my hand. Seconds after that, an empty glass. Three or four or ten—I'd lost count—drinks later, I looked over at Blane, needing to say something, but couldn't remember what, so I lowered my head to his shoulder and closed my eyes.

I stumbled off the plane. Blane wrapped his hand around my waist to keep me upright and helped me through baggage claim, then into my sister's car. Joy, one of the middle girls, stowed my bags in the trunk before she and Blane slid into the car. Faith sat in the passenger seat, eying me with enough animosity even my alcohol-induced peace shriveled. After her third over-the-shoulder glare at me, I leaned forward, my chin connecting painfully with the side of her headrest. "What? Do you have something to say?"

"Did you drink your way home?" She spat the words between the tight line of her lips.

"I did."

"And I guess you were out getting laid last night while Daddy was laying on that table dying, using his last breath to ask for you?"

Joy gasped. Blane sat back as though he'd been slapped, and I stared at her, the fury in her eyes flashing at me. "No, Faith. I wasn't getting laid." *Not for lack of trying*, my one sober brain cell chimed in.

"You brought your boyfriend home with you. What does that say, Grace?" Never before had my name sounded as much like a swear word.

"He's not my boyfriend. He's freaking married, smarty pants. So, turn around and mind your business." I pushed her cheek until she faced forward and slapped my hand away.

"Married? Jesus, Grace. That's a new low for even you."

"Go to hell, Faith."

Blane's fingers dug into my shoulder as he pulled me back against him. "Did Jamie tell you I'm married?" His warm breath tickled my ear, and I shoved my hair away, pulling my head back as I turned to face him.

"It doesn't matter who told me. It only matters who didn't." I slapped both hands against his chest and pushed off with enough force I slammed my head into the window. Rubbing the spot, I dropped an F-bomb with a bit of authority inspired by a lot of pain.

Joy checked me in the rearview mirror. "Are you okay?"

"No, Joy, I'm not *okay*. I'm not one bit *okay*." Suddenly, the words poured out of me. "How about you? How are you and grumpy Gus doing up there? Are you *okay*?"

"That's enough, Grace."

"Screw you, Faith."

She cocked her head to one side. "How will you ever have time when you're so busy screwing everyone else?"

I clenched my fists in my lap. "I swear to God I'm going to kick your ass."

Joy yanked the wheel hard and slammed on the brakes until the car came to a shuddering stop on the shoulder. She shoved the gear shifter into park, then turned in her seat to face me. "Stop it now. We get it. You're hurt, but so are we, and damn you, Grace, for trying to make this all about you. He loved you best, and this is one more time you let him down, but you deal with that on your own and stop taking it out on Faith and"—she turned to my sister—"you too. She can't help who she is. She doesn't hide it or try to excuse it, and when you need her, she always comes. Now, both of you rein it in or I'll be the one kicking ass here. Got it?"

Faith mumbled a reply as I nodded and Blane dragged my hand across the seat to rest on his lap.

I spent the rest of the ride battling motion sickness, holding my gaze on a single fixed point on the back of Joy's seat. The world around me spun as she drove. I leaned forward on my fists and stared at the floor, praying the nausea away. Before Joy brought the car to a complete stop in the driveway, I hopped out and headed for the nearest bush to throw up.

Charity rushed off the porch and pulled my hair back as all my insides battled to join the alcohol in the perfectly manicured hedge. "Just as she left, so she returns."

I gave her my best version of the drunken stink-eye, and she helped me up the porch steps. Blane brought our bags in and set them in the foyer. Instead of taking me upstairs, she pushed me onto the sofa and covered me with a blanket. Joy handed me two aspirins and a glass of water. This wasn't their first foray into dealing with drunken Grace. Faith shoved a trashcan at Blane and muttered, "Better keep this close."

"It was the car ride." I closed my eyes. "I'm not drunk. It was the car ride." Repeating it didn't make it anymore true.

Charity nodded. "Of course, it was. Lie down and take a nap. We'll talk when you wake up."

Chapter 16

I wiped the sleep from my eyes and used the back of the sofa to pull myself into a sitting position. With only the smallest movement, my head throbbed and my eyes threatened to explode right in their sockets.

As though they sensed I'd left the blissfulness of sleep, my sisters descended, bringing the sting of reality in concerned gazes, teary eyes, and tight-lined mouths. Charity sat next to me, Joy took a spot on the table, and Temperance stood with her back against the fireplace, arms crossed and eyes blinking a wariness I'd seen a few times before. Hope, Prudence, and Faith were absent, the older girls obviously taking the brunt of the responsibility for me.

"Did you guys send Blane away?"

"He's taking a shower. I think you might have thrown up on him in your sleep." Charity pushed her hands through her hair.

"I should probably apologize for that later." Their frowns all firmly in place said they neither found me cute nor funny. I swallowed hard, back to the business of dealing with a death. "What happened to Daddy?"

"We went out for breakfast yesterday morning, and he said he didn't feel right. I made him promise to call Doc Weber, and he said he would, but he didn't. When I tried to get a hold of him at lunch, he didn't answer. I called Faith, because she was off work yesterday, and she came over to check on him. She found him on the floor in the kitchen." Her voice thickened and tears streamed down her cheeks.

Temperance picked up where Charity left off. "She called nine-one-one and did CPR until the paramedics got here. He woke up yesterday afternoon, and they were going to take him to surgery, but he had another attack and didn't make it."

I leaned against Charity's shoulder, the act of holding my head up too much for me.

"He asked for you, Grace. His last thoughts were of you. Try to remember that." Charity ran her hand over mine, gripped my fingers, and gave them a little squeeze.

"Try to remember I wasn't here when he asked for me?"

She brushed her other hand along my back, up and down. "No, honey. That's not what I meant."

"But it's true. He died and I didn't say good-bye or tell him how much I love him. I was too busy"—I flipped my gaze to Joy—"trying to get laid."

Temperance sighed. "That guy?"

I shook my head. "It's complicated." Too complicated for a half-drunk to process, much less communicate to girls who didn't need law degrees to put judging on their resumes.

"We have an appointment at the funeral home tomorrow morning." Joy wiped her eyes and another round of guilt stabbed me in the heart.

The sun had long ago set, and rays of moonlight peeked in through the curtains. I stared out the window wishing for the heavens to open up and swallow me, taking me away from the ache in my heart. The clouds closed up. Another prayer unanswered.

"Where's Faith?" Not that I wanted another battle, but I always liked to know where my adversaries stood. The farther she stayed from me, the better.

"She went home." Faith had married right out of high school, and after college, started her own construction company with her husband. "Charity's staying here with you and Hope tonight. We'll all meet tomorrow morning."

I nodded.

"Grace, we're all planning to get up and talk about Daddy at the funeral. Do you want to?"

Talk about Daddy? I couldn't even think about him without dissolving into tears. "I don't know."

"Just think about it, and we can discuss it with the director tomorrow morning." Temperance stepped forward. "Don't drink tomorrow, okay, Grace?"

"You guys, I'm not like an alcoholic or anything. I don't drink every day."

Three sisters aimed their disbelieving gazes at me. With the taste of stale whiskey on my tongue and a hangover that wasn't yet an hour old, the picture I presented wasn't that of a girl scout, but I hadn't found the need for a twelve step program yet either. I threw my hands up, wished I hadn't, and lay back against the couch cushion. "Fine. I won't drink tomorrow." I pushed away from the couch, more rolled off to my knees, then stood as if in slow motion, one unbend at a time. "I'm going up to bed."

"Don't you want to eat?"

Shaking my head and hanging on to whatever was within reach, I made my way upstairs. I passed the room Charity and Temperance shared as girls, followed by Hope and Faith's, then Prudence and Patience's, before finally coming to mine and Joy's. Instead of opening my door and heading in to bed, I stared down the hall. His bed, his clothes, a world we knew nothing about hid behind that door and an army of tanks and wild animals couldn't have stopped me from turning the knob and going inside.

I took a deep breath. The smell of his cologne still hung on the air, and his pajamas were neatly folded on the corner of his bed. He kept a photo of Mom next to his reading glasses on the table by a copy of the Bible and a lamp made of antlers. I picked up his wallet, examined his driver's license picture and the folio of snapshots he kept bent inside…a picture of me at my college graduation, one of Hope from her senior prom, a photo of each of us at one important event in our life or another.

Blinking back the tears, I set the wallet down, smoothed the leather, and picked up his wedding ring, a simple silver band he'd worn all his life. It seemed wrong he was without it, and I tucked it into my pocket to bring to the funeral home. While it meant nothing to our mother, it had signified something to Daddy, and I knew he'd want it with him in his eternity.

I sat down and picked up the Bible, flashed on an image of God, his eyes wide in disbelief. The spine was worn, creased as though it had been opened often, the ends crinkled as though he'd clutched it in his hands, felt its strength. I put my hand on top and thought of the words I'd heard so often…"So, help you God." *Yeah. So, help me, God.* It wasn't a prayer, just a part of the ceremony of a court proceeding that I doubted too many of my clients ever noticed, but at that moment, I repeated the words aloud, begging for something to make the pain gripping my insides stop.

The tears streamed down my cheeks as I lay back on the bed, cradling his Bible, burying my face into his pillow to sob until I had no tears left, until my body had no more to give and I slept.

The next morning, I hid my swollen eyes behind a pair of big sunglasses, hid my vodka in a travel mug of orange juice, and my sadness behind a couple of Valium tablets I found in the back of the medicine cabinet. I sat quietly in the back of the room until the funeral director recommended we choose one sister to speak for all of us and all seven of my sisters turned to face me. I held up a hand. "Oh, no. Not me. I can't. One of you guys do it." Panic gripped my insides. How would I ever find the words to speak when I couldn't even hold my head up to meet their gazes and glares.

"Grace," Hope said, "you make speeches for a living."

Faith's hiss of hatred didn't miss its mark. "You owe this to him."

I blew out an alcohol-soaked breath and nodded, then stood by as they picked the flowers, the perfect color and style of casket, music, and remembrance cards. As one of the oldest daughters, I should have helped. Instead, I remained frozen in my little corner space, tucked in between a fake ficus and a table, sipping a drink that didn't stop the ache in my soul, didn't put conscious thoughts back in my mind.

I followed Charity out to the car, climbed in behind her, and tilted my head back. Tuning out the radio and the road noise, I ignored their somber chatter and fell into a dreamless, alcohol-induced sleep.

* * * *

The casket sat only a few feet in front of me. *Oh God.*

I cleared my throat, looked out at the back of the room, and did what I had always done…winged it. "There is a division of time in my family that divides our childhoods. The first is a time when we were one big happy family, all ten of us around a dinner table, laughing, smiling, telling the high points of our days, because there were always high points." Visions of those happier days came rushing forward and my voice cracked. "The second part is nine of us around the table laughing and smiling and telling the high points of our day. After we became nine, there were hard days... days I'm sure Daddy didn't like us much, or maybe wished he'd chosen a different path. I can't say for sure, because he never showed it. He never raised his voice or threatened us with more than a disappointed glance. And if anyone would know, if anyone had worked hard to try his patience, it would be me."

The door to the church, with its hundred-year-old hinges, squeaked open and my mother walked in. Every syllable caught in my throat. She walked up the center aisle and took a seat next to Hope.

"Um, I, um, I need a minute." I walked down the three steps to the pew where Hope's shell shock registered in her wide eyes and the hand over her lips. "You okay?" I leaned down with a hand on each of Hope's shoulders and waited for her to look up at me. When she nodded, I turned and walked back up to the podium. I blew out a breath, licked my lips, and pointed a glare at my mother. My strength came back in the form of angry disbelief. What the hell was she doing here? She'd broken him in life. My stomach clenched against the ball of anger rolling around inside it. She didn't have any business coming to see him in death.

"When our mom walked out, we didn't understand. It was too much for a bunch of little girls, and we couldn't imagine how a woman, our mom, could promise her life to Daddy, give birth to his kids, parent us for seventeen years, then disappear like we didn't matter. Like *he* didn't matter. As the days turned into months, and she didn't come back, Dad learned how to sew, to braid hair, and how to hold his head high no matter what we sent him to the drug store to buy. He baked birthday cakes, and they were terrible, but on his own, by himself, he raised eight girls into adulthood, and he never complained."

I pulled a deep, long breath in and blew it out slowly. "When I was seventeen, I went a little off my path." Charity smiled up at me and nodded. "My dad did everything he knew to do. He grounded me. Took every single privilege I had away. For one whole day, I wasn't allowed to speak, and for me, that was a punishment I would always remember, but it still wasn't enough." It had probably been more reward for him than punishment for me. "After a few days of my petulance and moping and cursing at him, he asked me to go for a ride." My heart ached as I pictured the disappointment in his eyes, the hurt I'd put there.

"I was sure he was gonna take me out to the woods and drop me off. I would have. Instead, he drove me to the nursing home where his mom was in a coma. We didn't go into the room. We stood at the door and watched my grandpa talk to her, hold her hand and love her like no one else in the world existed. She probably didn't know he was there, but he went everyday and spent all day with her.

"My dad didn't say a word, he just wiped his eyes, and we left. When we got in the car, he looked over at me and said"—I heard his voice as I spoke the words—"'every woman deserves a love like that. I wasn't that guy for your mom.' Then he drove me home." Tears pooled in my eyes and slipped down my cheeks. "After that day, I still acted up a little, but we figured it out. He had this magic thing. He knew what we needed without us telling him. Sometimes, it took him a while to get us there, but we always arrived eventually. The other girls probably have stories like that too. I don't know. I wasn't with my dad when he died."

Where the hell did that come from? "So, I never got to thank him for the man he was, the one he will forever be in my memory and in my heart." I looked down at Hope. Her shoulders shook, and my lips quivered as I drew in a deep breath and tried to imagine taking her pain away…the way he would have done. "Our dad is the man we will judge all others by, not because he didn't have faults, but because he did and he didn't hide them. He used them to be better, to make us better, and for that, we will always be grateful. So, I want to ask God to take care of our dad the way our dad took care of us. Completely, and with more love than we could have ever asked for."

I took my seat on the opposite side of Hope, shifted my body when my mother patted my shoulder. My pulse throbbed and my head ached. What I wouldn't have given for a drink right then.

Chapter 17

"Dinner? You want to have dinner with her?" Had the alcohol affected me so much I'd begun hearing things incorrectly?

"She invited all of us." Hope squeaked past me as she shuffled out of my room to cross the hall to her own. Her bare feet slapped against the hardwood, and I followed almost catching the backs of her heels in my hurry. She flung open her closet door, yanked out a pair of sandals, and slipped them on, then stood tall again to face me. Defiance? Aimed at me? From Hope? Oh, hell no.

"Hope, she left you. You were three, and she walked out on you like you didn't matter, like you wouldn't need her." Our mother was downstairs waiting for us to get ready. Even Charity had jumped on the mom bandwagon, ready to forgive and forget, to leave the past behind.

I couldn't have given one shit that she'd shown up to "help us through losing Daddy." She had a different reason, and damned sure I would figure out what it was. But first, I had to protect my baby sister.

"And she's here now."

"For how long? Until the going gets too tough, until her life seems too big and she leaves you again, broken-hearted and crying your eyes out? You don't remember, but I do. I was seventeen, and you were devastated. You balled every night you had to go to bed without her. Don't let her do that to you again."

"Grace. It was sixteen years ago. You've got to get over it." She slammed the door behind her. I listened for the telltale click of the lock, realized I wasn't in medieval England—our doors locked from the inside—then raced downstairs after her.

Blane and Faith sat next to our mother, one on each side. Charity leaned against the counter with her arms crossed, and Temperance had a carafe of iced tea ready to pour, complete with lemon slices. Joy's open mouth had yet to close since Mom strolled into church.

I walked to the table, yanked the chair out across from my mother, and plopped in. "What are you doing here?"

"I thought you girls might need a shoulder, someone to help you get through this."

I shook my head. "Lie. Try again." She'd had a thousand chances to be there when we needed her, and she'd never come home.

She cocked one eyebrow. "Your father and I never got divorced. I have every right to be here."

Oh. Now it all made sense. Blood roared in my ears. "So you're here for the house? His stuff?"

Hope's eyes widened. "That's enough, Grace."

I glared at my baby sister. "If she's not, let her say it, Hope. Let her look at you or me or one of the others and tell us why she's really here." I turned back to Mom. "Go ahead. Tell her you're here because you want the house. "

"That's enough, Grace. Maybe you should have a drink."

"Seriously?" I shook my head at Faith. "Yesterday I'm an alcoholic, and today you're telling me to have a drink?"

Mom stood and cupped Hope's cheek with her palm. "You girls are welcome to stay here any time, for as long as you want." Something evil flashed across her face when she looked at me. Her smirk said she had no intention of keeping the house beyond selling it for what it was worth. As soon as I saw it, it disappeared.

"Did you guys hear that?" I looked from one to another, trying to gage who sat on which side of the mom debate. "*We* can stay here for as long as we want. Damn right we can." I looked at Charity for support. Seeing none, I turned back to Mom. "He wouldn't want you here."

"Well, he's not here, now is he?"

Hope gasped. Charity inched forward, and Temperance slammed the tea onto the table hard enough it splashed onto Blane's shirt and my mother's dress.

"Mom?" The anguish in my baby sister's voice tore at my heart, and I pushed my chair back, rose to a height that dwarfed my mother, and leaned across the table until she backed away.

She wrapped Hope in a hug, smoothed her hair down her back, spoke in a tone that didn't match the aura of blackness surrounding her. "I'm here to help my girls through losing their daddy. We can worry about everything else later."

"Okay." I straightened up and winked at Charity. Just this once, I knew something they didn't. I tamped down on my inner glee and smiled over at Blane. "I gotta get some air. Wanna do a little sightseeing?"

He came around the table, took my hand in his, and smiled down at me. "Sure."

* * * *

Storybook Lake, Illinois. Not an average town by any means. Buildings looked more like children's toys than the brick and mortar cubes they'd once been.

"Wow. What is that?"

"It's a beauty shop." I smiled. The Little Shop of Hairs stood smack in the middle of town. The quirkiest of the buildings lining the main street, its two stories were shaped as a giant flowerpot with a plant stem and bloom reaching high into the sky.

"Sometime in the sixties, the town decided to capitalize on its location and make itself into a tourist destination. They started redoing the buildings, one by one, to reflect their mission statements." I pointed out a giant toy chest. "That was the first building they redid. It opened in just enough time for the Christmas season that year. Then, as new businesses came or decided to roll with it, they all underwent makeovers. The streets got renamed and Lakeland, Illinois became Storybook Lake."

"It is definitely touristy." He squeezed my hand as we walked past a tanning salon whose front was a giant sun. His tone, however, said it was an oddity he didn't fully appreciate, and I frowned. I loved everything about this town.

"Some of them only have decorative fronts, but others have taken their theme into every architectural element throughout."

"And you grew up here?" He stopped, did a full three hundred and sixty degree turn and grinned at me, then pulled me into his arms. "Is there some bottle shaped bar where we can get a drink?"

I stepped back, put a couple inches of space between us. "Um, I probably shouldn't drink right now. You know, with my mom and everything…"

He cocked his head to one side, batted his eyelashes. "Come on. One drink. It'll help you relax."

Never one to pass up a chance to drown my sorrows in a deep bottle of whiskey, and I had plenty of grief to drink away, I led him down the block to the most nondescript building on the street. Big Mike's. Mike had dug in his large, booted heel at turning the bar into a giant beer mug, and a normal square fronted building housed the only drinking establishment in the heart of town.

We pushed inside the glass door, then found seats at the bar. Carol Sundrup's eyes widened, and she rushed around the counter to throw her arms around me, crushing me against her large, mostly exposed chest. "As I live and breathe! Grace Wade." She pulled me back for a look, then yanked me close again. If I wanted any hope of ever breathing normally again, I would have to break free of her hold. I wriggled away.

Carol and Mike married long before I was old enough to drink, but her daughter sat for Hope while we were all in school and Daddy worked. I'd been a regular in the bar during school holidays and any time I was home from college.

"I'm sorry about Chance. He was a good man." I seldom heard anyone call him by his name and I smiled. It almost never occurred to me that he had friends outside our family.

"Thank you." I had no idea what to say to people, so I let her hug me again.

"Is this your young man?" And before he could blink, she released me and had Blane squished against her.

My reply choked in my throat, and Blane answered in his syrupy southern drawl. "Well, yes, ma'am. I'm anything she wants me to be. Blane Sheperd." Holding out his hand seemed kind of silly, since she had almost choked the life out him with her hug, but she shook it with an enthusiasm that had his arm pumping up and down like an electric hammer.

Carol smiled with a brightness that could have powered a city block as she rushed behind the bar. "What can I get you kids?"

"Jack and Coke for the lady, and I'll have a beer."

"Oh, no. I can't." It was barely lunchtime. I couldn't start with hard liquor.

"Baby"—he wrapped an arm around my waist and tucked me in at his side—"I'll take care of everything. A drink won't hurt."

As we sat again, Blane's hand came to rest on my knee, his pinky rubbing back and forth on the inside of my thigh. I ignored the sensation of friction-created heat and that damn cologne tickling my nose. Instead, I chugged the drink Carol sat on the coaster in front of me. She gave me a wink and went off for a refill.

Blane slipped the palm of his hand, the one not inching up my skirt, into my hair and tugged me close. He leaned in, and at the moment he would have pressed his lips to mine, I turned my head. Oh no. I wasn't walking down that path until he was divorced. No way. No how. At least not while I was busy wishing I'd gotten a hold of the other brother.

He studied me, his face giving away nothing. Leaning back, he dropped his hand. "Rory called you last night."

"I should call her. I left town and never even said anything."

"I told her you were taking it hard, and you would get a hold of her as soon as you could." I nodded my thanks and picked up the drink Carol brought. "My brother called too."

"Oh." The squeak of my voice did nothing to overpower the pounding of my heart. *Jamie*. His name brought a thousand images to mind…Jamie ready to kiss me by the lake…Jamie in that damn tuxedo, telling me the truth about our date…Jamie. My head was full of him and even shaking it and blinking like I had dust in my eye didn't work.

Get a grip, Grace. Maybe the whiskey would help. I drank it in one gulp.

"I let it go to voicemail." He took a swallow of his beer. "Then I deleted it."

He deleted my voicemail? I summoned anger from the spot where the alcohol had shoved it and glared at him.

"You can call him back, if it's so important to hear him lie to you." He nodded to Carol, pointed down at my glass, and turned back to me.

"Lie to me?" Honestly? He didn't have any business throwing those particular stones. I huffed out a scoff. "You lie to me, Mr. Married Man." I spun my head toward the bar, crossed my arms, and eyed my fresh drink with an unbridled appreciation.

He ducked his head. "I'm sorry, Grace. I just wanted…" He paused and sighed. "When we get back, we need to talk about some things. I know this isn't the right time, but there are things you need to know."

Mellowed by the alcohol fuzzing my brain, I turned to face him. "Like you're happily married with a dog called Skippy?" I had to quit drinking. Stupid things came out of mouth when Jack Daniels took control of my vocal chords.

"I'll explain everything when we get back. I promise. Just don't give up on me until you hear what I have to say." He traced my jaw, then ran his finger along the line of my bottom lip. "I know you and Jamie are getting close, I do, but he isn't right for you." His quiet murmur was enough ear candy for me to ignore the thoughts of his brother sneaking into my brain. "You need the danger and excitement. He's home in bed by ten o'clock every night. He isn't what you need."

Of course, if he continued to talk about Jamie, I would continue to think of him. "And you are?"

He nodded. "I've got plans, Grace, to get out of there and make a new life somewhere exotic. Somewhere we can be together and never have to worry about money or cases that put us against each other. I want to share it all with you, and I will, as soon as I get everything worked out, all lined up, and in place."

"Blane."

"One chance before you make a decision between me and my brother, give me one chance." I looked down at the ice in my drink. It must have been a family trait to know how to use words against a woman, to melt her heart, or make it beat extra hard. "Promise me?"

If his voice hadn't echoed with sincerity, his eyes not glistened with hope, I would have been able to walk away, but something about him… I couldn't wrap my mind around what it was, but whatever the trait, I nodded. Smiled.

"Seal it with a kiss?"

I shook my head. Alcohol or not, I wasn't ready to play kissy-face with a man who'd so blatantly lied to me, no matter how pretty he talked. And I dang sure wasn't about to do it after what happened with Jamie, after all I'd found out about Blane, or in a public bar mere hours after we buried my dad.

Taking a minute to compose my thoughts, I looked away from Blane, saw a familiar face, and smiled my first sincere smile since Daddy died. Sliding off my barstool, I grasped Blane's shoulder for support, then stepped two stools down. "Keaton Shaw."

I threw my arms around him, ignoring his ex-wife altogether. While I didn't personally have a problem with her, years of loyalty to Danielle hadn't washed away when I came home. And what the hell were Keaton and Jocelyn doing together? He pulled back and smiled. "It's good to see you, Grace."

His food smelled delicious, and I picked up his burger, then took a big bite. Jocelyn glared at me and I smiled. I hadn't had anything to eat in a while and didn't care what she thought. Through a half smile, I chewed and swallowed quickly. My God, that was good. I stopped ogling his food and tried to find a discreet way to figure out their new story. Obviously, their old one had undergone some serious revisions. "You two are you back together now?"

He nodded. "I came home a while back. I think Charity said you were up in Chicago then." He looked down at his plate. "I heard you're in Texas now."

"Yeah. Remember Rory from college? I think I brought her home once or twice on break. We opened a law firm." I wobbled and leaned heavily against the bar.

"Well, that's great." He eyed me up and down. Concern etched lines into his forehead. "You feeling all right, Grace? You might want to slow down." He intercepted his beer before I could get it to my lips for a quick swig.

"Oh, yeah. I'm great." I waved a hand through the air and reached in for another bite of his food. "How's Dani doing? I haven't talked to her in a while. I think the last I heard you guys were up in Canada somewhere."

His face colored a deep red, and Jocelyn whipped her head toward me. "Uh, I"—he shook his head—"I haven't talked to her in a while."

"That's a shame. I miss her. I was hoping she'd be home while I was here." Well, this had turned awkward.

"Is that your husband?" He tilted his head toward Blane and cocked one eyebrow. After years of knowing Keaton, I recognized his in-your-face look.

"No. He's just a…" A what? "…a friend, I guess."

"Will he look after you while you're like this?"

I didn't know. Would he? Even if he didn't, I was perfectly capable of looking after myself. "I don't need him. I'm fine."

"Grace."

"Seriously, Keats. I'm fine." I performed a half-spin before staggering into his shoulder. "Mostly."

Before I could manage an apology, Blane was at my side. "Whoa, there, sweetheart. You okay?"

"Oh, yeah. Just reminiscing with friends. Blane, this is Keaton and Jocelyn. This is Blane. He's from Texas. Go on talk. Show them your accent." I moved between Keaton and Joss as Blane and Keaton shook hands. Something sparkly caught my eye, and I snatched Jocelyn's French fry holding hand away from her mouth. "Wow. That is some ring. Like, what? Twenty, thirty karats? Are you guys getting married again?" I wondered how that had happened. He left town a few years earlier because she'd dumped him on his ass. I would have to remember to call Danielle and get all *that* dirt.

"In a few weeks." Keaton winked at Joss as Blane's arms circled me from behind. I wriggled away and eyed Jocelyn's fries. Jocelyn Hunter had never been one of my favorite people, and a guy like Keaton could do much better, but if she made him happy…whatever. I could love and let love.

He looked over at me, his playfulness dehydrated with his glance. "I'm sorry about your dad."

Next to him, Jocelyn agreed. "He was a good man. He came to the bakery every morning."

I nodded and looked down at my shoes, barely able to push a breath out past the lump in my throat. The mere mention of my dad broke something in me and I shriveled.

"Thanks." Grief squeezed my heart. "We should let you eat. It's been great seeing you guys, and congratulations." I gave them a dorky thumbs-up, spun a little too quickly into Blane's chest, then shook him off. The last thing I wanted to do was fall apart in front of the perfectly put together Jocelyn.

"They seemed happy to see you."

"Him, maybe. Not her."

"Old boyfriend?"

I plopped back down on my seat and resisted an eye roll at the jealousy in his tone. "No. He went out with my best friend in high school. Then he started dating *her*." I jerked a thumb over my shoulder. "My dad used to go to her bakery every morning." Something about that made me sad. Maybe that he would never go again?

"I'm sure he's in a better place."

How? How was he sure? Instead of arguing the point, I nodded, trying to blink away the urge to cry.

"You okay?" He caught the first tear and brushed it away, then the one that followed.

Of course I wasn't okay. Three sheets to a gale force wind on the day my dad got buried—what was he thinking? "Okay" was a state of being I aspired to find. Thinking of him brought tears to my eyes. Knowing I would never again feel one of those daddy bear hugs he saved for special occasions or hear the deep bass of his voice almost doubled me over in agony.

"I'm fine." I emptied my glass, pointed to Carol for another, and ignored her frown.

"I might have something that could help you. If you want." He patted the pocket on his hip.

"Something to help me?" Was he offering me drugs? That was his solution for my broken heart? "What are you talking about?"

A frown turned on his lips, and he shook his head. "I meant a hug, silly. You need someone to take care of you for a while." He pulled me into his arms and cradled me against his chest. He was right. I wanted to be held, loved enough that the pain in my chest subsided, even if only for a few minutes.

Burying my head in the slope of his neck, I inhaled the scent of his cologne, Jamie's cologne, and pressed a kiss along his pulse point. I'd only meant it as a thank-you, but with a fingertip under my chin, he tilted my face up to meet his and pressed his lips against mine. Powerless to do much more than be held, I parted my lips at the gentle insistence of his tongue.

The kiss deepened, his hand brushing down the side of my breast to rest underneath. A moan that started at my toes and worked its way up, escaped into his mouth, and he tugged me closer, broke the kiss to nibble his way down my neck. As long as he didn't talk, I could pretend it was Jamie. They looked the same, felt the same….*Jamie.*

As I turned my head to give him better access, I caught a glimpse of Jocelyn in the mirror, her eyes wide and her mouth set in a grim line. She shook her head, and I closed my eyes, but the image of her judging me wouldn't fade.

Her look mirrored my thoughts. What the hell was I doing? This was absolutely not Jamie. This man had a wife somewhere and I was in a bar.

I broke the kiss, pushed on his shoulder. "Blane, stop."

He rested his forehead against my throat and exhaled deeply against my sensitized skin. "I don't know what it is when I'm around you. I lose all control." He scooted my drink closer. "Here you go, baby. Drink up."

I was on my third, maybe fourth, drink and he'd barely touched his beer. "I should get back home, Blane. No telling what havoc my mom is causing while I'm gone."

"One more drink." He gave me the puppy dog eyes and I folded.

"Okay. But only one."

Chapter 18

Three drinks later, I stumbled out the door. God. I was drunk. How the hell did that happen? Hadn't we only stopped for one? Fortunately, the whiskey made me not care as much that Jamie, no, Blane had to swing me into his arms to get me back down the block to my car. Instead, I enjoyed snuggling against him, running my tongue along the shell of his ear, whispering naughty things against his skin. He smelled good—not as good as the night of a thousand roses and poetry, but good.

I wanted to kiss him again. For a few minutes, so the pain went away, so my heart knew a moment's happiness even if my mind wanted something else.

As he lowered me to my seat, he seared my lips with a kiss and snaked his hand down the front of my dress, inside my bra to tease my nipple with his fingers. "Is there somewhere we can go?"

"I have a bed at my dad's."

"No. Somewhere closer."

I couldn't think with all the pinching, then soothing going on. Not Jamie, I reminded myself, but not bad and not enough to make the difference matter. "Yes."

He raced around the front of the car and climbed in. A few minutes later, I'd directed him to a farm road between two fields. He shoved the shifter into park, then climbed out to come help me out.

Before I had both heels sinking into the soft dirt, he had my dress yanked up and my panties torn off. His lips melded to mine, his tongue thrusting in and out of my mouth as I gasped for breath. He spun me around, bent me over the hood, and grasped my shoulder as he pushed into me with such force I cried out. "Jamie, stop. You're hurting me."

I couldn't wrap my head around a rhythm or believe what I'd said. *Blane* pulled away to fumble for his ringing phone.

"What?" he barked, slapping it against his ear with a thwack that made me smile. "It's under control. Don't worry about it. No one is going to jail." My ears perked up, and I swayed a little closer than necessary. He raised his gaze, lifted his eyebrows, and turned his back to me. "I have to go now. I'll call you later. Stop freaking out. I have it taken care of."

He ushered me around the still open door and all but pushed me into the seat. "Let's get you home."

"Seriously? That's it?" I wanted to say something, to ask if there was more to come, to find out about the phone call and who wasn't going to jail, but the alcohol sloshing in my stomach, coupled with its effects on my brain, robbed me of the ability to do more than sit back and breathe.

"So, it's my brother you think of when you close your eyes." He drew lazy circles on my knee with his finger. "We'll have to see what we can do about that."

"Blah, blah, blah." Words somehow evaded me. Important words. Ones I wanted to hurl at him and at myself. My stomach lurched sideways and back again. I squinted to clear my blurred vision.

Who was on that call? Who wasn't going to jail? Daddy dead. Mom in town. A country road? So many things. *Jamie.*

The car lurched to a stop, and he climbed out, opened my door, then leaned in. He carried me inside the house and set me on my wobbly feet in front of Joy. "Goddammit, Grace." With one hand clasping mine and the other arm around me, she helped me up the stairs. "We have to do the will in an hour. What the hell is the matter with you?"

A voice behind me said, "I told her to slow down."

I whirled, almost causing a domino of three falling down the steps. "You did not. You got me drunk so you could take me out on a country road and screw me." I looked at Joy. "Yeah. That's right. Country road." Over my shoulder I added, "Speedy."

"You need to sleep it off, Grace." Blane's tone lost the good-old-boy melody, and instead he bit out every word.

I raised my hands and yanked away from my sister. "I can take care of myself." I tried to run up the stairs away from them, tripped, and settled for crawling to my room.

Before I had the opportunity to enjoy the bed I flopped on, Joy tugged me up by both arms and shoved me across the hall into the bathroom. She stripped me and pushed me into a cold shower. After a few minutes, I flipped the dial to warm up the water. Somewhat more stable, I stepped out and wrapped the towel she handed over around me. "Your boyfriend is pissed."

"He's not my boyfriend."

"Well, whatever he is. Smoke is pouring off him."

I rolled my eyes and swayed. "Damn."

Instead of getting dressed, I flung open the bathroom door, holding my towel shut, and found Blane sitting on my bed. He glared as I sat beside him. "Sorry."

"You're a mean drunk, Grace."

"I am what I am." And I didn't care what he thought. I lay back, wanting nothing more than to close my eyes, escape the day and the memories of it. Fortunately, they were whiskey soaked and would be much fuzzier, I hoped, later on.

"You're gonna have to learn to be a little nicer when we're drinking or your rewards aren't gonna be so good." He leaned over me, kissed my cheek, my jaw, worked his way around to my lips as his hand parted the towel and slid down my belly.

"Rewards?"

"Mm-hmm." He nipped at my collarbone. "Rewards like I could finish what we started." He lifted his head and met my gaze. "Or at least, help you finish."

He inched his fingers lower, nudged my legs apart, and teased me for a second before he slipped two inside. My eyelids fluttered shut as he took my nipple between his teeth and tugged while his fingers worked in and out, building a pressure inside me begging to be released. As I neared the edge, his phone on my bedside table rang, and he withdrew, then reached for it. "Shit." Forget alcohol. This man had a serious phone addiction that was starting to piss me off.

He slid the bar then said, "Hey."

I shuffled off the bed, stood semi-straight. Sober me knew with one hundred percent of my working brain cells that Blane was not Jamie. Drunk me didn't have a freaking clue, nor did she seem to care that sober me only wanted Jamie. I snatched a pair of jeans out of my suitcase.

After I finished dressing, I stomped down the stairs, barefoot and not at all interested in reading a will. My sisters had gathered at the table with Dad's lawyer, waiting for me and Mother, who stood at the counter, to take our seats.

We reached for a chair at the same time, and I yanked my hand away. "You take it." I moved to sit across from her, watching.

"Are we all here?" Fred McIntosh was a lawyer older than Moses and smarter than Einstein. In all the years I'd known him, he had a long, furry Santa look and wild curly hair he tried to shove under a hat. I'd worked for him the first three years after I passed the bar, but he'd been Daddy's friend since before Mother left.

He nodded and pulled out the will along with a stack of envelopes he passed out. When he skipped over my mother, I hid a smile behind a closed fist at my mouth. Charity elbowed me hard, and I dropped my hand, holding the envelope on its top corners.

McIntosh read slowly, stopping to explain every caveat and line in the will. Dad left us almost everything and gave Mother only enough that contesting would be difficult—a thousand dollars. She fluffed her hair, smoothed her hands across the tabletop. "I have nowhere to go."

Still drunk enough not to care, I said, "There's a really nice overpass on route fifty-seven."

Hope squared her shoulders, sat up straighter, and glared at me. "You can stay here with me, Mom."

"What about your job in Texas? With Jamie?" Saying his name sent a shiver of treason through me. I had to get that whole brother situation worked out, but first to deal with my mother and the veil of worship my sister had shielding her from Mom's faults. "What about your classes?"

"Who's Jamie?" Charity's eyebrows launched up her forehead.

"Blane's brother. Twin brother." Hope sat back, crossed her arms, and wiggled her eyebrows at me as though she'd tattle-taled.

"He's too old for her." Faith, who'd remained silent through the whole ordeal, shot me her best version of Dad's disapproving gaze, and I shook my head.

"They aren't dating. They work at a restaurant together." I ignored them all and focused on Hope. "Daddy wouldn't want this, Hope. Not at all."

"How do you know what your father wanted?" Mom toyed with her nails but looked up at me.

"Stay out of it." Prudence, the quietest of our group, took Hope's hand in hers. "Listen, honey." Prudence was only a year older than Hope, but an entire world of wisdom shone in her eyes. "For all you know about her, she could be an ax murderer who left us to avoid police capture."

"I most certainly am not."

Prudence shot daggers out her eyes. "How would we know? You never so much as called us or sent one birthday card."

"Your father wouldn't allow it."

"Bull. Shit." Prudence never spoke out. She was the eternal hippie, the guitar playing peace lover who didn't smoke, drink, or swear. Ever. "You walked away and never looked back. For what? A man? A better deal than living in Storybook Lake with your eight daughters and a husband who worshiped you? Go ahead. Now's your big chance. Explain it for us. Make us see why you walked out."

"Now, is not the time."

Temperance stood and led Fred to the door while I waited for my chance to pounce. "You're right, Mom. The time to explain would have been before you left. Now, it's too little, too late."

"No." Hope stood, walked around the table, and put a hand on our mother's shoulder. "She is our mom, and I would think after losing Daddy you'd all be thrilled to have her here, but no. All you're worried about is yourselves. He left her nothing."

"What did she deserve, Hope? What do you give a person who walks out and leaves you with two toddlers and a bunch of teenagers to raise by yourself?" My head throbbed and my heart ached, but I plunged on. "What is fair? Was it fair you had to grow up without your mom? That you cried yourself to sleep at night? That Charity had to go with you and Faith to mother-daughter day at summer camp because we had no idea how to find her?" I stabbed a finger at my mom. She jerked back as though I'd slapped her. "Tell me, Hope. What should he have left her?"

Mom stood. "I'm going back to my hotel. I'll call you later, Hope."

"I wouldn't hold my breath," I muttered to my sister.

Hope chased her to the door, and Prudence glanced from me to Charity to Temperance. Joy continued the pacing she started during my tirade.

"We need to do something." Joy stopped, pounded her hands on the countertop. "What the hell is she doing anyway? It's not like we inherited the Taj Mahal. It's a five bedroom in Storybook Lake and maybe enough money to pay off our student loans. Well, not Grace, but everyone else."

I'd spent longer in school than my sisters had between screwing around the first two years and the added years law school tacked on.

Charity shook her head. "When I tracked her down a few years ago, she was living with some guy in Montana, didn't want me there."

I whipped my head toward her. "You tracked her down? And you never said anything?"

She shrugged, traced her finger over the smooth letters of her name on the envelope in front of her. "I wasn't sure I could find her, and I used work resources so I couldn't tell anyway. The point is, I found her and she didn't want anything to do with us. She sent me away."

"And now all the sudden she's here?" Prudence didn't buy it either. "Why?"

They didn't spend the time working with the ugly side of life that Charity and I saw every day in our jobs, so their life-experience didn't provide them with a defense mechanism for our mother's brand of evil. I sighed, hating that I had to enlighten them further to her sins. "Because he died. Because she thought she would inherit it all, since they're still married." Luckily, Dad had taken steps to make sure she didn't.

"Did you know he cut her out?" Temperance glanced at me when I nodded. She motioned to the doorway. "You need to take care of that?"

I turned to find Blane leaning against the wall. Instead of answering, I walked to where he stood holding my phone. "You have a call." Instead of waiting for me to answer, he picked up his luggage and stalked outside. I checked the screen—Jamie—hit ignore with a shaking finger, and shoved it in my pocket.

Dealing with my guilt over my country-road escapades with Blane and hiding it from Jamie while I still sat on the wrong side of tipsy was not a good plan. The screen door banged as I stepped onto the porch.

"Hey. Where you going?"

"I'm flying home."

"What?" He'd told me we were staying two more days.

"You've ignored me since we got here."

"What do you want me to say, Blane? This trip isn't about our alone time or lack of it. I have a little bit going on." Selfish, inconsiderate—selfish…

"And instead of dealing with it, with me, all you do is drink. I don't have time to be your babysitter. I have to get home."

I grabbed his shoulder, yanked until he faced me. "To your wife, right?"

"Not now, Grace. Sober up first." His whisper, just out of earshot of my sisters, did nothing to mask the contempt I couldn't believe I'd earned.

"What the hell are you talking about? You're the one who kept ordering me drinks, and you're the one who—"

"I want to love you, Grace, but you make it difficult." He opened the door to the waiting taxi and climbed inside.

I closed my eyes and blew out a big breath. I'd had about enough. Heading back to Texas sounded good to me too.

Chapter 19

The phone ringing in my pocket, the sweat pouring down my back, and the headache pounding against my temples, all needed to be dealt with, but I decided to deal with the easiest to tackle first. I pulled out my cell, answered, and waited.

"Grace? Oh my gosh. I'm sorry about your dad."

Rory. Someone sane. "It all happened too fast. I should have called, but Blane made all the arrangements and I failed to think."

"I understand. Don't worry about it." She paused. "Things are happening here, with the case and with a bunch of others. When do you think you'll be back?"

"I was planning on leaving tomorrow and driving through the day. It takes about fourteen hours, so tomorrow night?" I hadn't planned anything. "Why? What's going on?"

"You sure you want to talk about it now?" Her voice dripped with concern I couldn't bear to hear.

"Absolutely. I need some normalcy. Go. Tell."

"The State's Attorney's office is being investigated. Everything from witness intimidation to jury tampering. Jamie told me about it this morning."

I shook my head. "He told me he was leaving because of my drinking. He never mentioned this." What a liar. My stomach rolled, whether from the alcohol or the anger, I couldn't say.

"Leaving? Who was leaving?"

"Blane." I bit my lip, wishing I could organize my thoughts into some semblance of sanity.

"He was with you? I thought he just had your phone for some reason."

"No, he was here until about five minutes ago." I chewed my nail as she peppered questions at me like a machine gun. Instead of responding, I changed the subject. "I need to sleep for a little while, but I'm leaving tonight. I'll be back in the morning." Nothing like a little work to calm my bleeding heart and mind.

"Let me know when you get here, and we can head to the office. This is big. If we can prove there's any flaw in the case, the judge will have no choice but to drop it."

I had news for her. I wouldn't be winning by default. I would win because it was the right thing. Or I wouldn't win at all.

* * * *

"You're leaving?" Temperance frowned. I'd stowed the last of my bags into the trunk of Daddy's car and slammed it shut as my sisters crowded around the car.

"I have to go. I have a case. There's nothing more I can do here anyway. Hope has to figure it out on her own. Like we did." That little piece of wisdom came during a long nap that afternoon. "All we can do is help her through it when Mom lets her down."

I hugged Prudence, then Temperance and Joy.

Charity stepped forward. I'd explained the issues I had with the Quinns, the evidence I'd seen, and what was missing. "I'll be there in a couple days. I have to wrap up some things at work then I'll fly out Saturday morning."

"Sounds great."

She pulled me in. "I'm bringing Hope back with me," she whispered. "I'll need your help to keep her there. Away from Mom."

"I don't know if she'll listen to me."

"She didn't run to any of the rest of us."

I sighed and stepped back. "Right."

Hope pulled up in a cute little sports car she hadn't owned that morning and threw her arms around me. "I'll miss you."

I hugged her tight, sad for what I knew she'd go through if she stayed with our mother. "You could come back with me. Help me work, see Jamie, finish your classes."

She pulled back, held me by the tops of my arms, and smiled. "I know you're worried, but I'm not a little girl. I won't let her hurt me."

"Call me a lot. Let me know you're okay."

She nodded. "I love you, Gracie."

"Take care of yourself. I love you too."

I hopped in Daddy's car, and with a last look in the rearview at my sisters gathered in the yard, I drove away. Stomping down the sadness that everything had changed, I focused on getting back to Texas. I wasn't sure how Rory's news would affect my case, but my gut feeling said it would be good for Gabrielle Quinn.

* * * *

A fourteen hour drive, by myself, with no one to chat with or to keep me awake might not have been my best plan, but after eight cups of coffee, two energy drinks, and a soda, I made it, pulling up in front of my apartment right before lunch.

The flowers on my stoop had been cleared away, and I dragged myself up the steps. I sent Rory a text telling her I'd returned, then received one in reply telling me she would be right over. When the doorbell rang and I answered, I expected to see a petite blond woman instead of a tall, dark, and dreamy sheriff.

His uniform fit exactly as I remembered, in a way that emphasized every good thing about his body. Black pants hugged his long legs as a gun belt hung low on one hip. His dark T-shirt highlighted the wide span of his shoulders and tapered where it tucked in at his slender waist.

Wow. Some genius woman had definitely designed that uniform with Jamie in mind. "Hi."

His mouth compressed, thinned to almost nothing while his eyes flashed an angry fire. "Can I come in?"

I stepped back. "What's up?"

He walked past me, turned, a frown tugging at his lips. "You called Blane when your dad died?"

"He had your phone, Jamie. I tried to call you." I hadn't expected Blane to answer Jamie's phone, but hadn't fought to speak to Jamie either. Since the information wouldn't help my position, in true lawyer fashion I kept it to myself behind closed lips.

"But you knew he had my phone. I told you."

I had an explanation, but the set of his mouth, the hard anger in his eyes said he didn't care, and I was past the point of finding the motivation to defend myself.

"He couldn't wait to get back here to tell me how you dragged him out to a country road and gave yourself to him on the hood of a car."

I winced and he stepped back. When I reached out a hand and laid it on his crossed arms, he flinched away.

"The hood of a car." His whisper echoed with disbelief that chipped away at my apathy.

"It wasn't like that, Jamie. I was drunk and stupid." I stepped closer. "Please, let me explain. I couldn't separate the you from the him." *Oh, if only I could make this worse.* Even my brain shouted sarcasm at me. How could I make that mistake? What the hell had I done?

"I thought we were working on something."

"We are. Please. I made a mistake." I blinked back the tears for a full four seconds before they won the battle and slipped down my cheeks. "Jamie, I made a mistake."

He shook his head. "I can't do this right now." He brushed past me and paused at the door. Without bothering to turn and look at me, he said, "I'm sorry about your dad." Before I could reply or beg him to hear me out, he squeezed around Rory as she walked in the still open front door.

I pinched the bridge of my nose and shut the door behind him.

"What was that?"

"Long story." I shook it off for later inspection, dried my cheeks with clammy hands, and turned to her. "Tell me about this investigation."

She opened her shoulder bag, full of files and folders, and spread them out onto the table. "Okay. I don't have all the details, but there is some sort of corruption going on in the office, and Blane is taking some serious heat right now. There are investigators here from the Texas Bar Association and the Attorney General's office. I saw him at lunch and he looks a little flustered."

Served him right, in my book. "What does it mean for Gabrielle Quinn?"

"It means we need to go over every piece of evidence, examine the chain of custody, and we need to check the interrogation videos and techniques. No mistake is too small for us to pick at. We're looking for anything we can use to scar up his work."

"What about the police department? Are they involved?" Were both brothers in on it? My stomach twisted, and my head ached at the thought.

She shrugged. "I haven't heard anything, but I wouldn't be surprised."

"You think Jamie is involved too?"

"Think about it, Grace. They're brothers. Twins. What do you think?"

* * * *

We worked through the evening, long into the night, until Jack called and she rushed home not realizing the late hour. Exhausted, I tumbled onto the sofa with every intention of resting, possibly even sleeping, until I could figure out what to do about the disarray in my life. Despite my best intentions, the shambles I'd made of everything brought forth images of my dad shaking his head, that same disappointed frown on his face whenever he tried to help me straighten out what I'd made crooked. All I had to do was figure out what wonderful words of wisdom he would impart to get my life back together.

Without the ability to talk to him, I couldn't hear his voice, and a batch of tears floated over the edge of my lashes. I cried until the sun started peeking over the horizon then I traipsed down the hallway and fell into my bed.

Before I closed my eyes, I picked up my phone to call Jamie. I wanted to set things right, to beg forgiveness, but instead, I set the alarm for two hours later.

Chapter 20

The text *Meet me in my office at 11* offered no clues as to what he wanted, and I could only guess…dropping the case against Gabrielle? Well, if so, it was a meeting I didn't want to miss.

I dressed in my lucky verdict suit, spritzed on an expensive perfume, and walked out of my apartment minutes before my command performance. The skirt, long enough to be respectable, but short enough it elongated my legs, hugged my ass as I climbed the steps to his office.

His secretary's desk was unattended—she'd left her door guarding post?—and I lifted a hand to knock. The door swung open, and in a barely audible whisper, he said, "Keep your mouth shut."

I raised my eyebrows and followed him to a seat next to a woman whose coffee colored hair was pulled back so tight she'd never need plastic surgery. Her skirt fell past her knees and her shoes were the same make and model as the sensible ones my grandma wore as a nurse. The entire ensemble was the same shade of brown as the piles left in the dog park back home.

"Grace Wade, this is Valerie Chelsior. She's going to be taking over the Quinn case for me until I can get this investigation sorted out."

Instead of taking the hand I extended, she stood and stalked her way behind Blane's chair. I let my hand fall to my side, cocked my head, and regarded her with a haze of uh-oh surrounding me.

She braced both hands on the high leather back and shot me one of those looks meant to kill.

"Miss Wade." Her voice was tight, not concealing an anger I hadn't yet earned. "Before we get too friendly, I want you to know I have looked at the evidence in this case." Had I somehow wronged her? I'd heard that tone often enough to recognize the hostility and scorn. "I won't be offering a plea bargain of any kind."

One of the first things I'd learned in law school was to never underestimate my opponent. The second was to not make unnecessary enemies. Well, I'd become good at one because I always seemed to fail at the other.

I glanced from Valerie to Blane and back. "Okay. Since we're exchanging love letters here, I have a couple things I'd like to say. First, I don't see us getting friendly at all. Not that you don't look like a fun person." She didn't. "But I have plenty of friends. I just don't have room on my calendar for another." I ignored Blane's narrowed eyes, the glare transforming his normally handsome features into something worthy of a scary movie villain. "Second, plea bargains are cheats and I lose." I cocked my head to the side. "Make no mistake, Miss Chelsior, I don't have to cheat, and I never lose."

"Well, maybe that's because you only take cases any lawyer with a matchbook degree could win. Maybe that's because Illinois is a place where the law isn't upheld to as high a standard. But this is Texas, *Miss Wade*"—Good God, what was it with these people and their hatred for the single ladies—"and you can't use your perky little body or your bought and paid for assets"—she pointed a finger at my semi-obvious, but tastefully designed chest—"to win. I know you came here hoping to ride Rory Allden's coattails to victory, but in Texas, our murderers go to jail no matter how attractive their lawyers are."

Match book degree? Rory's coattails? What the hell had I done to this woman?

"I also know you have a thing for my husband. He had to take his brother's phone in order to get you to leave him alone? That's pathetic. We're having a baby. Stay out of our lives or you're going to have more to worry about than losing a case."

Blane's skin flashed scarlet, and my blood boiled. I wouldn't have expected him to tell her the truth, to say how he'd come on to me, but I couldn't control my wide-eyed shock. "A baby?"

"That's right. A baby. And we don't need some white trash Yankee slut coming in the way of the vows we took before God and all of our family and friends." Her left hand, adorned with a ring that had more carats than a farmer's market, slipped off the back of the chair to rest on Blane's shoulder.

"Well, cue the happy music." I stood.

"Honey…" Blane turned his head, picked up her hand, and pressed a kiss into her palm. "I need to speak to Grace alone."

"For what?"

Seriously? Could the man make it any worse? "No, Blane. She's right. There's nothing you could say I'd want to hear."

He looked up at his wife—even thinking the word while seeing her in more than abstract thought form curled a ball of guilt into my stomach. "Please, Val."

"Fine." She glared at me, her eyes never straying even as she passed by me.

When the door slammed behind her, I whirled to face him. "Wife *and* pregnant. Nice, Blane."

"We were separated when I met you. She came home because of the baby." His voice, no longer the curved sounds that pleased my ears, dropped to a beaten growl as though he'd been boxed into a corner.

"When?"

"When what?"

"When did she come home?" Oh, did it even matter? Maybe.

"A few days ago."

"Before you went to my dad's funeral with me?"

He nodded, toyed with a pen on his desk, rolling it between his long fingers.

"You screwed me knowing you were coming home to her? Your wife and your cookie cutter family?" I wasn't sure what upset me more. That he'd known he was coming home to her, or that he knew it and had sex with me anyway.

On the hood of a car. On a field road.

His eyes flashed and his other personality, the one I'd briefly glimpsed when he left Illinois, came out to play. "Like I'm the first married man you spread your legs for."

I flinched as though his words reached out and slapped me. "Wife, Blane. As in till death do us part."

He opened his mouth to speak.

"And you better be careful, pal, because you're awful close."

"What do you want me to say, Grace?"

"Well, I don't know, Blane. What did you want to be alone with me to say?"

He looked up, shook his head. "I wouldn't be staying with her if there wasn't a baby on the way."

I laughed, though the feeling never quite reached the happy place that normally inspired the sound. "Does she know that?"

He shook his head once more.

"Wow." I rooted around in my bag. "Well, in that case, Rory and I are probably gonna branch out, start taking on divorce cases. Here's my card." I slapped it onto his desk blotter and stalked my way to the door. "Tell little Susie Scorned I'll see her in court. And I hope it all works out for you."

As my hand twisted the knob to leave, he spoke. "Grace."

I paused then turned in slow motion. "What?"

"I need you to keep quiet about what happened in Illinois. She doesn't know I was there with you."

Shame snapped in every cell of my body, followed by a quick synapse of anger. "We'll see."

With the agility of a panther, the speed of a bullet, and the fear of a man about to be ratted out to his wife, he shot around the desk. He snatched my arm away from the door, pushed me against the wall, and crowded me into the corner.

I met his dark, glittering gaze. My mouth twisted. "Get the hell off me."

His body pressed into mine and his hand wrapped around the base of my throat. Panic and fear raced through my veins as his grip tightened, fingers squeezed, and I struggled for oxygen. He leaned in close, mouth against my ear, his voice low and calm. The tone belonged to a serial killer, not the Blane who'd consoled me after Daddy died. "You're not going to say anything."

I shook my head as my chest burned and breathing became more difficult. Struggling to get away, I wrapped my fingers around his and tried to pry them free.

He was one second away from a painful kick between his legs. His fingers fell away, but his body remained tight against mine.

I gulped in a huge swallow of air then coughed in his face for the effort. "Get off of me."

His thumbs brushed down the sides of my breasts as he palmed my ribs. "I never did get to enjoy these much."

Bracing both hands against his chest, I shoved with every ounce of energy I could muster. "You son of a bitch. Stay the hell away from me."

Flinging the door open, I made my escape. My jelly legs carried me to the steps, then down before I collapsed onto a park bench outside the police station.

I looked up and down the block, and there, like a beacon calling out to me, neon lights in a window, an open sign, my salvation from a day I should never have started. As soon as my legs would carry me, I hobbled down the street, and for a moment, when I reached the door, I stood back in appreciation of the name. Mom's House. I imagined for a quick second the arguments saved by the name. *Where you going? Mom's House*. No one lied. No one got unhappy.

With a chuckle that escaped on a choking cough, I pulled the old wooden door open and stood back in the doorway, letting my eyes adjust to the quiet interior. Some old timers sat at the bar sucking suds from schooners while a TV blared in the corner. I perched on a stool two away from anyone else and waited…and waited…"Excuse me. Can I get a drink?"

"We don't serve your kind in here."

"My kind?" What the hell? Had word spread so quickly?

"Lawyers."

I ripped open my wallet and slapped four one hundred dollar bills onto the bar. "Lawyers make a shit load of money. And we drink a lot."

He shuffled down to stand in front of me. "What can I get you, honey?"

"Jack and Coke with a shot of tequila."

A few drinks later, me, the bartender, Joe, and my money had all become best friends. I'd almost forgotten about the incident in Blane's office. Then an interruption to our regularly scheduled program on the bar's ancient TV announced the Texas Attorney General's office reopened seven cases prosecuted by Blane Sheperd. They had gathered evidence that he or members of his staff participated in widespread jury tampering, including threatening members of the families of jurors seated on the cases. I flipped my glance back to the melting ice cubes in my drink. "Hey, Joe. What the hell? My drink is empty."

He chuckled. "Never met a pretty little thing like you who could put away the whiskey like you do."

I wiggled my finger and leaned in close. "Wanna know my secret?"

He nodded.

"Practice. Lots and lots of practice." I laughed as though I'd never before heard a joke and found that one uproariously funny. "What time is it?"

He checked a clock on the wall behind him that had a few too many hands, then turned to face me again. "Six fifteen."

"The night is young."

Soon, the Friday after work crowd piled in, couples and singles elbowed for space as Joe got off work and a college-aged kid started pouring drinks. "What's your name?"

"I'm Tyler. You must be Grace."

"How do you know?"

"Everybody knows about Grace Wade, and I know everybody."

"Yeah? Let's test that theory. You know the Quinns?" Hey. Even tipsy, I could do my job. Too bad none of my friends could be there to see it. My mind musings forced a smile I hid behind the rim of my glass.

He nodded. "Nathan. Quiet guy. Drinks vodka on the rocks."

"What about his wife?"

"No. Never met her. I saw her in town with the kids before, but she don't come in here." He picked up my glass. "You need another drink, darlin'?"

I nodded. He walked away, and before he returned, my chair spun toward the dance floor, almost throwing me out. "Hello, beautiful. My name's Sam, and I would love to buy you a drink." He tipped a snow white cowboy hat. I took it off his head and smacked it onto mine.

"That sounds wonderful."

Sam turned out to be a great dancer, a fun drinker, and semi-good karaoke singer. When he dedicated some eighties hair band rock anthem to me, I couldn't help but climb up on the bar and dance.

A hand reached out for me and I smiled, slipping my fingers into his. My smile didn't fade until the moment I caught a glimpse of the black T-shirt and cargo pants. "Shit."

I stepped onto the bar stool as Jamie clasped his hands around my waist and lifted me to the floor. Unable to bear the look on his face, the hurt I'd put there, I turned away. I could see disappointment anytime I wanted. *Just hand me a mirror*. There was no way I was going to let him ruin a buzz that cost me four hundred bucks. Shaking my moneymaker as Sam belted out the chorus and half the bar clapped along, I ignored Jamie and his damn cologne.

"What happened to your neck?" He shouted over the music, his voice losing none of its sexiness for the act.

I didn't turn to face him. "Someone gave me enough rope." I laughed at what I thought was the funniest joke ever told.

"Come on, funny girl. You don't belong here." His fingers curled around my forearm, gently tugging while his thumb soothed the skin on the inside of my bicep as he pressured me around to face him.

I pushed against his chest, tired of being manhandled by the Sheperd men. "I don't want to leave, Jamie. I've had a hard week and I am sick and tired of people telling me what to do. So, go away and let me have some fun."

He nodded to Jeb, an old-timer who'd come to sit by me halfway through my day. I'd poured out my troubles on his slightly hunched shoulders and he'd smiled. We spent the afternoon chatting and he imparted some fine words of wisdom. *Hang in there* and *buck up*, and, *for the love of God, don't trust men who take you out on a country road and bend you over the hood of a car*. He'd said it with a down-home slur that softened the words and made me like him even more. Oh, if Jeb had only been about fifty years younger…

Jeb stood. "Take care of her, Sheriff. Your brother did a number on her." I didn't miss the affection in his wink or his tone as he moved toward the door, leaving a seat open for Jamie.

"What are you doing, Grace?" Again with the disappointment and I shoved my fingers into the sides of my mouth and whistled at Sam who'd commandeered the stage to bellow out a second song.

I waved my newly emptied glass in front of Tyler. "And get the sheriff here a ginger ale or would you prefer a Shirley Temple? What do straight-laced good boys drink?"

I had no experience with his kind and tried to picture Jamie drinking. He'd only done it the one time in front of me, and he hadn't been very good at it. Now, the only image I could conjure came in a teacup and had a lemon floating inside. It had to be the accent clouding my thought process.

Jamie nodded to Tyler and said, "Beer."

"Oh, look at the good brother being all bad ass and drinking in uniform." I tsked him before turning back to my drink.

"Did Blane do that to you?" He ran his hand along my throat, his gaze following the path as I turned back toward him. "God, Grace." His eyelids closed for a second and I waited for whatever else he might say.

When no sounds came, I brushed him away. "Doesn't matter. I got mixed up in something I shouldn't have and I learned. That's what my life is all about, Jamie. Learning from my mistakes." I hid behind the veil of my hair. "Fortunately, I get to do it a lot. You'd think I'd be darn near genius by now."

He took a swig of his beer and looked straight ahead into the mirror behind the hard liquor bottles on shelves at the backside of the bar. I don't know what decision he made as his eyes raked over my face in that mirror, but he smiled a soft smile and turned to me. "Dance with me?"

"Why? You hated me yesterday. What changed between then and now?"

"I think you did." He held out his hand and wiggled his fingers. "Come on."

Swaying as I stood, I grasped hold of him then squeezed through people until he stopped and drew me into his arms.

"You know what he said to me?" I knew the rules for dating. Don't talk about one guy to another. But my mouth had a mind of its own, and I didn't try to stop the words as they tumbled out.

"What?" His chin rested on my head and I pulled back to look up at him.

"That he wouldn't be staying with her if she wasn't pregnant." I nodded. "That just means he knew he was married."

"Do you love him, Grace?"

"No." So what if he'd helped me get through the worst day of my life. He also used my body as his own personal pounding ground. So what if he held me while I cried into my pillow. He was married to a vicious little woman who had his bun in her oven. "Definitely, no."

"Good. You're too good for him."

I reached a hand up and cupped his cheek. "Did I hurt you, Jamie?"

"No."

"Liar." I pulled his head down for a kiss that stopped the motion of our bodies, scorched the air around us, and burned its way through my veins. His soft lips parted and his hands clenched the back of my blouse in a fist as our tongues mated inside his mouth. The kiss lasted for minutes or hours, I couldn't be sure, but the world slipped away. In this version, no Blane existed. We weren't standing on a dance floor in a bar with bad country music playing on an antique jukebox. Gabrielle Quinn didn't exist and no one in the world mattered but Jamie. When he pulled away to lean his forehead against mine, I could do little more than hang on to him and gasp for breath.

I'd made a mistake with Blane and hurt Jamie to do it. Even in my alcoholic haze, I wanted to make it right. Because unlike his brother, Jamie was…he was…

"To be loved completely, flaws and all," I whispered, wondering if he'd be able to make the connection.

He smiled. "Your birthday wish?" He kissed the sore spot on my neck. "I don't want to be the guy you run to when he hurts you."

"Then what do you want to be?" I kept my mental fingers crossed.

He pressed his lips against the top of my head. "The guy who loves you completely, flaws and all."

"There are a lot of flaws."

He pulled back then ran his finger down my cheek. "Admitting it's half the battle."

Chapter 21

I flung the alarm clock across the bedroom, snuggled back into Jamie's warm chest, and pulled his arm over me. Nestled closer, I moaned in sheer delight, quite happy to forget whatever reason I'd thought to set an alarm for seven on a Saturday morning.

Later, with a dull throbbing behind my eyes and a louder pounding on my front door, I rolled over to find the spot next to me cold, empty. I flipped a pillow over my head and yanked the blanket up.

Muted voices disturbed my pending death by over-indulgence. I slipped into my robe and stumbled out to the living room. Charity, Faith, and Jamie stood in the doorway discussing his new accent.

"He's not Blane, you big dopes. He's the other one." *The one*. My brain screamed at my heart to shut the hell up, and I couldn't decide which stance I wanted to take on the matter, so I shut up.

"Another late night, Grace?" Faith's anger broke through my headache and I remembered the exact reason I'd meant to be up early.

"Yes." No point in denying it.

Instead of pouncing as I expected, she ran her hands through her hair and said, "You owe me a hundred and seventy dollars for the cab ride here."

I waved a hand toward the coffee table. "It's in my wallet."

She stalked across the room. After snatching my purse off the table, she looked inside, then turned my wallet upside down. "There's nothing in here."

I scanned back through the memories I had of the night before. "Oh, yeah. I spent four hundred dollars on a Jack and Coke." Three sets of wide eyes stared at me in disbelief. "I needed a drink."

I threw up my hands and stepped around Charity, and her open mouth, to the kitchen.

"It would have been cheaper to have an IV line set up." Faith plopped on the sofa, her glare following me as I made coffee. Great. Just what

I needed—the sister least happy to spend time with me plopped on my couch, judging things she knew nothing about.

"Not as much fun." My words came at a pounding price and I spared no extras. I did wink at Jamie and smiled when he ducked his head.

"I should go." He had one hand on the door before I thought to move.

"No. Wait." I followed him outside. "Don't."

"Grace…"

"Come on. I probably need police protection now more than ever." I waved a hand toward the door and grimaced.

He tucked my hair behind my ear and leaned down. "I'll check on you later."

I sighed. "I know this is horrible, but I don't know how I got home, and I was wondering…did we—"

He shook his head. "You fell asleep at the bar and I brought you home. You asked me to marry you, did one hell of a strip tease, then fell asleep again."

I looked away to avoid whatever emotion I would see in his eyes. "I'm kind of a mess."

He got to the bottom step before he spoke. "I'll call you later."

I watched him walk across the street, the sway of his hips, the long gait of his legs.

"Marry him?" I mouthed the words then walked back inside to face an inquisition that would put the Spanish to shame.

* * * *

Crafty enough to get around their questions without giving too much away, I turned the conversation back to why Hope stayed in Illinois and Faith came in her place.

"Hope and Mom are redecorating." Faith narrowed her eyes and sank farther into the sofa.

"Dad's house?"

Charity nodded as she took a sip of orange juice I didn't know I had. "The kitchen, new appliances, new cabinets and countertops. Then she bought new furniture and a big screen TV. She's blowing through her money like she has an infinite supply."

"And Mom's encouraging it." Faith didn't bother to look up as she spoke.

I rolled my eyes. "Of course, she is. She's getting the house all prettied up so she can sue us for it."

"Can she do that?"

I shrugged. "Dad had her name taken off, but anything is possible. We'll have to wait until she makes her move." I had enough on my plate without having to play watchdog for them. I'd step in when we rolled around to the courtroom. They could handle it until then. "Now, about my case. Did you have a chance to look over the notes I sent you, the reports?"

Charity nodded and Faith flipped open a magazine buried under case files I'd combed through with Rory. "Yes. I think your problem is in the victim herself. Your biggest challenge will be to answer the question of why her. Out of all the people in the house, why kill her? You answer that, and you'll find your murderer."

She wasn't exactly spilling headline news. "I know, but so far, I can't figure the answer. If you could have seen her mom, no one could fake that kind of genuine sadness."

Charity shook her head. "You would be surprised what guilty people can do."

I shrugged. I'd never been surprised before. "Okay, but I'd rather have some proof one way or the other, and there is none. They have no murder weapon, no blood on the mom. Dad was covered in it, a sick amount, and he's walking around free."

Charity glanced up at me, curious. "I thought she was all tucked in when they found her."

"From what I was able to gather, Dad found her, picked her up, and was holding her when he called for Mom."

She nodded. "Tell me about the hair in her hand. I couldn't find a DNA report."

"That's because there isn't one. The hair was lost, mislabeled, I don't know. It won't get into court anyway." In a strange and not at all good for my client kind of way, I wished it would. At least then I'd know one way or the other.

"Let's go to the house. I want to have a look around." This was the Charity I needed. Not the motherly figure who groused if I enjoyed a beer or ten, not the sister who wanted to chat about my love life until it was dissected like a tenth grade science project, and not the social butterfly who wanted me to give her every detail of every person I'd met in town.

As I drove, she flipped through Emily's medical records along with photos of the injuries. Faith sat quietly in the back filing her nails. "She had a broken leg when she was two. Fell down the stairs."

"And?"

Charity shrugged. "Could be a sign of prior abuse."

I rolled my eyes. Whose side was she on, anyway? "Or it could be a sign she fell down the steps."

"Maybe."

I focused on the road, ignored her huffing and puffing as she turned pages, compared one to another, shuffled photos back and forth.

"Where's the actual injury part of the autopsy report? The one that details the wounds."

Come to think of it, I hadn't seen one of those. "I don't know."

She slapped the cover of the folder shut and twisted her body, fighting the seatbelt to face me. "Grace! That is a vital piece of evidence. I shouldn't have to tell you that. It shows trajectory of the wounds, the kind of blade used… all the stuff that would convict or clear your client."

She was right. I hadn't exactly been focused on the case, given it the undivided attention it deserved. Instead, I'd been too busy wallowing in my own personal crap.

"You're right." I doubted Valerie would give up any single piece of paper without a Congressional order, so I made a mental note to draft a motion. I called Rory and left a voicemail asking her to meet us at the house if she could.

The house hadn't changed much since the last time I'd been there. The lawn had been mowed, the toys were put onto the porch, and all traces of crime scene tape had been cleared away, but a spooky feeling still loomed. On my first visit, I hadn't notice the small memorial underneath a large oak tree in the center of the front lawn. Teddy bears and candles, hand-drawn pictures, a statue of an angel, and a few balloons no longer holding air had weathered under the bright Texas sun.

I walked past to the steps and opened the unlocked door.

Faith took a sniff of the stale air, walked to the center of the room. "This is creepy."

I nodded. "Yes, that kind of observation is very helpful. Thank you." My hangover had yet to ebb and I wasn't in the mood for her immature commentary. I needed her to do the job she'd come for. As the most hands-on of my sisters, she'd put on a pair of overalls with her tank top and carried a shiny red toolbox in one hand. There were drains to be disassembled and she was the girl for the job.

"I'm just saying, it's weird to be in a house where a little girl died, scoping it out."

"Well, it's why you're here." I pointed over my shoulder to the steps while Charity compared the room to the photos in her hands. "Bathroom, upstairs in the master bedroom."

She smoothed her hand along a crack in the drywall running alongside the steps. "This is some shoddy workmanship, here, let me tell you."

"Well, master craftsman, I'll find the contractor and let him know."

She squinted one eye over her shoulder at me, then continued making her way up, tracing the crack with her index finger as she walked.

I turned to Charity. "Anything?"

She shook her head. "Let's see the little girl's room."

Faith was right. Seeing the house in the cold light of day, comparing it to the photos, imagining the horror, definitely fell into the creepy category, bordering on scary movie.

Charity pushed the door open, walked inside, and looked around. "So far away from the master bedroom. I wonder why that is." She slapped some clothes out of the way in the closet to investigate the wall behind as she continued to spout her musings aloud. "I mean, I'd want my baby's room right next to mine, not down the hall and so close to the steps."

I nodded. I'd thought the same thing. "Maybe they didn't want to disrupt the little boy's life by moving his room. You know, make him resent her by taking away his room to give it to her?" I had no clue how parents thought and made a note on my legal pad to ask. If I'd noticed, and my sister noticed, the prosecutor would too.

She clucked her tongue. "Safety is always an issue with little kids. Parents worry about it. That's why there's a whole retail industry dedicated to it."

What had Rory said? "I talked to someone with kids, well, a kid, and she said the first one is all safety and good hygiene. By the second kid, it's more relaxed, more laid back."

"Maybe, but this kid opens the door and her foot is practically on the top step."

I couldn't form a good argument until I spoke to the Quinns and discovered why they allowed the geography of her bedroom to put her in hypothetical peril. "Okay. Aside from that, is there anything in here that isn't right?"

She inspected the doorframe, then the door. "Yes." She waved a hand behind her as she tucked the folder under one arm. "Look." She pointed to the doorknob, a plain Jane lockset.

I bent in to have my own look, straightened, and shrugged. "What?"

"The lock is on the outside."

I leaned in again. "Well, I'll be damned." She turned, walked out of the room down the hall to the little boy's room. I remained staring at the door as though it alone held the mystery of all that happened in the house the night Emily died.

"Aha! Grace." I jumped at Charity's bellow. She poked her head out the door and glared at me. "Get in here."

I trudged down the hall to a room that had no bearing on my case, not quite understanding why she found this so important. "Look." Stacked next to the TV, a tower of DVDs wobbled as she ran her finger up them. She popped open the DVD player, slipped a movie free from the slot, and held it up for me to see. "What would an eight or nine year old boy be doing watching *Cinderella*?" She rushed to the bed, flung back the blankets, and gazed down. "Two pillows."

"So?"

"Good Lord, Grace." How did I suddenly become the stupid sister? "The little girl didn't sleep in that room. I would bet any money on it." She set the folder down on the dresser, reached into her pocket, then pulled out a pair of blue vinyl gloves. "You don't touch anything. Got it?" She was in full work mode—stern line of her mouth, eyes boring into details I hadn't noticed, hands deftly collecting the sheets and pillow slips from the bed. "Go downstairs and see if you can find an unused garbage bag. Don't take it off the roll. Bring me the whole thing."

"What if there are none?"

"Look for those plastic freezer bags, and whatever you do, don't touch them inside."

I nodded and raced from the room to the kitchen where I checked every cabinet, every drawer, and found nothing. As I leaned back against the counter, in front of me, like a gleaming beacon of light, a door marked pantry mocked me. "I'm hungover, okay?" Speaking to no one in particular, I pushed off and stepped inside. A plethora of food and utility supplies stared at me from floor to ceiling shelves. I looked up and mouthed "Thank you" before grabbing both kinds of bags she'd mentioned and rushing back to her.

She placed the pillowcases each into their own Ziploc bag. I handed her a garbage bag, and she carefully stuffed the fitted sheet inside, then stuffed the blanket into yet another. "I have a friend who will test these, but we have to get them in the mail. And I need a DNA sample from everyone in the house. Find me hairbrushes, tooth brushes, and take pictures before you touch anything. You need it from close-up and wide angles."

"I didn't bring a camera."

"Use your phone. Or my phone." She reached in her pocket, whipped out her cell, and snapped pictures of every single thing inside the room, then handed it to me along with my own pair of ugly blue gloves. "Don't touch anything without these on."

"Evidence collection is not my specialty."

She shook her head and looked me up and down. "I have no clue how you won all those cases."

"I had a whole team back home. They brought me stuff and I made it work."

"Grace, the things we've found are all bad news for your client."

I nodded. "I know. If the little girl slept in here, that means everything that morning was staged, but at least I'll know what I'm up against." A tiny smile crept up from my toes to my lips. "As a bonus, if the police or the prosecutor knew this, they would have taken the sheets already."

"Well, that's your half to deal with." When she had all the parcels sealed, she turned to me. "Call the hottie in the uniform from this morning."

"Right." I needed someone official to sign off on the items she was busy listing on the outside of the folder. Once I dialed his number, I tapped my foot against the carpet and breathed a sigh of relief when a decidedly British accent answered. "Are you working?"

"Yes."

"Good. I need you to get to the Quinn's house." I gave him the necessary details, what I needed him to do, then hung up to wait.

Charity stood next to me. "Give me a dollar."

I knew the deal. To ensure the validity of the reports, which wouldn't be an issue if not for our family ties, I had to hire her. I checked my pocket. "All I have is a twenty."

She snatched it out of my hand and shoved it down the front of her shirt. "It'll do. Now, I work for you." I nodded at her smirk. "And I'm flying home tonight with this stuff so I can personally test it. I'll be back with your results as soon as I can." God bless her for taking up forensic science as a life career. "I don't want to trust it to anyone else."

Her incessant finger drumming as she stood over Faith's shoulder, watching our younger sister carefully removed the bathtub to get to its drain, then the shower floor, made me want to slap her, but I bit my tongue and waited.

"Why didn't the CSU guys take the drains out already?"

I shrugged. "I don't know."

"Who's in charge of this rinky-dink operation?" Charity's work ethic surpassed anyone I'd ever met, and her shock that others didn't comply with her high standards was genuine. Her brows knitted together and her eyes narrowed as she asked.

Jamie picked that moment to appear in the doorway. "I am."

Charity turned, her cheeks flushing a bright shade of red.

Faith looked up a drain trap in her hand, cradled as though it were the Holy Grail.

I smiled in spite of myself. It may have only been a few hours since I'd seen him, but I had missed him. "Don't mind her. She thinks the whole world should be taken apart, examined, and put back together before a case is made one way or the other."

She glared at me. "Yes, I do when someone's life is at stake." She crossed her arms. "Science can prove one way or the other that a person is inherently evil or absolutely innocent. Only science can do that."

That wasn't bait I planned to rise to except to say, "You're wrong. Along with science, I have that power. It's my super hero thing." I shrugged a shoulder at her, buffed my nails against my shirt.

Jamie chuckled. "I'll bet growing up in your house was—"

In one voice, my sisters and I answered, "Loud."

Chapter 22

I followed Jamie downstairs to the front porch. As he headed to his car, I laid my hand in the center of his back between his shoulder blades. His heart thumped and I smiled. There were some things his cool, quiet-guy demeanor couldn't hide. "Thank you for taking care of me last night."

He turned, leaned down, and kissed my cheek. "Can I see you tonight?"

I considered that for a minute. A short minute. "Yes." I stood there, my hands itching to slip under his shirt, feel his skin unadorned against mine. My mind's eye envisioned all the things we could end up doing and my skin heated.

"I could bring some take-out and a movie?"

I frowned. "Afraid I'll embarrass you in public?" Not that the concept was unheard of when it concerned me and relationships, but I had an entirely different idea as to what the night could be.

He moved closer, crowded me against the side of his SUV. "More afraid I'll have to share you."

My fingers crept up to his shoulders, brushed up the side of his neck. "You say the best stuff."

"You inspire me."

His lips brushed against my jaw then my mouth. My breath stalled as I waited for more that didn't come. He stepped away, but ran his thumb along the line of my mouth as he stared at me, a world of mystery behind his eyes.

"I should get back to work." His voice cracked and he ducked his head.

"I wish we were alone in a better place." My mouth did not have permission to make that kind of statement.

As he lowered his head once more, Charity cleared her throat, breaking the spell he'd cast over me. I took a step back, but stayed within touching distance in case the opportunity presented itself.

"If the love fest is finished down here, I need to go back to the apartment and get my stuff so I can fly home."

I squinted one eye and shook my head, spinning to flip her off. Jamie chuckled, the sound at my back ringing through me, heightening my awareness of his close proximity.

A moment later, gravel crunched under his tires as he pulled out of the driveway onto the street. I walked back to the porch.

Faith, toolbox in one hand and a couple of bags in the other, came off the porch in a blaze of energy. "I've never worked this upfront on one of your cases before." She shoved her stuff into the trunk and turned. "It's exciting. Definitely better than sitting on the sidelines listening to you guys rant on about witness this and jury that. Building houses might not be able to compete anymore."

I shrugged. "I haven't taken a case this big before. Usually, I know exactly what I'm getting into, but this one is more…" I didn't have a good word to describe the turmoil rolling around in my stomach whenever I considered the facts of this case, and tried to fit them together into a working picture.

Charity rested a hand on my shoulder. "No worries, glory girl. You can figure this out."

I rolled my eyes. "You know, I've never liked when you call me that."

She stepped around me and hopped into the driver seat. "Can you deny that you love it when reporters are shoving microphones in your face and congratulating you on a win no one thought would happen?"

Okay, she had a point, but she didn't have to emphasize it with a nickname that made me sound like I chased the reporters down for their praise, especially when the truth of it was contrary to the image.

I climbed into the car and she pulled away from the house. While I knew she probably hadn't meant anything by it, I considered her words. "Do you guys think about me like that?"

"Self-doubt? Isn't it a little late for all of that now, Grace?" Faith's edges had always been sharp, and her words swiped at me with an axe that struck another nick into our relationship.

"Maybe."

"I don't think you're bad for it, Grace." Charity cast a sideways glance as she turned the wrong way at a crossroad. "I think the things you put yourself in the middle of might be the reason you drink too much and party too long. But I also think you have a cloud of karmic good luck surrounding you."

Luck? And when did this turn into an episode of *Dr. Phil*? "I work my ass off. I deserve to have fun when I'm not knee deep in drug dealers and shady husbands who put anti-freeze in their wives coffee in the morning instead of the usual two cubes of sugar."

"You shouldn't ask questions if you don't want the answer." Faith's helpful input from the backseat earned her one of my go-to-hell scowls.

I could live without the backseat backbiting. "Thank you, Confucius. I'll try to remember that." Actually a rule of good lawyers everywhere, I lived by the concept in the courtroom. In a supposedly safe conversation with my sisters, I shouldn't have needed to consider it.

"That's why you bought new boobs?" Charity reached a pointy finger and poked my left breast. "To console yourself after a bad case?"

"No. I defended a plastic surgeon and he couldn't afford to pay me. It was either this or a nose job. And I like my nose."

"Don't be flip. We're worried about you." She'd morphed from slightly older sister to mother figure in the space of another left hand turn. "You drink too much. You forgot to pick us up from the airport. You're involved with identical men. Did I mention you drink too much?"

"Alcohol kills brain cells and you're two margaritas away from becoming a talking monkey."

I turned to glare at Faith, the seatbelt saving her from my arm pounding her in the head. "I appreciate your input. I'll take it under advisement." Thankfully, my cell jingled a melody in my pocket and I checked the screen before answering. Blane? What did he want? "Hello?"

"We need to talk." His voice, on the gravelly side of its usually curved sounds, grated through the speaker.

"About what?"

"Come on, Grace. Just come talk to me."

I shook my head. "No."

"I miss you, Grace. Please. Everything isn't the way you think it is."

"Are you still married?"

"Yes." His pained whisper choked at my heart.

"Still having a baby?" Not that I would have wished anything to change it for them. My voice broke as I asked the question.

"Please, Grace. Meet me tonight."

"I can't. I have plans." With someone who genuinely seemed to care about me, whose face lit up when I walked into a room. Who didn't use my body and toss me aside for the next ring of his cell phone. With a man who made me tingle just by looking at me, not because of the way he looked, but because of the way he treated me, touched me.

"He's not what you think he is. He's a liar and a thief." There was the bitterness I expected.

"He's not married." I disconnected the call and fogged the window with a huff of my breath.

Charity's voice snapped me out of the funk Blane's call wrapped me in. "Where the hell am I?"

Somehow, in the minutes I'd been ignoring the trip, she found a country road lined only with trees and no telltale signs or buildings. "I haven't got a clue." I whipped my head toward her. "Why are you driving anyway?"

She slammed on the brakes. "You were all wrapped up in top cop and I wanted to get back to your apartment."

"Turn around and go back the way you came."

After a few swearwords as she attempted a three point turn that ended up being a fifteen pointer on the narrow road, and a quick consult with cellular GPS, she finally angled the car onto the street in front of my apartment. Within minutes of our return, she'd booked a flight for herself and Faith, dumped out a whole bottle of vodka and one half full of wine, arranged my apartment into a semi-working living space, and unpacked most of the boxes still towering over my sofa.

"Jeez. Lay off the caffeine, Char." But I had to admit, thanks to the speed and verve with which she found homes for all my things, she'd provided me with room to move and work I had been without.

Chapter 23

I made the two hour round trip to the airport, shoved them and my evidence onto a plane, and returned home as Jamie walked up my front steps. "Hey."

He rewarded me with a bone-melting smile. "Hello. I thought you'd forgotten about me."

Forget him? Seriously? The man obviously didn't have a clue. "Nope. Had to get rid of my sisters."

He frowned.

"Not like with a shovel and a shallow grave. Think airplane."

"My line of work makes me hear things a little differently."

"See crime where there is none?"

"It's a character flaw." He grinned just a little and looked at me from under a veil of thick eyelashes. "Or maybe it's my super hero thing."

I unlocked the door and he followed me in. In one hand, he held a small bouquet of wildflowers he'd obviously picked from someone's garden as they still had globs of dirt at the base of the stems, and a movie. In the other, a box of microwave popcorn. He looked around the now wide-open space of my home, turned in a full circle, and raised both eyebrows. "Wow. You do this for me?"

I lowered my eyes. "If I say yes and it's a lie, even if I want it to be true, is that bad?"

His nose wrinkled as he nodded.

"Okay. My sister did it. I have no clue where she put anything."

"She didn't leave a map?"

I shook my head. "She'll be back in a couple days. I only have to survive until then."

Together we popped the popcorn then he hooked up the television to the DVD player. We sat back on the sofa watching bubbles of static roll across the screen. "Are all the cords in the right places?"

He shook his head. "I haven't a clue. I'm not mechanical."

I laughed. A real laugh for the first time in a long time. "Why didn't you say so?" I snapped the power button to the TV. "We could talk."

"Okay."

To buy a little time, I chewed the inside of my cheek. I didn't want to tell him about the phone call with Blane, but…"Your brother called me today."

He nodded and looked away. "Did he?"

"He said he wants to talk."

"Do you?" He pointed those beautiful eyes at me. "Want to talk to him?"

I took the bowl of popcorn off the space between us and set it in my lap then scooted closer. "No." I wrapped my hand around the back of his neck and tugged until his lips hovered an inch above mine. "I want to stay right here with you."

I leaned forward and kissed him softly, slowly, drawing out the touch into minutes rather than the quick second I'd planned. He wrapped his arm around my shoulders, caressed the side of my throat with his thumb, the touch almost as erotic as his tongue teasing the inside of my mouth. I wanted more, to touch him, feel his body against mine, and hear him whisper my name in a way only he ever had. I had it bad.

When we parted, popcorn spilled all over my carpet and, as he leaned down to pick it up, his hand brushed my leg. Someone had forgotten to tell my hormones we were still in kissing only mode.

I stood and walked to the TV. "I'll try to fix this."

His total focus on popcorn retrieval gave me a full minute to admire his form. With each reach of his arm, his muscles bunched and relaxed. He worked with such a fixed concentration, hunting under the sofa for wayward kernels, sliding his hand over the cream colored area rug to locate ones that blended in well enough the naked eye could have missed them. An army of dancers could probably have spun their way across the floor and I wouldn't have been able to tear my gaze away from him.

After a lovely few moments of adoring his body, I checked my chin for drool and began dealing with a sailor's knot of wires. With a few new swear words under my belt, I stepped back and turned the TV back on. Sounds and light filled the room as the symphony of music set to motion picture filled the air.

"Shall I make more popcorn?"

He rose to his full height, bowl in hand, and I shook my head, grabbed a throw off the chair, and advanced toward him. With his head cocked to one side, he looked down at me as I lay on the sofa and patted the spot behind me. "There's room for two." If we squished together, mashed our bodies in tight, and he held me from falling off the edge.

Without a sound, he rolled in behind me, wrapped both arms around me, and spooned his legs with mine. "You smell nice. Like flowers and sunshine."

I pressed a kiss against the bend of his arm and wiggled my bottom against him. "Stop distracting me. I'm watching a movie."

By the end, I'd shifted and squirmed enough that every cell in my body stood at full alert. He'd tried moving away, but the back of the sofa provided little refuge. As the credits of the most ignored movie ever played in my living room rolled across the screen, there was no hiding how badly he wanted me. I spun around, flung my leg over his hip, and waited.

"Did you like the movie?"

"I don't know." His hoarse whisper thrilled the little seductress inside me, and I rubbed against him again. His eyes closed and his fingers curled into the back of my shirt. "You are making it difficult not to carry you into your bedroom."

"Good." I couldn't move any closer without crawling into his clothes with him.

He tucked a piece of hair behind my ear then let his finger trail down my chin and up to trace my lower lip. "I don't want to just fall into bed with you. I want to know you, build something to last longer than a few hours in your bedroom."

"A few hours?" My throat slammed shut and my brain focused on the promise behind those words.

Hours. Not minutes. A bed. Not a car or a car hood.

"I'm extremely thorough."

Oh, God. "Well, I'm all about put up or shut up. It's a personal motto actually."

"Grace…"

I countered with a breathy, "Jamie."

Our lips came together in an explosion of fire, a collapse of the space-time continuum. Suspended in minutes, hours, days, a world passing by that didn't include me. I lost myself in the sensation of pressing intimately against him.

Spurred on by the moan against my throat, I slid my hands under the warm cotton of his shirt, walking my fingers up his abs to his chest. His lips branded my skin. His body caressed mine.

He lifted the hem of my T-shirt, and tired of waiting for him to do more than brush his knuckles across my skin, I yanked it over my head.

"So impatient." He grinned as I pawed his skin, shoved his shirt out of the way. He caught my hand, brought it to his lips, and ran his tongue along the inside of my palm. A symphony of sound erupted in my ears, drumbeats of passion mixed with strings of awareness. Every touch, every kiss plunged me deeper into the sensations created by his body, his taste, the way he inspired my complete and total surrender.

I quivered in places I didn't know had the capability, and when he swept his fingers over my collarbone down to the swell of my breast, then followed the trail with his mouth, I threw my head back, pushing into him, wishing the barrier of clothing between us would evaporate or melt away.

He pulled back, breathed softly against my skin, and whispered, "Have you ever been with someone who loves you so completely you're the only thing they can think of? Someone who needs to see your smile? Who dreams of you even when he's awake?"

I opened my lids to find him staring at me, desire burning behind his eyes. Mesmerized by the soft tone of his voice, I shook my head.

"Then tonight will be a first for both of us." I swallowed hard and he continued. "I've never felt this way before, Grace."

He captured my reply with a kiss, and in a move inspired by some Victorian romance novel, swooped me into his arms without breaking the contact, then carried me to the bedroom. I slid down his body until my toes curled into the plush carpet beside my bed.

His eyes raked over my body as he tugged me forward by a belt loop. "I'm not my brother, Grace. If he's the one you want…"

I shushed his words with a finger over his lips. "I don't want him. I want you. Right here. Right now. And tomorrow and the next day."

"And after that?"

"Yes." My heart thumped an erratic beat so loud I wanted to cover it to shush the pounding. Instead, I closed my eyes as he lowered his head, brushed my hair away from my neck, and kissed each of the light bruises left there.

"I'm sorry he hurt you."

"I'm sorry I hurt you."

"No." His soft smile preceded a softer kiss. "It brought us here, to this moment. You are worth every minute." He captured my mouth, then claimed it, branded me with his lips, his hands, his eyes.

I reached for the button on his jeans, and he caught my hands between his. "No. Tonight is for you."

I grinned, appreciating the sentiment, not so much the timing. "Well, the equipment I require is in there." I pointed a gaze at the bulge in his pants.

He shook his head, a cat-who-ate-the kibble grin tilting his lips. "We'll get there."

I'd never known such reverence or tenderness, such worship as that which shone through his eyes as he explored my body with his hands, his eyes, his mouth. With slow, agonizing steps, he stripped me of the rest of my clothes, then stretched out beside me, tracing a finger down my stomach, circling my belly button before trailing lower. My body burned beneath the surface of my skin. I ached for more.

I reached out to prod him along and he stopped, held my hand to his lips, and pressed a kiss against the inside of my wrist. "Be still. Let me take my time with you, know you." He raised his eyebrows in question and I nodded.

Every touch took an eternity of anticipation as each moment passed into the next and he continued to tease me into an oblivion where only he existed. His mouth blazed a path from my collarbone to my hips, kissing and swirling his tongue over my skin in white hot passes. As I was almost ready to beg for more, he lowered his head between my legs, and I couldn't form a thought. I writhed beneath him, and he braced a hand on each side of me, holding me still as he continued making magic with his mouth.

Unable to do more than pant, my world narrowed to pinpoints of light followed by starbursts and an explosion of my every atom. His name rang in my ears, and when I could finally form a thought, he lowered his head again.

This time, he moved slower, making love with his tongue, his fingers. His soft moans vibrated against me as he lapped and suckled at my skin. I couldn't hold still, begged for more. I needed so much I hadn't realized until that moment. With the blanket fisted in my hands, I struggled to remain still. I shattered into a million pieces, and finally, he shoved his pants away.

When he covered my body with his, I could do no more than cling to him, hang on to the precious minutes of being cherished, caressed, and massaged until the frenzy of desire took over. Even then, I held on to him, heart pounding, breaths coming in short gasps, as desire consumed me, pushed me over the edge, and I cried out, more intense, more alive than I'd ever felt.

I shuddered and floated back to my body as he trembled over me.

He kissed my shoulder and rolled away, sliding an arm under my neck, tucking me in at his side.

"Very thorough."

He closed his eyes. "I'm not finished with you. Not near finished."

I drew a nail over the line of hair trailing down his stomach, then moved back toward his chest. "Tell me something about you only I'll know."

"Our secret code?"

"If I need it, maybe."

He trapped my hand under his, held it there on his stomach. "Okay. Something no one else knows." I nodded. "I went to law school at the same time Blane did."

I shook my head. "I think Blane probably knows that, and your law professors, maybe even a few other students." A hundred girls with a sleazy twin fantasy?

His hair mussed against my pillow as he nodded. "Yes. That isn't my big secret."

"Sorry."

"I had to take a test, a big one. And I was in this place in my mind where I had no idea what I wanted to be. I'd only gone into law because of Blane. He wanted to do it together and start our own firm. He had our lives planned, beginning to end." His thumb stroked my palm as he spoke and he stared at a spot on the wall. "He blames me for quitting, for failing that test, for his being a prosecutor instead of raking in the big money."

"Why does he blame you?"

"I ruined his dreams." His lips twisted and he waited a moment before speaking again. "But I didn't fail. I used that test, that lie, to get out of law school, but the truth is I passed."

"And you never told him?"

He shook his head. "Now, tell me your secrets."

I laughed a bubbly little sound that came out more giggle than usual. "I drink too much to have secrets. I'm chatty."

"I know."

Uh-oh. "You know?" This could be bad for me. I sat up, closed my eyes, and said a quick prayer. "What do you know?"

"Many, many things I bet you don't remember telling me. Things that make me like you more."

Heat seared its way through my veins, congregating in my cheeks. "And less, I suspect."

"No."

"For example?"

His mouth twitched from side to side. "This is supposed to be you telling me things."

"My boobs are fake." I nodded. "Probably not a big secret, but I didn't take a billboard out to advertise the idea, either. Now, tell me all the things I told you while I was too drunk to know better."

"Well, you did tell me that. You didn't tell me what compelled you to get them."

Damn me for bringing that up. "It's a long story."

"I'm not leaving."

"Okay. Here it is. I've always been tall, with these ridiculous long arms"—I held them out in front of me—"no curves, flat chest. I was pathetic. I never wore makeup or dresses. The only shoes I had were meant for running and everything from here up"—I moved my hand from my waist toward my neck—"was as flat as Illinois farmland."

"I'm not sure I believe that."

"Oh, it's true. I was so busy in college trying to be the best in my class, I didn't care. All my friends deserted me, so I didn't have to compete with anyone. I had my sisters, but they probably love me more without makeup or good hair. Anyway, after law school, I worked for this guy back home. My first case was a plastic surgeon getting divorced. He didn't want to part with his money. So, I fought like I was protecting a kid or something and I won. As he left the courthouse the last day, he slipped a business card into my hand and said since I'd helped him, he'd be happy to return the favor."

"And a fairy god mother came into your room one night and transformed you into what you are now?"

"No. I was completely freaked out about that *help me* thing. I'd always been a pretty happy girl my whole life, but if a complete stranger thought I needed help, maybe there was something to it. I looked in the mirror, really looked. My clothes fit wrong, my hair was scraggly and this color of blonde that wasn't actually blonde, but too light to be brown, just icky. So, I celebrated my first win with a makeover. Then, not completely happy with my new look, I called that client and made an appointment. A couple weeks later, I bought my first bra that wasn't a trainer."

I gasped as he moved his hand up, caressed my nipple through the sheet. "Then, with my new look, I needed a new wardrobe. Suddenly, I had some confidence. Sometimes, I still see that scraggly mess in the mirror." Maybe that explained why I'd easily fallen into bed with Blane, even though he treated me as nothing more than a body to use for his amusement. "Anyway, that's my big secret." My words broke as he replaced his fingers with his mouth. Story time was over.

* * * *

I stretched, rolled my head around on my neck, and sat up, pulling more than my share of the blanket with me. Memories of the night flooded back to me, talking, touching, kissing. I had a lot to smile about.

He sat up, leaned on one hand, his chest against my back, and kissed my shoulder.

"Good morning."

"It's afternoon, love. We didn't make it to sleep until morning."

"I love lazy Sundays." His lips skimmed my cheek as I turned into his kiss. "Do you have to work today?"

"Not so far."

"Wanna go for a run?" Rejuvenated by my overnight athletics, I had a hankering to feel the sun on my face, to breathe some fresh air.

"It's raining."

As if cued by his words, a loud clap of thunder split the air, and I jumped. He tugged me back toward the pillow, wrapped his arm around me, and I snuggled in close.

"Okay, staying in is fine with me."

"Mmm. Me too." He ran his hand down my arm and laced our fingers together.

"I could make us some breakfast."

"Or we can shower together and I can buy us breakfast."

"What happened to staying in?" I puffed my lower lip out and wiggled my eyebrows.

He chuckled as I crawled on top of him, kissed my way from his ear to his collarbone.

"You are a very persuasive woman."

Chapter 24

Spending the night with Jamie, connecting with him, falling for him, scared me on many levels. I'd never experienced this kind of magnetic pull toward another person, never wanted to be connected, but something about him made me yearn for more. Not just the sex, although, I would never say no to that. I enjoyed every part of our night, the talking and laughing, not to mention the cuddling and silliness between go rounds.

He pushed his bowl away. "That was the worst oatmeal I've ever tasted." But he said it with a smile.

"Well, that's because they were mashed potatoes. I didn't have oatmeal." I shrugged as I cleared the dishes to the sink. "I thought I owed you food after that shower." Long, soapy, and steamy from more than the heat of the water.

As I rinsed the dishes, he stood behind me, nuzzling his chin into the bend at my neck. He wrapped his arms wrapped around my waist. "You don't cook much?"

"No." I turned around, put my wet hands on his chest, leaving damp prints as I slid them up to clasp behind his neck. "That's bad, right?"

"I happen to be a wonderful chef. And my mum owns a restaurant. You won't starve."

"You are a man of many talents."

He walked backward to a kitchen chair and sat, pulling me on top of him. His lips teased mine as his hands skimmed my side, landed on my hips, and pulled me more fully into place.

"I can't get enough of you." His ragged breath blew back my hair as I kissed my way across his neck to his shoulder and rocked my body against his. I didn't want him to ever feel like he'd had enough, because God knew I never would.

Scooting back the tiniest fraction I could manage, I unfastened his jeans and shoved my hand inside. He let his head fall back, his eyes close.

After a minute, I moved off him, pulled him to his feet. He looked down at me and sucked in a loud breath as I dropped to my knees to tug his pants down, never taking my gaze from his.

He gripped the table behind him as I took him into my mouth, swirling my tongue over the moist tip.

"Grace." He moaned my name as his hand fisted in my hair, holding me in place. I increased the pace, then slowed, teasing until he blew apart and his body sagged. When I swept a kiss across the inside of his thigh and he jumped, I giggled like a giddy schoolgirl.

"So sensitive." I towed his jeans up as I stood and pressed my lips to his cheek, then grinned as he wrinkled his nose and wiped his cheek.

He pulled me in close, buried his face in the crook of my neck, and nipped gently at my throat. "That was amazing."

"You inspired me."

Pulling back, he framed my face with his hands, kissed me softly. "You're more than I could have ever imagined. More than I probably deserve." The sadness in his eyes didn't match the moment. I opened my mouth to ask about it, but he quickly cut me off. "How about I take us out for a real meal?"

"You didn't love my mashed potatoes?"

He grinned. "They, like you, were perfect, but after last night and now, I need to replenish my energy supply."

"I'll go change."

After the quickest quick-change I'd ever managed, I stepped out of the bathroom to find him on the phone, his back to me.

"That's ridiculous, Blane. She'll never believe you." I stepped behind the wall, the busy body in me always on duty. "Well, that's your problem with your wife. Leave her out of it. Leave me out of it."

He gripped the phone in both hands as though trying to choke the life out of it, then pressed it back to his ear. Anger radiated off him as he lowered his voice. "I can't pretend to be you and I won't. Not anymore. I care about this girl, and I'm not messing it up to help you out of a jam you never should have been in." He ran a hand through his hair and stepped out of my line of sight. "No. I don't want to see Mum get hurt." I leaned in to hear better. "Fine. I'll be there in a little while." He ran his finger over the screen, and his shoulders rose high with a deep breath he whooshed out as I laid a hand in the middle of his back.

"You okay?"

"Yeah." He wrapped me in his arms, rested his cheek on the top of my head. "Just a work thing. Nothing to worry about."

I nodded and stepped back. We'd had all the sex I could manage for the day, and I couldn't think of a single activity inside my house that wouldn't lead us back to my bedroom. A ray of light snuck its way in through the curtains at the window. "How about that walk now?"

"It was a run earlier."

"I changed my mind." I shrugged. "Maybe I want to hold your hand, walk next to you and talk."

But the air in the room changed. No longer light and playful, he'd gone dark, shielded himself with a moody cloud. "I should go."

Almost willing to beg him not to lie to me, to stay with me, I nodded. "Okay."

I followed him to the door, leaned against the edge with one hand over my head after he stepped through. On my front porch, he turned, cupped my face with his hand. "I meant everything I said to you, Grace."

"You could blow off work." The bubbles in the pit of my stomach told me almost as much as the sadness in his eyes, and desperation crawled into my heart. "You don't have to go."

He closed his eyes, and when he opened them, he drew away and turned to leave. Without so much as a look back or even a wave over his shoulder, he strolled across the street, climbed into a police car, and drove away. I shut the door and plopped onto the couch.

The walls in my house grew smaller for every minute I sat in them. I grabbed my shoulder bag, stuck my case file, phone, and a couple notepads inside, then set off to do what I did best—ignore the things that bugged me.

* * * *

I drove through town to the outskirts, maneuvered onto the highway, and picked up speed. Life would have been much better had this pitiful town had its own Starbucks. I needed a double shot mocha, something served by a barista who didn't care about the day, the week, or the month I'd had. Just served the coffee and waited on the next customer without the personal chit chat of a mom and pop diner. I drove into Dallas, commandeered a table at the first Starbucks I saw, and lifted my overstuffed bag onto the table.

No one cared that I buried myself in the files spread out on the table for four. Three hours later, I had two tablets full of notes and questions for the Quinns. I had Post-its stuck to the photos, and no matter how many times I looked at it, something about that closet bothered me. It gnawed at me until I finally brought the photo closer to my face, held it up and examined it from every angle. Then it hit me.

                              Melissa Shirley

I shoved everything back into my bag and raced outside as though the devil himself aimed his pitchfork at my ass.

More than an hour later, I pulled up in front of the Quinn house and left the car door open as I raced inside, phone in one hand, picture in the other. I dialed Charity, excited about my discovery.

Taking the stairs two at a time, I ran down the hallway, bypassing the other doors until I stood in front of his closet. I shoved an overflowing toy box to the side and there, in the space behind it, a wooden panel with a key hole. "Son of a bitch."

I tried prying it open with my fingernails, but the clasp stuck like it had been nailed into place. Shoving a bobby pin into the key slot, I prayed the tumblers would give, but to no avail. With no other choice, I shoved the clothes on the rod over my head out of the way and kicked, thankful for the running shoes I'd worn. After about ten minutes of putting all my strength into an attack, the wood splintered enough that I could grab it and pull, leaving a hole. I shuffled out of the closet, reached into my bag for a pair of gloves—Charity insisted I have my own supply—then shoved my hand inside the hole I'd kicked through. Using the light on my phone, I lit up the dim space. "Oh no."

With the clothes on my lap, I leaned back and wished it had been anything else hidden in the false wall of the closet. I laid them on the floor and used my phone to photograph them, front and back, together, then each piece separately. Every minute I sat there inside the closet, every picture I snapped, choked a new piece of life out of me. The caked blood had cracked over time, and the clothes had hardened. I closed my eyes and said a prayer. Life had taken a turn for the worse, and this time, winning would break me.

* * * *

After parking in front of my apartment, I couldn't stand the thought of being alone and walked down the street. I strolled first away from the bar, then toward it, with steps much quicker than a few minutes earlier. As I walked, the horror of Emily Quinn's last thoughts, the last thing she realized, slammed into me with full force, the eyes she'd looked into as she took her last breath, the terror she must have felt.

I opened the door and walked straight to the bar. Ignored, yet again, I leaned over, grabbed my own glass and a bottle of whiskey, the cheap kind, and poured a big shot before anyone noticed.

"You can't do that." A bartender I'd never met and didn't care to win over with my bubbly personality snatched the bottle off the counter and held out his hand for money.

I rooted around in my purse, pulled out my American Express, and slapped it into his hand. "Now, put the bottle down and walk away."

He shoved the card next to the cash register then resumed ignoring me as though I wore a leper's shroud rather than designer jeans and a Bon Jovi T-shirt.

As I drank, it became easier to forget all I knew, easier to lose myself in the bottom of my glass, right up to the moment someone tapped my shoulder. I peered up through one open eye. "Oh, we have to stop meeting like this." I smiled and ran a finger down his bare arm.

His twangy voice told me I'd been mistaken. "Well, sweetheart, you don't leave me much choice when you won't take my calls."

With a hand at my back, he spun the stool until my knees were rested at the top of his thighs. He put a hand on each side of my waist and lifted. "Let's get you out of here."

I hugged my messenger bag with the evidence I'd taken from the Quinn house to my chest. "Where are we going?"

"Just getting some air, sweetheart. Then I'll tuck you into bed, and you can pretend I'm my brother and give me some of what you gave him last night." He guided me to the door and helped me outside with a hand on my back.

I pushed him off me, stumbled, and caught myself with the backrest of a bench along the sidewalk. "You've had enough of me. Go home to your wife."

"Oh, I will, but first we need to talk."

"I'm with Jamie now."

He pursed his lips, nodded twice. "Of course you are." He wrapped his fingers around my arm and squeezed, pain radiating up through my shoulder, down to my wrist. "Let's go."

"I don't have anything to say, Blane."

His eyes narrowed, and his mouth compressed as he bent at the waist to put his nose against mine. To anyone passing, we probably looked like lovers about to share a kiss, but there was something sinister in his stance, in his eyes. "Then you'll listen. Drop this case or someone is going to get hurt."

Even without the ability to stand on my own or hold my head straight on my shoulders, I recognized the danger behind his words. "If that's a threat, Blane, I'm not scared. You're nothing but some pathetic married guy who has no idea how to satisfy a woman." Shaking with anger, I pushed him back again and stood, almost straight. "No wonder your wife left you. And for your information, you could take a lesson or two from your brother. I'm sure Valerie would appreciate it."

He stepped closer, tangled his fingers in my hair, then gave it a little yank. "He's a liar, Grace, and you're too stupid to see it. He's the one tampering with juries and planting evidence. He wears my suits and sleeps in bed with my wife trying to be me. Then he leaves my house, calls you up, and takes you to bed like the cheap whore you are."

"Careful there, Tex. Your charm's fading."

"And my brother's not your knight in shining armor. We're the same, me and him, right down to our DNA."

"Bullshit, Blane. He's twice the man you are."

"Where do you think he's at right now? Call him. See if he doesn't answer his phone in my voice so my wife has no clue which one of us she's fucking."

My gaze wobbled but found his as I pulled out my cell, then punched a number into the screen.

"Oh, you have him on speed dial. That's sweet."

I shoved against his chest, but he held on as Jamie answered. "Hello." I closed my eyes as his lilt adopted a slur. "Hello?" I hit end. Shit. Jamie. What had he said into the phone that morning when he spoke to Blane? It escaped me, just out of my reach.

"He's with my wife right now, pretending to be me."

I closed my eyes and the world spiraled. His hand, still fisted against my scalp, held me upright. "Let go of me, Blane, or I'll scream. I mean it."

With one last jerk, he let me go, pushed me forward, and I fell to my knees.

"Gutter's right over there waiting for you, Grace." He squeezed my cheek, forced me to look at the curb. "Why don't you go crawl into it and save me the trouble of kicking you there."

"Fuck. You. Blane."

He walked away laughing before I stood, shoved my phone into my back pocket, gathered my bag onto my shoulder, and weaved my way home.

Chapter 25

The shrill beep of my alarm clock—no, I'd broken that. I sat up, coughing and sputtering in a thick haze of smoke billowing under the door to my bedroom. What was the rule? A child's song came to mind. Head and shoulders, knees and toes. No. That wasn't it. Stop, drop, and roll. It had something to do with fire, I rolled across the floor to the door, felt the knob, singed my skin on the metal. Shit.

The spaces in my room containing pure air shrunk by the second, and I couldn't think, couldn't figure a way out. "Help!" My pathetic rasp went unheard as I struggled to the window, reached a hand out, and fought to get closer. Still inches, or feet, maybe miles short of my goal, I hacked until I couldn't raise a hand. I laid flat against the floor, knowing death waited for me, had finally caught up with me. My mind screamed for me to get up and run, to find a place where the air was thinner and I could breathe, but my limbs weighed me down. I couldn't move. My heart ached for the things I would never do, the wedding I would never have, the children I would never carry. I said a quick prayer for whatever sins I committed and resigned myself to my fate.

* * * *

"She's waking up." The voice broke into my death and pulled me back. My chest hurt, my arm ached, and a blur of white noise rang through my ears.

I tried to speak, held up a hand that weighed too much. My eyes stayed blissfully shut, blocking out the thousand sounds whirring around me. I sank back against a pillow, wishing I could block out everything.

"Grace, can you open your eyes for me?" A soothing voice I didn't recognize spoke through the clouds of fog in my mind.

I tried, struggled to pull them up through sheer strength of will, to see what was happening all around me, Pain splintered through my head. My voice choked on a cough caught by the mask on my face. I pulled it off my mouth and sat up, the violence in my chest hacking out my throat.

"You're okay, Grace. You have a bad burn on your arm and you inhaled a lot of smoke."

"Is everybody else, okay?" My voice adopted a smoked-too-many-Marlboros rasp.

"The fire was contained mostly in your apartment. The people upstairs weren't home and the people next door have some water damage. The sheriff broke his wrist when he carried you out. Try to relax and we'll get you both to the hospital in a second."

"Jamie saved me?"

The EMT, a girl I guessed to be about twelve, pushed my shoulder back against the gurney. "He's fine. He's getting his wrist braced right now then we'll take you both in."

"How did my apartment start on fire?"

"I don't know, hon. The arson investigator is in there with the fire chief. You're a lucky girl."

Yeah. I was feeling rather lucky, not counting my house burning down, my hangover clashing horribly with smoke inhalation, and the agony that had replaced my left arm. All of that, along with the fact that Jamie had posed as Blane once again to fool yet another unassuming woman, crashed in on me. Definitely lucky.

I would have rolled my eyes at my own thoughts, but I couldn't believe they would be able to fight their way back to the front. Imagining a blank canvas, I tried to clear my mind, then watched it fill up with words…liar, cheat, drunk, death, murder… and my personal favorite… arson.

With a jolt, I was loaded into the ambulance with an oxygen mask wheezing air into my lungs. Shivers rippled down my body as a sudden cold chill enveloped me and Jamie climbed into the ambulance. "Are you okay?"

I turned my head, faced the cold white wall. His voice, the warmth, the sincerity, the concern, floated over me, and for a minute, I couldn't block him out. For a minute.

"Please, Grace. Talk to me…please." I tuned out the sound of his voice, ignored the pleading. "At least let me know you're okay."

The pain in his voice softened my anger enough that I decided to answer. "I'm fine." But the words choked out accompanied by a hacking cough.

"Your arm is burnt."

I lifted the mask off my face and held it away from the EMT trying to wrestle it from my grasp and snap it back in place. "Stop. I can breathe."

I struggled against the restraint keeping me flat, and finding no release from it, turned to face Jamie. "You lied to me. Over and over."

"Once."

"Where were you tonight?"

"Home. I smelled the smoke and came to save you." I rolled my head away. "I saved you, Grace."

"I called your phone. Heard you answer in Blane's accent while you were with his wife."

He shook his head, ran a hand over my hair, smoothing it back. "No. It wasn't me. I don't have my phone. I lost it this afternoon at the diner."

"I heard it, Jamie. I called you and I heard you answer." A tear I neither expected or welcomed slipped out the corner of my eye.

"It wasn't me, Grace."

I shook my head, closed my eyes. "It doesn't matter."

"It matters to me."

"Not now."

He continued to stroke the top of my head until we arrived and he climbed out. Separated by more than the flimsy curtains between our cubicles, I strained to hear his voice as he explained how he'd banged his arm on my doorframe as he carried me out. He coughed twice and I resisted the urge to climb from my bed and throw myself into his arms. He'd lied to me. I needed to keep reminding myself or I'd end up being some piece in the game he played with his brother.

The whir of the oxygen blowing up my nose, the beep of the monitor attached to me measuring my air quality levels, did nothing to drown out the sadness in his tone. After a few minutes, a nurse pushed back the curtain, edged toward the bed. With a tube of cream in one hand and a pair of scissors in the other, she took a seat next to the bed. After a couple of attempts at small talk—did I have any idea how the fire started, would I like her to call someone for me, I was a lucky girl—she gave up and worked quietly.

Removing the bandage, she exposed my charred, peeling skin. I turned away as she cleaned the wound, then spread the cream gingerly over my wrist. It would scar, but I hadn't died, so a little scarring didn't bother me so much.

After a few hours, Dr. Too-young-to-have-served-his-time-in-med-school signed my release papers and I was free to go home. With a sinking heart, I realized I had nowhere to go, no home, no clothes other than the smoke soaked ones I had on. My cash, whatever I had left, my credit cards, and my ID, along with the evidence I'd collected at the Quinn's had all burned up in the fire. The evidence to clear my client was gone. *Shit.*

A hundred or more swear words floated around my mind and I brushed them all back. Logic. I needed a big fat dose of logic, someone to help me put this mess I'd made into perspective. What I needed was a plan.

I stepped out into the waiting room and Rory shot up from her seat, rushed forward, and threw her arms around me. "Oh my God. Are you okay?"

"Yes. I'm fine, aside from smelling like I slept in a barbeque grill." She pulled me through the door, but I dug my heels in, stopping our progress outside the emergency room entrance. "I have to talk to you about the Quinn case. It isn't what I thought."

"Okay, but let's get you home where you can relax."

I shook my head. "No. I can't. I need to call my sister, go see Gabby, talk to Blane's wife. Gabby's innocent." Well, mostly. She had helped cover up a crime, but considering the circumstances, I could argue extenuating circumstances, capacity diminished by grief…oh hell. Either way, the situation plain old sucked.

"Okay. We'll talk about it, but let's get out of here."

I followed her to her car, climbed in, and waited as she backed out. "I went to the house, Gabby's house, today. In the closet behind the toy box in the boy's bedroom, I found a panel." No one I'd ever met used decorative wall coverings in closets. It was what bothered me about the room.

I reached into my back pocket, pulled out my cell, and smiled. "Oh, thank God. I forgot I put it there." I scrolled through the pictures, found what I was looking for, and held it up for her to see. "Look. She didn't do it."

Rory glanced at the screen, whipped the car onto the shoulder of the road, and grabbed my phone from my hand. "I would bet any money she'd rather go to jail than tell what happened in that house, pictures or not." She frowned. "Where are the pajamas now?"

"Burned up in the fire, is my guess."

"You took them from the house?" I nodded. "Jesus, Grace. There's no chain of custody, no way to establish they existed before you walked in there and took them."

I shrugged. "I think you're right about her. There's no way. Even if they would have been admissible she would never let us use them. Would you?"

She shook her head.

"Let's go to the jail."

"It's three o'clock in the morning, Grace."

She was right. "Okay. Tomorrow.

Chapter 26

I woke up to a text and the idea I could somehow convince Gabrielle Quinn to save herself at the cost of her child.

The text from Jamie, either he'd found his phone or lied about losing it, simply said, *Meet me. I need to see you.*

I typed quickly. *Where'd you find it?*

Jamie: In the place I left it. Meet me.

Me: When?

Jamie: Now? At the lake.

He'd lied, one way or another, but even the cynic in me wanted to know why. What was behind the switches that put him with Blane's wife?

I shook off the hurt, left a note for Rory, and borrowed her car for a quick drive. The sky, to the east, was full of orange and gold as the sun peeked over the horizon. On the other side, darkness and stars. I pulled into the lot where I always parked and made my way to the trail.

The tall grasses brushed across my legs as I battled the semi-dark while wearing Rory's shoes and a pair of sweatpants that left my calves bare. Frogs, flipping fish, crickets, the sounds that made scary movies scary, sent shivers along my skin. I didn't concentrate on the eeriness of the moment, but focused, instead, on not falling face first into the mud.

He stood at the edge of the water, facing down into it. He threw a rock with his right arm, the one that should have been in a cast. It wasn't Jamie. He stood too casually, trying too hard to suppress the subtle differences between them.

Fear screamed through me, begging me to run away. I turned to walk back to the car as he called out. "Going somewhere?"

I stopped, his accent didn't quite mesh with the one that whispered such sweet words in my ears. "Nope. Just wondering why here?"

"I wanted to be alone with you."

"Why here?" I stalled, took two steps toward my car as he advanced toward me.

"To make sure you're okay. That fire was rather scary. I thought I'd lost you."

This slipped over the border to plain ridiculous, his bad Dick Van Dyke in *Mary Poppins* accent, the super-secret meeting, and the full moon glittering through the fog. I smiled in spite of myself. Jamie could fake being Blane, but that road only traveled one way. "I guess you haven't seen or talked to your brother. When he carried me out of my apartment, Jamie broke his wrist."

He chuckled. "Did he? He didn't mention it." He'd dropped the charade and his regular voice mingled with the melodies of nature.

"Yes. So, you should have a cast on if you want to play him with any kind of conviction." I shook my head as he lowered his, almost appearing bashful. "Why not call me and ask me to meet you? Why pretend to be him?"

"Would you have come? If I'd been the one who called?"

I shrugged. "I don't know. Probably not."

"Because of him?" Something about the way he'd shoved his hands in his pockets, kicked at the grass, and peered up at me from beneath long lashes, said the answer meant something to him.

"Because of Valerie."

"I was honest with you about that. She left me, Grace, and she didn't come back until they took my cases away and brought her back to town."

"You only told me because you had to, because you didn't have a choice." Someday, I would sit back and decide how I felt about it, but I had a feeling he hadn't called me out there to discuss the end of our one minute affair. "It doesn't matter, Blane."

"It mattered. You mattered to me. More than you know. More than I showed you." He stepped close enough to run his fingers though my hair, to cup my cheek, to force me to look into his eyes. "When your daddy died, I was with Val. She came home, wanted to be with me, and all I could think about was you, you hurting, you alone. It took me two days to realize you'd called Jamie, not me." His eyes changed. "Everybody calls Jamie."

Shaking off the clouds wrapped around my brain, I stepped back, shifted away. He hadn't done a single thing to make me want him, no romance, simply a few quick interludes that had left me unsatisfied, but he piqued my curiosity. I wanted closure to this whole nasty little redneck love triangle. I wanted to be free to see Jamie, at least, hear his explanation for answering his phone as Blane.

He sighed and backed off. "He's the one, my brother?"

"Maybe. Maybe not."

"But not me." I almost believed the sadness in his voice. Until he looked up. His face twisted, his mouth pulled taut. "Never me. Always Jamie. Better basketball player. Better grades. Always better." The air around us changed. I reeled back a few steps. The ice in his stare chilled me and fear gripped my heart.

"Why am I here, Blane? What do you want?" I silently willed him not to notice the falter in my bravado, to ignore the waver in my voice.

He closed the distance between us quickly, grabbed me by the wrist, squeezed, and pulled me forward. "I know what you found in the house. I can't let you use it to free Gabby Quinn. I gave my word."

Maybe it was the terror, or the pain in my wrist, or maybe the fact he'd lied to me to get me out there, but… "Your word? Your word means shit, Blane."

"That's not nice."

"I've had a rough couple days, and you keep toying with me."

"I'm not toying with you. I meant what I said."

I shrugged, not believing one damned thing that came out of his mouth. "Well, then let's chalk it up to my life falling apart one piece at a time ever since I got here."

"I know. Dad died, house burned down, one boyfriend is a big fat liar and the other is married with a baby on the way. Poor, poor Grace."

He clucked his tongue and I struggled against his grip. The hold tightened. He pulled me forward until we were chest to chest and his aura of evil glowed bright in the moonlight mixing with the sunrise. My emotional pendulum swung between anger and fear and his words grated on me. "He's playing you. He's a liar and he's trying to take me down with him. I didn't plant evidence. I hid it for him. I helped him, because he's my brother, but he's the one, Grace."

"Get away from me." I jerked away hard, fully prepared to make a run for it, but he reached out, dug his fingers into the bandage covering my burn. "I don't believe you. You can't lie well enough to make me believe he is the bad one and you're the one protecting him. I've been with both of you enough to know who the asshole is and isn't."

"Asshole?"

"That's right. And if you can't bluff any better than this, I would have kicked your ass in court." I jerked free, bit back a whimper, maybe a scream, of pain and called on all my confidence to see me through.

"You know what I think?" At that point, even I had no clue what was going to come pouring out of my mouth. "I think you're jealous of everything about your brother. He's good, and clearly you're not. He's kind, and let's face facts, Tex, you're anything but kind. You're selfish and, I'm thinking, kind of evil." I shrugged a nonchalant shoulder. "But, I don't know if you're smart enough to pull this off without him. I mean"—and this was only a guess—"you had to cheat off him through law school, right? You weren't pissed off he ruined your happily ever after with your brother by your side. You were pissed you were gonna have to do a little studying yourself. You couldn't have planned it without him, because you wouldn't have been able to figure out how." I wasn't sure if I believed my words or had resorted to baiting him to buy precious moments before my own impending death.

"You think you're so smart."

"Oh, Blane. I am so smart." I shook my head in mock disappointment driven by real fear. "And I don't hear you denying anything."

"I don't need my brother to plan anything."

"Really? You need him to pretend to be you with your wife."

"Oh, you are gullible, aren't you?" He yanked Jamie's phone from his pocket. "I recorded a voicemail, set your calls to go straight there." He tinkered with the screen for a moment, then held it at arm's length, speaker on. "Hello…hello." It disconnected after a second. "Now, who's the dumbass?"

"Oh, bravo. It doesn't take a genius to pull the wool over the eyes of a semi-drunk." Lord, the things my mouth came up with. It was a wonder *I'd* ever won a case.

"Nothing halfway about you. You're actually a full-blown drunk."

"But I'm not going to jail." I looked around for an escape route that would get me the hell away from him. He blocked my way back to the car, and it was too dark under the canopy of trees to haul ass into the woods. "I might be a drunk, but you're a bad man, Blane. And in my world, bad men suffer."

"Ooh, that's real scary coming from someone who can't keep her lips off a bottle for more than a couple hours a day."

"Hey, we've already established I might have a drinking problem. No need to beat it to death." While it might not have been the time to haul out the humor, I didn't see a reason to back off, just yet.

"Witty. I'm gonna be sorry to see you go."

"Joke's on you, bud. I'm not going anywhere."

"We'll see."

"Unless you have a weapon and a shovel, I'm pretty sure the only place I'm going is home tonight."

"You don't have a home." He lowered his gaze, looked up at me from beneath batting eyelashes. "Sorry about that."

"You? You burned my house down?" I should have known. My first real, honest-to-goodness moment of panic flared through me, and my heart pulsed fear through my veins. He'd burned my apartment down with me inside. Clearly, he didn't bring me out here for fun and games.

He shrugged and a knot of apprehension tightened in my stomach. I already knew the answer, but I needed to hear the words.

I yelped as he drew me in close enough I could smell his cologne. "I can't let the boy go to jail, Grace. Nathan Quinn is a vital part of my operation. How the hell do you think that piece of hair disappeared?"

"You did that too?" Evil didn't begin to describe this asshat.

He nodded. "I had to. If the Quinn kid goes to jail, Nathan will spill the beans on this whole thing. Do you have any idea how long it took to get everything in place? The right people on each end, the scouting, the man hours I have invested in this whole enterprise?"

"Did you bring me out here to brag about your frequent flyer miles or is there something you want from me?" Pretend courage was still courage, right?

His chuckle turned vicious. "Oh, I don't want anything from you. Had my fill. Remember?"

I'd fallen for some dumb tricks in my life, things that shamed me and my self-proclaimed brilliance, but not seeing through to his inner devil provided the exclamation point at the end of my stupidity. Seriously. Some counselor, somewhere, was rubbing her hands together with glee at the thought of getting a hold of the turmoil in my brain. "How could I forget the most unpleasant fifteen seconds of my life?"

As a reward for my sarcasm, he hauled me in close, pressed his lips against mine. I pushed with everything I had, and he didn't budge. Another uh-oh feeling crawled in my stomach.

"You taste kind of smoky. Probably all that fiery air you inhaled." With one hand still wrapped around my arm, the other pushed a piece of hair behind my ear. "We could have been great together. I wanted to share all of this with you. All of it. The money, the things it can buy. When you strolled into town, all hell-bent for justice, it was my love at first sight moment. I don't believe in that crap, but I saw you, and somehow, I couldn't imagine another day without you."

"So you burn my house down? Wow. That's not exactly country music kind of love. It's sick. The holy-crap-you-need-therapy-and-a-bedroom-that-has-padding-on-the-walls kind."

He blinked his answer as he slipped both arms around my waist, pressed me against him in a hug that felt anything but tender. "I like that you're thinking about my bedroom." His chin rested against the top of my head, and I fought the urge to resist. I didn't have the strength to break free on my own and needed him to release me so I could run away.

"Don't flatter yourself."

"It's nothing personal, Grace, but I need Nathan Quinn on his game. His kid goes to the big house, I lose my shipping coordinator. Can't have that." He pulled back a few fractions and looked down at me. His wolfish smile tore the beauty of his face into one half decidedly evil and the other plain mean. "You're right, though. I am a bad man."

"Tell your priest, pal. I don't care." I shoved him again, but he only tightened his arms around me. Air pushed out of my lungs along with a yelp as he gave a hard squeeze, then relaxed.

I couldn't break free, and the darkness in his eyes caused a shiver to skitter over my skin. "You couldn't leave well enough alone. I thought the gods smiled on me when your daddy died and you rushed back home. But no, you couldn't wait to get back to Texas. You were so sure you could get Gabby out of jail. I can't have that, Grace. She has to go away. Or my goody-goody brother will keep the case open. He doesn't believe she did it either. God, that was a battle." He shook his head, dropped one hand, and pulled a small pistol from his waistband. "It's not personal, but now that the kid's clothes are gone, you're the last loose end I have."

He kept a hand wrapped around my arm, hauled me toward the lake path. My stomach flopped and my mind raced. I had to get away from him, had to. This situation, yet another result of my poor decision making skills, had spiraled right out of control. "I was kidding about the weapon and the shovel."

"Too bad I'm a good planner."

"Blane, you don't have to do this. I'll be quiet and step away from Gabby's case."

"No, you won't. You can't. I blame it on all that Midwest honor. It's such a shame. We could have been great together." He raised the gun, aimed at my chest.

I swallowed hard. "You're pretty calm for a guy who plans to shoot someone." There had never been a day in my life where I censored my words, worried about the trouble my big mouth could get me into. But, in the moment, standing toe to toe with death, I would have thought I could control myself. "People will miss me, look for me, and figure out your little scheme."

Death nodded. "You know, I thought about that, but you're a drunk, darlin'. Everybody knows you can't turn down a drink, and you've been depressed since your dad died."

I let that one pass, but if I survived this, I was never touching another drop of alcohol as long as I lived. Well, at least until he was handcuffed and stowed into the backseat of a police car.

I needed to think and fast. He was starting to get twitchy. As soon as the answer came to me, with its little ray of hope attached, I blurted the words. "It'll never work, Blane. I left a note for Rory saying I was coming to meet Jamie at the lake. She's going to come all fire and ice to get her car back and probably kick my ass."

As though he couldn't believe I'd been smart enough to leave a note, which I had, he dropped his mouth open, shook his head.

"I didn't want her reporting her car stolen."

"Even better. I was gonna take the gun along, clean it, put it back in his little lock box, but this way I get rid of both of you. She'll find your body, my brother's gun, and she'll demand the swift justice only Texas law can provide."

"Oh, God bless Texas. What is it with you people and your pride in Texas law? We all have laws against murder, Einstein." I couldn't seem to stop myself.

He turned away from me for a second, relaxing his guard, playing at sadness. "It will be hard, but my dedication to making sure the person who killed you goes to prison will demand I prosecute my brother to the fullest extent of the law." He grinned. "Thank you. And it will be much easier to convince everyone that he was the one screwing with my cases too."

"So, you have it all figured out?"

Lord, why hadn't I recorded it on my cell? Well, because I thought in terms of a defense attorney, and we, as a rule, hated taped conversations. They never seemed to work out well for us. Damn it all anyway. I would have had sole ownership of a confession to his involvement in the dirty side of the investigation against him, as well as his half-baked conspiracy to commit murder, *mine, and* frame his brother for it.

I stood, a hostage to my own idiocy, and all I could think of was confession tapes and my general dislike for them. Out of body experience maybe? Ill-timed Attention Deficit Disorder, more likely.

I had to think, stop kicking myself and get it together, because I was afraid his trigger finger would get itchy and I would end up in a slump with blood pouring out of my body. My heart pounded, my hands trembled, and my stomach ached.

"This is far enough." He pulled up short at the edge of the water.

Oh, Lord. I didn't want to meet my maker in Rory's sweatpants and tank top. I clenched my fists and held up a hand as he leveled the gun toward me again. "Wait."

"What?"

"Okay, you win, all right. You get to shoot me, frame your brother, whatever." I rolled my eyes as though none of it mattered. "But what happened to Emily? I know her brother did it, but why?"

He cocked his head to one side. "Really? Now?"

I shrugged. "Yeah. I'm not going to be around to see how it all plays out, right?"

He tilted his head to one side. "They came home, just like they said. Checked on the kids, took the sitter home. Middle of the night, they wake up to a horrible screaming. The boy was covered in blood, holding a knife. The little girl was on the garage floor. She was already gone. Nothing they could do. Nathan called me, begging for my help. He couldn't lose them both. He and Gabby were on the skids, his drug use too much for her to handle. She didn't want the kid to go to jail, and he didn't want her anymore. This was perfect and you screwed it up."

How had I not noticed? Thinking back, he'd come in wild-eyed, demanding to see Rory, and I'd brushed it off as anguish, the agony of losing his daughter, seeing his wife in an interrogation room. I wanted to kick myself.

"So, he promised her he would get Rory as her lawyer and she would get off if she took the blame. I wasn't worried about Rory. Even if she took the case, she would have fallen apart. I left her that binder to make sure. Then, my dumbass brother stepped in, and you showed up, and it all started getting out of hand. Thanks to you, I can't control Nathan. He's talking to the investigators and trying to get out from under his responsibilities to me because his wife is convinced you can save her. All the sudden, he's back in love with her. The fool is even talking rehab and getting clean." He shook his head. "And every single one of them is putting their money on a drunk to save them. Go ahead. Save them all." He shook his head again and raised the gun, this time sighting in my head. "But who's gonna save you, Grace?"

"I don't need anyone to save me. I can save myself."

"Really?" He pulled back the hammer with a click of metal sliding against metal, but a flash of movement from behind him caught my eye as Rory stepped out into full view.

"Or maybe she will." I pointed over his left shoulder and he chuckled. "Nice try."

I breathed a sigh of relief as Jamie joined Rory, along with four police officers, weapons drawn, and Valerie?

"Blane?" Valerie's voice was soft, and he turned, then moved to position his body at an angle to all of us.

"You really left a note?" Blane flipped an irritated, open-mouthed glance my way.

"I stole Rory's car." It explained things in my mind, but he looked down at his shoes, taking his eyes off me long enough that I dashed around him to stand beside Rory. Relief powered through me, weakened my knees, and I sagged against her. I couldn't have been more grateful for the trio of badly dressed superheroes, not a cape among them, and the uniformed cops.

"I thought you were bluffing." He shook his head.

"Put the gun down, Blane." Jamie's voice held a note of calm, but anger danced behind his eyes. "Think this through."

"You have everything. Do you have to have her too? You let her come between us."

"She didn't come between us. Life did. Your extracurricular business ventures came between us." Jamie shook his head. "We had it all. The whole town worshiped us. *We're* their heroes. I catch them, and you put them away. Wasn't that enough for you?" Softer he added, "Why wasn't it enough?"

"It was never about you and me together. It was about you always being better, having more. I was smarter"—he looked at me and grimaced—"and they all liked you better." Blane waved the small pistol around as though directing an orchestra. "It's always been about Jamie and how fucking perfect you are."

"Blane."

"Even the drunk likes you better." He nodded his head at me.

"Seriously. Let it go, Blane." I took one step forward and Rory's nails in my arm dragged me back to her side.

"You know what? You can keep her, but you'll always know I had her first. I was the one holding her when her daddy died. Me, not you."

Jamie gulped back whatever emotion might have been bubbling to the surface. "Just put the gun down, Blane. We can work everything else out."

"I'm not going to jail, Jamie. They'll kill me. I put most of them in there. I won't make it to my cell without some punk, hell-bent on revenge, sticking his sharpened toothbrush in my back."

"Blane," Valerie's southern twang softened the hostility as she stepped around me to stand in front of her husband. "Please, put the gun down. For us. For the baby."

"Val. It's too late for all of that."

She wrapped a hand around his neck, pulled his face close to hers. "It's never too late, Blane. I've loved you my whole life, since we were little kids, then in high school and college." Tears streamed down her cheeks. If this was an act, she deserved her own red carpet walk and one of those shiny, gold man trophies. "We've made it through so much, but I won't be able to forgive you if you make me raise this baby without you. Please, Blane, put it down."

"They'll put me in jail, Val." He stopped pointing the gun at me and turned it on himself, shoving the barrel against his temple.

"No. You're a pillar in this town, a man people respect and love. You served them, protected them. A judge is going to see that." I couldn't be sure how much she heard before they all appeared, but I had to believe she'd heard enough to know we hadn't been platonically taking a stroll. "We'll get a lawyer, a good one, and no matter what happens, we'll work it out. I love you so much. Please."

She ran her hand up his arm to the pistol still clutched in his hand. He shook her off. "It's not enough, Val. I've never been enough."

"To me, you've always been everything." A tear slipped down his cheek, lit up by the increasing dawn. "Please, put the gun down."

"I can't."

"Yes, you can. You can put the gun down and walk out of here with me by your side every minute. We'll get one of these hotshot chicks to represent you, and we can get through this together. The way it's always been meant to be." She had a stand by her man vibe I couldn't fathom considering all she'd seen and heard.

I could do little more than watch, wait for the resolution.

Jamie circled to the side, his gun resting against his thigh. "Blane, think about Mum. If something happens to you, it will kill her. And that'll be your fault."

"Shut up, Jamie." Blane swung the gun away from himself and pointed it at Jamie. The weapon wavered, and he seemed to think better of it, then pressed it back against his own head.

"Please, Blane. Don't do this. I need you. I love you." Valerie reached to lay her hand over Blane's. After a few long minutes of looking into her face, he lowered his gun. "We'll get through this together. I promise."

He nodded, pulled her against his chest, then raised his arm and leveled it at Jamie. This was one smart Texan. He'd helped himself to a human shield. No one would risk firing a shot while he held a pregnant woman in front of him.

I struggled to free myself from Rory's strong-arm grasp. For barely being five feet tall, she had upper body strength that rivaled anyone else who'd tried to stop me from doing what I wanted.

The officers moved forward, coming at him from all sides, but no one stood between his gun and Jamie. If he fired, he wouldn't miss, not at this close distance. *Shit.*

Rory pulled me behind her body and stepped forward, blocking Blane's view of his brother. "I'll defend you, Blane. I'll do it. Don't make it worse. Don't do anything they can use against you later."

He closed his eyes, breathing deeply, his nose buried in his wife's hair.

"Come on, Blane. It's a good deal. I don't lose unless I want to. You've been my friend for a long time. I won't want to lose your case."

Well, all right then. We've evened out in the taking-cases-that-made-the-other cringe category of our relationship. I held back my huff of disbelief behind clamped lips.

He shook his head, dropped the gun to the ground, and waited.

An officer on each side grabbed one of Blane's hands and pulled them behind his back as another led a struggling Valerie to safety. "I'll meet you at the police station. I love you, Blane."

Without further incident, an officer walked Blane calmly to the car, and every ounce of adrenaline my body produced caught up with me all at once. I shook, knees wobbling, heart pounding, as Rory pulled me into a hug. "I was so worried. When we pulled up and he had that gun…I'm glad you're okay."

I doubted she would feel that way after I got finished with her. "Seriously? He burned down my house. Tried to kill me. And you're promising to be his lawyer?" This whole partnership thing was not at all what I imagined it would be. Where was the glamour? The camaraderie? The mid-day shopping trips while clients went out and proved their own innocence?

She nodded and pulled me close again. "And he didn't shoot your boyfriend." She nodded at Jamie. "You're welcome." She released me from her Hulkish grip and walked away, toward the police car where Blane awaited his transport and Valerie stood sobbing outside.

Jamie cocked his head to the side, a ghost of a smile almost turning his lips. "Hey, you."

I blew out a short breath. "Hey."

"Are you hurt?"

"My pride, maybe. My arm, a little."

"What about your heart?" He moved closer.

"It's fine." I shook my head. "What about yours?"

He shook his head, grasped the back of his neck, and looked at me. "I don't know yet." Somehow, whether I moved or he did, the space between us shortened. "I hate what he did to you."

I nodded and waited as his good hand reached out to clasp mine. "I hate what he did to me. And most of all, I hate what he's done to us."

"We're okay."

"Yeah?"

"Aren't we?" He gave my fingers a squeeze and I looked down. I hadn't planned on a big admission, but I wanted to start off on the right foot. For this to work, I couldn't hide and neither could he. "Ever since I got here, it's been… I feel like I'm falling into something and I don't know… I'm scared, Jamie."

He nodded. "If you fall, I will always be here to catch you, to save you from whatever haunts you." With a finger under my chin, he tilted my head up to meet his gaze. "From the first minute I saw you when he brought you to the diner, I knew. You're the girl I've dreamt of my whole life. And now you're here. I'll wait if you need time to process all of this, but you're the girl I want to marry, the one I want to wake up with every morning, and sleep next to every night. If you're gonna fall Grace, fall with me."

"Have you been practicing that whole speech?"

He nodded and breathed out a small sigh. "I didn't know if I would ever get to say it."

He cradled me against his chest, and the wild beat of his heart thumped under my cheek. "I don't need to process anything." I lifted my head, pressed my lips against his, and waited. The world didn't implode around me. The sky didn't open up and dispense a swarm of locusts. No sign from the universe warned me away from him. Of course, I'd gotten no clue about Blane, none that I paid attention to anyway. How had I not noticed that his brother was the bad seed? It didn't matter. Being in Jamie's arms, holding him close, looking into the clear depths of his eyes, all caused a fluttering in my stomach. "I'm in, Jamie. With you. I love you."

He grinned, brushed his lips across mine, then trailed across my cheek to whisper, "I love you, Grace. I think I always have."

"Just say you always will."

"I always will."

Meet the Author

As an author, Melissa Shirley believes in fairytales, happily ever after, and destiny. Born and raised in Illinois, and a mother of eight, she lives with her husband and three youngest children in a quiet town in the southern part of the state where she spends her time writing and watching her children grow into the people she has always dreamed. Please visit her at http://melissashirley2.wix.com/melissashirleyauthor.

Be sure not to miss Melissa Shirley's sequel to Falling Grace:

Simon Says

Read on for a special sneak peek of the next book in the Storybook Lake
series!

Learn more about Melissa Shirley
http://www.kensingtonbooks.com/author.aspx/31684

Chapter 1

Present—Opening Statements

"All rise!"

Being on trial for my life taught me two things. One, when the bailiff says "All rise," everyone in the courtroom should immediately shut up and stand. Two, the business end of being on trial and the tremors associated with it did not couple well with coffee drinking and wearing silk blouses.

I blotted at my shirt while my lawyer leaned in close to advise me, yet again, of the possible outcomes of the case should I lose. She turned to face me head-on and recommended I, at least, consider the prosecutions deal of life in prison with the possibility of parole in twenty-five years. Twenty-five years? I decided to gamble on a jury trial and a possible life sentence. Surely, at least one of the twelve people would realize I didn't kill Sean, no matter how badly I wanted to and no matter how much unwavering gratitude, (trial talk taboo), I harbored for the person who'd actually done the job.

The jurors filed into the courtroom, seven women between the ages of thirty and late sixties and five men from early twenties to late forties. There was a school teacher, bus driver, street sweeper, an accountant, landscaper, college student, and three food service professionals— translation: waiters and waitresses—a dog trainer, boutique owner, and a hairdresser. Somehow, being accused of murder changed how I evaluated my *peers*, especially since I had no choice but to put my life in their hands.

Calvin Coolidge Connor, the prosecutor and apparent love child of Beetlejuice and Mr. Frodo with dark black hair, a slender waist, and suits that swallowed him almost whole, looked over at me with slits for eyes and a grim smirk on his lips. As green as any other small town thirty-five year-old prosecutor and eager to make a name for himself, he probably jumped at the chance to take this case. He'd been an opportunist in high school too, but as friends back then, I'd been able to overlook it. In this moment, with a gallery full of TV cameras, former friends, and reporters with pens poised to capture every detail, I hated him for it.

My attorney, the only lawyer I'd ever met, had been my best friend growing up and, though ten years had passed since we did more than make small talk on the phone, she took my case, no questions asked. Even though Grace Wade had been career dormant as of late, I sat next to her not at all worried. She'd always been wrapped in some karmically blessed aura of greatness. At least, that's what I told myself that morning before I dressed for trial.

She smoothed her skirt as we sat and waited for the prosecutor to begin his opening statement. At seventeen months older than me, Grace had movie-star beauty. Along with her dramatic good looks, she capitalized on her porn star figure by wearing short, mostly respectable skirts and blouses opened at the throat, thoroughly enhancing her pushed up C cup.

Without looking at me, checking her notes or picking up a pen, she stared at the troll and waited. To anyone else, she appeared calm, poised for battle, but her fingers trembled as they sat idle against the table. A light sheen of sweat dotted her forehead and upper lip. We ignored the whirring of cameras, crinkling of papers, muffled coughs, hushed whispers in the court room, and most of our childhood friends on the witness list. For a former glory hound like Grace, ignoring it all said something.

As much as I'd come to love Storybook Lake over the last year, we weren't holding the trial at home. Storybook Lake would never let something so tainted as murder touch its cobblestoned, gas-lit streets. The proceedings had been transferred to neighboring Bloomington, and my friends and former neighbors, all with ready-formed opinions as to my innocence or guilt, elbowed for space in the tiny courtroom.

Cal, whose grades in high school mirrored his initials, stood and walked to the center of the room, facing the jury, his back to me. While I understood it was the little troll's job to prosecute me, it irked me that he'd been able to start without as much as a glance at the pile of notes on his table. Executing a perfect military turn in his too-shiny clown shoes, he took three paces toward the judge parallel to the jury, executed a military left turn, and stalked back to his original spot. He stopped abruptly and faced the twelve people prepared to hang on his every word.

"Good morning, ladies and gentlemen. My name is Calvin Connor and I represent you, the good people of the State of Illinois." I nudged Grace and mouthed the words, "suck up." She shot me a glare and turned back to Cal. "Storybook Lake, Illinois is an innocent little tourist town with a quiet character based on works of literary greatness. Its existence celebrates the lives of those who let us borrow their words to transport ourselves through whatever carefully woven life they have created in their pages. On June fourth, this woman"—he pointed at me without ever turning around—"shattered the calm that normally floats over the quiet little city. She lured her husband away from his home in California with the promise he would get to see the son she kidnapped away from him."

I looked around for the Academy Award presenters and shrugged when no little gold statue appeared.

Grace leaped to her feet. "Objection, Your Honor. Mrs. Turner had, and continues to have, sole custody of the child. There was no kidnapping involved and absolutely no evidence Mrs. Turner lured her husband here. In fact, all evidence points otherwise." Grace turned to me, eyes wide, the hint of a smile on her lips as she waited for the judge to answer.

The judge shifted her attention to Cal. "Mr. Cooper?"

He simply lifted one shoulder, cocked his head toward it with an off-handed smile, offering no explanation. "Sustained."

The judge shot him a dirty look.

He turned back to the jury and continued. "This woman, the defendant, is a cold, calculating killer who was involved in a relationship with another man while still married to Sean Turner. She knew in order to be free to be with the love of her life"—*Air quotes?*—"and raise her son with him, she needed to get rid of her husband. She had to make sure he wasn't around to interfere. So, what did she do? She took a knife and stabbed Sean Turner not once, not twice, but seven times. And, just like that, she was free of the burden of marriage." He shook his head and clucked his tongue. "But then, she wasn't. Sean Turner refused to die, to let her take his son away and live with another man, refused to give up the tenuous hold on his wife and on his life, he was clinging to. She couldn't let him live, especially not now. Attempted murder? She would have lost her son anyway. So, she ran to her purse, took out the gun she stole from her boyfriend, a former chief of police, and she shot Mr. Turner in the face." He made a pistol with his fingers, flicked his arm out in aim, and *shot* me. "She lied to investigators, not once, but three times. She lied to her friends, her family, and to her son."

Grace shot out of her chair again. "Objection, Your Honor. May we approach?" Without waiting for an answer, she stomped to the front of the courtroom and stood, hands on hips, feet apart. Grace Wade, princess warrior, ready for battle.

After an animated discussion—her hands flailing, his head bobbing, and the judge jerking her head back and forth ping pong style—she returned to her seat next to mine and picked up her pen. She scribbled, "No worries. I got this."

I aspired to worried.

The judge looked at Cal, then the jury. "The objection is sustained. Ladies and gentleman, there is no evidence the gun used to shoot Mr. Turner was, in fact, the same gun that belonged to Simon Hunter." Cal was the recipient of his second stink-eye from the judge in a matter of minutes. "Proceed, Mr. Connor."

"The point isn't who this defendant lied to or whose gun she used, or why Sean Turner was here in Illinois. The point is she lied and she lied a lot. She left Mr. Turner in his hotel room bleeding to death."

Nope. By the time I arrived, he'd been stabbed and shot and died alone. The way I always knew he would.

"The relationship between the defendant and Mr. Turner was born in the back of a limousine where the defendant conceived the couple's child. After trying unsuccessfully to dupe Keaton Shaw into believing the child was his, a DNA test confirmed she lied to him and the baby actually belonged to Mr. Turner. Another lie in her long list. She sought out Sean Turner and married him, then quit her job."

I hadn't quit my job. My job didn't require a desk or an office, just a pen and piece of paper. I designed kids' clothes for a living.

"Then she moved to California to be with her husband. After a few months of fighting and quibbling over money, she left the marital home, taking the child with her. When she returned, over the Christmas holiday, she visited Storybook Lake with her husband, and while they were there, together, as a couple, she flaunted her desire to be with Mr. Hunter in Sean Turner's face."

We had been fighting over my money and the way Sean spent it in big fat wads, but the tone of Cal's voice suggested I was the greedy one. And for his information, during that trip, Sean found me talking to Simon for the sum total of one minute, then hauled me back to the hotel and hit me with such force my eyes rolled back. I thought he'd literally broken my face. The next morning, he'd cried like a baby, said he couldn't stand the thought of losing me. I went home with him because he'd been *sorry* and because he promised to start over with me and make a life with me and Kieran. Plus, Simon went to the New Year's party with Kelly Devlin, the big shot magazine writer he'd broken up with me to date.

"Mr. Turner, by this defendant's own admission, cried, begged, and pleaded for her to return to him so he could share in the life of their child. Reluctantly, by another of her own admissions, she returned home to Mr. Turner where the real fighting began."

Rage at the injustice behind Cal's half-truths welled up inside me. Grace covered my fingers with her own squeezing hard, probably to stop the drumming against the table top. The fighting began because Sean was sleeping with every stripper in his employ, as well as some who worked for other clubs. Jeez! Where was a tiny-headed voodoo doll when I needed one?

"By the time she was done with him, Sean Turner was as ready to be rid of his wife as she was to be gone, but not his son. Oh no. Within hours of her leaving, he filed papers for custody of his child."

Sean had only done that to lure me back. I resisted the urge to roll my eyes. Grace had been forthright about how I should behave and eye rolling topped the no-no list.

"But did this defendant call the police after the body was found to tell them she had, in fact, been in Mr. Turner's hotel room that night? No. Did she one time mention her fable that Mr. Turner had been stalking her, taunting her, having her followed? No. Instead, she pretended she'd had no contact with him since she'd taken their son and run home to Storybook Lake some seven months earlier." He shook his head and his pacing in front of the jury continued.

"When investigators discovered otherwise, her story changed again, tailored to fit the evidence. She finally concocted this story of abuse toward not only her, but the child. She, in her desperation to stay out of jail, involved their four-year-old son in her web of lies." He looked down most of the time, presumably to make sure his ugly, brown, clown shoes didn't catch on one another and cause him to topple head over feet. "Danielle Turner is the worst kind of predator. She uses her beauty"—he looked up at the jury and stabbed a bony finger through the air in my direction—"to snare men into her web of lies."

His words curdled my blood.

"She used her over-average intelligence to try to outwit cops and investigators. And she used her son as a weapon to get her way. In this case, her way was to kill Mr. Turner so she could embark on her new life with Simon Hunter in a town that celebrates its fiction. Don't lump her in with the likes of Shakespeare, Mark Twain, or even Dr. Seuss. Show her that her fiction is as unbelievable as the evidence will prove it to be." With a smirk, he raised one eyebrow at Grace and went back to his chair, needing a copy of the yellow pages on his seat to properly see over the top of his table. Without it, he seemed to have tucked himself almost underneath the smooth flat surface holding the mountain of notes and binders on the case.

Grace stood and smoothed her skirt. "Mr. Connor." She shook her head, long, blonde hair swinging along her back, soft curls dancing. "Shame on you."

"Your Honor." Calvin shoved his legs against the fabric of his cushioned chair, shooting it backward into the short wall dividing us from the gallery. The clatter echoed throughout the high-ceilinged room. "Ms. Wade needs to speak to the jury, not the prosecutor."

The judge smiled at Grace. "Miss Wade, I know you know better."

Grace nodded, her lips pursing as she tried to wipe the smile from her face. "Yes, Your Honor." She turned back to the jury and introduced herself, then began. "Mrs. Turner didn't lure her husband to Storybook Lake. That was the last thing she wanted. Since the day of their wedding, Sean tortured Danielle, beating her and their son. There is irrefutable evidence to prove it."

She turned to Cal, with another quick shake of her head as though reprimanding him for his lie. "As soon as the private detective Sean Turner hired to hunt Danielle found her, bad, scary, dangerous things started to happen. Her home was vandalized then broken into. She received countless texts on numerous cell phones indicating Sean knew where she was and what she was doing. And the week he died, Sean bought a plane ticket and flew to Storybook Lake to step up his efforts to intimidate my client, her friends, and her family. The evidence will show you Danielle did not kill Mr. Turner. She was aware Mr. Turner was stalking her, but she didn't kill him.

"The evidence will show you that Sean Turner taunted her, threatened her life repeatedly, not only over that week, but during the entire course of their relationship. What the evidence will not show you is that she had a single thing to do with his murder. The prosecutor has no murder weapon, no eye witness, not a single, tangible thing to prove Danielle had so much as an inkling Sean Turner was in Storybook Lake."

She paused for a moment, looked from me to the jury. "You are going to hear things about Sean Turner that will make it seem as though he's the one on trial, about his behavior, his job, and his sex life. Make no mistake. We're not trying to smear Sean Turner's name, but this is all information you need to walk into the jury room with a full picture of the events leading up to the night Danielle left her husband and returned home to the safety of Storybook Lake.

"Danielle had the most to lose and nothing to gain by Sean Turner's death. All she would inherit when he died was an almost bankrupt strip club and a pile of debt he ran up in the months since she'd left. She had an army of friends surrounding her to keep her safe from Sean and his henchmen, and because of the man Sean was, there were many, many people who wanted him dead. Danielle did not kill him, and Mr. Cooper cannot prove otherwise."

Grace smiled once more at the jury then came to sit beside me as Calvin stood. "Your Honor," he said, with enough glee in his voice I imagined him about to spring into cartwheels. "I call Mr. Keaton Shaw."

Ugh. Keaton was no longer indebted to me and, no matter what he said about forgiving me, I had no idea what he would say or do on the stand. He raised his right hand, swore to tell the truth, and took his seat to the left of the judge. After he stated his name for the record, he shot me a half smile. I hoped against all other hope it was a good sign.

When Keaton straightened his tie, adjusted his jacket then pointed a straight-forward gaze at the jury, several of the female jurors sat up straighter. His beauty inspired the same reaction wherever he went.

"Mr. Shaw." Calvin walked from his seat to the podium, almost wringing his hands together in evil merriment. This was his every nerd dream. He had the captain of every sports team in our graduating class sitting in front of him testifying against the homecoming queen. It played out like an after school special gone wrong. "How do you know Mrs. Turner?"

Keaton's eyebrows knitted together as though he'd never heard a question more stupid. "We all grew up together." His tone clearly indicated he included Calvin in the group.

Calvin chuckled. "Right. We did." Though I'm sure Cal remembered growing up outside their circle a little differently than Keaton remembered growing up surrounded by Gatlin, Joss, Simon, Kelly, and Luke. "During that time, how well did you get to know Mrs. Turner?"

Keaton smiled. "We were friends, then we dated in high school, and after high school we lived together for a while."

"And when you were living together, was it while you were still married?"

Uh-oh. "I was in the process of getting divorced."

"But you were still married?"

Cal's question left Keaton no room to wiggle out of the answer. "Yes." He ground out the word as one eyebrow cocked on his forehead, daring Cal to take it further.

A bubble of anger formed in the pit in my stomach as Calvin asked, "And was that divorce precipitated by your involvement with Mrs. Turner?"

Oh good Lord. I nudged Grace. *Object, dammit.* She'd never been good at hearing my mind messages, so I kicked her shin. She whirled to look at me and tilted her head. "Stop."

"My wife thought I was having an affair." *Explain, explain, explain,* I silently commanded, hoping Keaton had the gift of telepathy Grace did not. Unfortunately, he remained sitting, hands clasped in his lap, waiting for the next question.

Calvin continued grinding his ugly little axe to a razor sharp point. "During the time you lived with Mrs. Turner, was there any drug or alcohol use?"

"Yes." He looked at me and frowned.

"By both of you?"

"We didn't do drugs."

I closed my eyes as memories of those days washed over me, well, dim, alcohol-fogged memories.

"And it was during that time Mrs. Turner became pregnant?"

I wanted to smack Cal's self-satisfied smile right off his smarmy, thin lips. If eye rolling was a no-no, then smacking the prosecutor was off limits, but the desire itched inside my palm.

"Yes." Well…

"And she let you believe the child was yours for how long?"

"It wasn't like she did it on purpose. We lived together like couples live together." I guessed that was his way of saying we'd had some sex. He was lying to defend me? Knowing Joss was seated a few rows behind me. I couldn't decide if his untruth was helpful or hurtful. "She didn't know he wasn't mine, either." Keaton frowned. Mr. Proper-grammar-at-all-times never liked the double negative.

Calvin looked at the judge. "Your Honor, the witness is non-responsive."

The judge glared back at Calvin. "And your question was leading. Rephrase." She shot a lifted brow look at Grace.

"How long did Mrs. Turner let you believe the child was yours?"

Grace stood up. "Objection. Relevance and foundation."

The judge looked at Grace, a half smile crooking her lips. "Sustained."

Calvin clarified the details. When had we lived together and where? How long after we began living together did I become pregnant? How long after I told him did I have the baby? Then he asked, "Did you believe the baby was yours?"

"In the beginning? Yes."

"And how long was it before you discovered he belonged to someone else?"

Grace stood again. "Objection, relevance."

"Your honor, it goes to her motive for seeking out Mr. Turner in the first place."

Grace almost popped her hip out of place coming around the desk, and for a split second, I thought she might wrap her hands around his neck instead of punching them against her waist. "Your Honor, we believed Mr. Shaw was going to be called because he was a first responder to the scene."

"She can't tell me what to ask my witness." Calvin's voice climbed to a child-like whine.

The judge cocked her head. "Approach, please." They walked to the front of the courtroom, and I sat back in my chair, remembering.